Reading Lady Chatterley
in Africa

John Samson

TSL Publications

First published in Great Britain in 2018
By TSL Publications, Rickmansworth

Copyright © 2018 John Samson

ISBN / 978-1-912416-09-7

When I am dead
Cry for me a little
Think of me sometimes
But not too much.
Think of me now and again
As I was in life
At some moments it's pleasant to recall
But not for long.
Leave me in peace
And I shall leave you in peace
And while you live
Let your thoughts be with the living

Traditional Indian Prayer of the
Native American Ishi People of the Pacific Northwest

ONE

She had expected the heat, but not like this. The morning sun, unhindered by clouds, coiled its tentacles around her naked forearms in a clammy embrace, welcoming her to this new, strange clime. The white concrete glared angrily, jealous of the attention the sun had gained. Mary blinked, momentarily taking in the heat, then the glare then, as she began to descend the rickety steps from the plane, she breathed in the foreign air.

Wood smoke danced on the light breeze and vied for her attention, loosening slightly the grip that the sun's rays had on her. The sweet scent caught in her nostril and stoked memories as she walked across the airport apron. She didn't want the memories – she had come here to forget – but the hidden fires from somewhere on the other side of the airport fence secreted a powerful fetish that demanded her mind to think back to those evenings by the fireside, cold winter nights when a dark blanket was thrown over the land and Mary and George had sat, snug in the front room, staring into the fire as it popped and stuttered its message of warmth, the orange glow dancing wild tangos across newlywed faces. No, she did not want to remember those nights and she fumbled in her handbag for her sunglasses to hide away from the smells, as if the olfactory attack was somehow allied with the brightness.

The terminal building squatted behind a low barrier of azaleas that was broken only by a faded red path which led to the glass doors. It was cooler inside, marginally, and the wood smoke was banned from entering by the reek of officialdom which manifested itself in inkpads, yellowing forms and a large, uniformed man who was melting over the armrests of a chair that was too small to protest at its load, but too polite to break.

The drops of sweat on the man's dark brow scattered as it creased, some making suicidal dives down his temples while a smile of genuine warmth climbed from his mouth to his eyes.

'Welcome to Africa, Madam. May I please see your passport?'
The voice, deep and booming though it was, seemed to coat the
words in a musky scent.

Mary dug in her handbag again, only now realising that the
dull light in the building was a result of her still wearing her
sunglasses, but she did not want to remove them for fear of
showing the passport official the apprehension she knew was
etched there. Why had she agreed to come here?

'Please can you remove your sunglasses? Thank you.' He
seemed not to notice her concern as she complied with the
request, 'and may I see your yellow fever certificate too, please?'
The glow of the smile had faded slightly, not from anything he
had seen in the passport, but because it had done its duty and
could relax a little till the next white face stepped up. His fat
fingers paged through the small red book, found the visa page
and, while Mary located the documentary proof of the jabs she
had obtained at a travel clinic in London, he vigorously thudded
his stamp twice on the inkpad before crashing it down onto her
passport, carrying with it all the force of his office.

Merskine. That was the name on the certificate. Mary Merskine. It had been George's name, she thought as she handed the
bit of paper over to the man, and she had never really liked it.
It sounded oily and rodent like, not that George had been like
that. George had been...

'Thank you very much, enjoy your stay.' The smile saluted
dutifully again as passport and yellow fever certificate were
offered back to Mary. She took them quickly, nodded her thanks
and moved past the small cubicle that the man occupied, shov-
ing her sunglasses deep into her bag and burying her embarrassment that she had not been more polite to the passport man.

Baggage retrieval was a sparse hall where paint was slowly
divorcing itself from the two toned walls and gloom hung silently like a watchful sloth over the travellers. A faded beer advert
blushed silently next to a vibrant mobile phone poster, while a
grainy elephant trumpeted a muted welcome to the continent.
A few grey fans turned lazily as they hung from the ceiling, too
hot and tired to build up any burst of speed.

Mary eyed her fellow travellers as they began to congregate
around the stagnant conveyor belt and hoped it would deliver

her luggage. A young couple in khaki twittered like weaver birds, excited at the prospect of their safari, a tall dark man in a western suit spoke on his mobile as his eyes watched for any sign of movement on the carousel. His words were alien, holding secret meanings that Mary dared not even guess at. The heat leaked into the room, building up to a claustrophobic level and still the conveyor belt did not deign to move.

Mary wiped her brow with a wet wipe and this seemed to trigger a reaction in the belt as it clunked to life, then set about building up a squeaky rhythm as it limped slowly round the room. Mary watched a brown mud stain pass by her twice before the first bag appeared and then had to wait for this to do two laps of honour before her suitcase came. She struggled to lift it from the carousel and the man in the suit who was walking by with his own bag, leaned over, hoisted it off onto the floor and continued on his way as Mary's 'Thank you,' scurried after him.

'There's nothing to it, the place practically runs itself. Come. It'll do you the world of good.' The email from James had sat read, but uncontemplated when it first arrived. She had been too miserable then to even seriously consider its invite, but that had been in the comfort of her own living room where she could soak in her unhappiness, undisturbed by outside forces. She had closed down her computer, made another cup of tea and sobbed quietly to herself as she squeezed what warmth she could out of the steaming mug that she clutched in both hands.

Shelia Cobbler had seen her coming and had deliberately made a show of crossing to the other side of the road. Sarah Slater had been decidedly uncomfortable talking to her in Tescos and she was almost sure that Amanda Hazell had actually tried to run her over as she crossed the road on her way home.

Once inside, she flung down the bag of groceries, cracking the eggs and splitting the milk bottle. She screamed, only cutting herself short at the thought that Mrs Tindall next door would probably be relishing her distress. She cursed George. This was all his fault. She stared at the gathering pool of milk on the kitchen floor and refusing to cry again, made her mind up about Africa.

'Did you fly well, Mrs Mary?' The young man threw her suitcase into the back of the 4x4 and shoved the piece of paper, which had 'Marry Merskine' written on it, in with the bag. Mary had been tempted to tell the sign bearer that she had and look where it had got her, but as quickly as the humour surfaced it sank again. Besides he would never have understood.

In the cab the young man, who had introduced himself as Caiaphas and who had refused to stop smiling, spoke with a confidence that bordered on cocky. Too familiar, Mary thought, but politely nodded and watched the black tar of the road hurtle beneath the hood of the bonnet. She held tightly on to the handle above the window as Caiaphas negotiated his way through a crowded market that lay on either side of the road about a mile from the airport. The car's horn parted the mass of people and caused panic-stricken hens to flap their feathers frantically at the approaching wheels, before deciding that they may come off second best should they hang around.

Caiaphas seemed unaware of the tension that was growing inside her as he swung the steering wheel from side to side with one hand, while the other flapped nonchalantly outside the window at the obstacles, as if too lazy to really warn them of the imminent danger. A bead of sweat trickled down Mary's back then dived headfirst into the pool that was forming at her trouser waist.

Once clear of the market, they sped up again and the breeze through the window cooled and calmed her enough to make her realise that Caiaphas was looking at her expectantly.

She felt rude asking him to repeat the question, but what else could she do? She was hot, tired and in no mood for conversation. Could he not see that?

'Mr...er...James,' her own use of that manner of referring to someone annoyed her, but she was caught between being too formal and calling him Mr Carling, or encouraging informality by simply referring to her friend as James. Although, god knew, this Caiaphas fellow already seemed too casual. 'Mr James said that he would probably be away for about three months. I am to look after the lodge until he gets back.'

It sounded strange saying it out loud for the first time. 'Look after the lodge.' Toby hadn't even called to discuss it when she had sent the email to inform him of her plans.

'*Okay, mum. Let me know if you need anything.*'

Her son's promise of help in his hastily typed reply was as hollow as her life felt just then and she had prepared for the trip on her own. No further query of how she was doing came from Toby who was too busy to care.

Mary watched a large bird swoop down onto the road ahead to peck at some road kill, then her gaze followed it as it flapped off again, frightened by the car thundering towards it.

'Bwana Afia,' Caiaphas informed her.

'I beg your pardon?'

'Bwana Afia, the health officer.'

Mary stared at Caiaphas who laughed.

'That big bird, we call it Bwana Afia, the health officer, because he cleans up the rubbish off the road.'

The smile was one of acknowledgement and was aimed at trying to stop the conversation. It worked, but left Mary feeling annoyed with herself. The silence in the cab was suddenly unwelcome and she willed Caiaphas to continue talking, but he had given up on this stupid white woman who took no interest in him, his way of life, or his country. She sighed inwardly. What had she become? She hadn't been like this when George was around.

The road curved gently as they made their way down a slight incline towards a dry river bed. Mary cleared her throat and scratched round in her mind for something to say to get Caiaphas talking again. They sped over the bridge that crossed the sandy river and began to climb up the slight slope on the other side.

'Is it much further?' She felt glad of the banal question that fell from her mouth.

'No, not too far now.' His reply was sullen.

Three hours later she woke as they stopped in Kilimbati. Caiaphas grinned as if to say, 'Poor white woman, she cannot cope with our long journeys here,' but all he did say was that he needed to get some supplies before heading up to the lodge.

Mary sat up slightly dazed. She took a moment to orientate herself, then looked round. They were parked under a large tree that had strange purple blossoms. They must be the jacaranda that James spoke of, she thought as her eyes followed the lilac line that meandered down the side of the road. A crude pavement tried to attract customers, but most of the passers-by shunned it to walk on the smoother tar of the road. She watched Caiaphas' back disappear into the dusty building that advertised Coke and swallowed away the dry heat that scratched at her throat.

A cold drink would go down well, but what could she do? She couldn't leave the car as she had no keys to lock it with and she didn't want to risk losing her bags; they may as well represent everything she owned. All her other worldly goods were sitting lonely and isolated in a slightly run down house in England. 'House', not 'home' she thought bitterly, trying to dispel the thirst that threatened to consume her. It had been a home once. There had been good times there. If she just thought hard enough she would remember them, but she hadn't had the energy for a good while now to be up to that task.

A tap at the window snatched her away from her self-pity and replaced it with shock as a severely deformed face pleaded for small change. One eye was iced over while the other tried to wriggle out of its socket as it sought out the perfect expression of helplessness. A large scar divided the nose and split the lip that was drawn back to reveal a single tooth that sat like a lonely gravestone on the red, raw bottom gum. The man's tongue lolled slightly as he tried, unsuccessfully, to stem the tide of spittle that broke cover and cascaded down his chin, creating a shiny path in the dust that caked not only his face, but his whole being. It hung as a suspended strand before finally snapping and plummeting to the ground.

It took Mary an instant to take in the grotesqueness of the man, another beat for her face to express disgust and far too long, she felt, to hide her feelings. She shook her head quickly to indicate that she had nothing to give him and then stared resolutely out the front window, her heartbeat, kick started by her fright at seeing the man, showing no signs of slowing.

The window was tapped again and she turned her head further away.

I've got nothing to give him, honestly, I haven't had a chance to get any local currency.

She felt her cheeks burn at how lame her excuse sounded, and then slowly hardened her mind, calmed her heart and shut the tapping that continued on the window out of her thoughts. *Where the hell is Caiaphas? Why is he taking so long?*

There were looks now from those passing by, bemused grins and one or two fingers pointing as jovial voices laughed at her discomfort. It had been a mistake to come. Why had she agreed? She should have stayed at home where at least she was familiar with the embarrassments and jibes she had had to cope with there.

The rear door of the vehicle opened, allowing a snatch of cool air in. Mary turned and watched Caiaphas squash a large cardboard box between her bags. He shut the door, dug in his pocket and handed over what Mary presumed were a few coins to the hideous man who slurred a word and gave a crooked hand salute before limping away.

She expected Caiaphas to be judgemental of her lack of charity and braced herself for a look, or even worse, a word, but none came. He just jumped into the front seat and cheerfully announced that they could now head up to the lodge.

The air cooled noticeably as the car moved smoothly up the side of the mountain towards the lodge. Mary turned her thoughts to what was going to be home for the next few months and, while taking in the beauty of the scenery, she couldn't help wondering what other nasty surprises lay in store for her there.

TWO

'You should have seen her face, it was like she had looked up and seen a lion,' Caiaphas broke off and pulled an exaggerated face of fear.

Esther hid her smile behind the dish towel she was holding, but that failed to stifle the noise of her joyful laughter. Her eyes, laughing quietly at Caiaphas' tales of the white woman, now watered slightly and her fresh, young face glowed.

'Ai, Caiaphas, you are terrible,' she tried to bring her laughter under control, but it was set off again as Caiaphas continued his story.

'Old Man Mawenzi was just standing knocking on the window, like he always does.' He distorted his face and mouth as best he could to imitate the disfiguration that had startled Mary earlier, and then hobbled around begging from the wood stove and the large basin.

Esther doubled over laughing now, holding on to the back of a wooden chair for support.

'Stop it, Caiaphas,' she chided.

The imitator knocked hopefully on an imaginary car window, then sucked heavily on his spit, lolled his tongue for an extra laugh, which he got, then morphed into a frightened white woman again, hands shaking next to his face, eyes wide. He started to flap a nervous hand at the grotesque beggar then slowly stopped as he realised that he had lost his audience.

Esther was furiously wiping a clean plate with her dish towel, her eyes downcast, firmly fixed on the object of her labour.

Caiaphas took a moment to recover, then flicked his hand again and muttered, 'These flies!' Without turning, he picked up the broom that was nearby and began to swipe at the spotless floor.

The shadow in the doorway waited a few seconds before stepping slowly into the kitchen. Beneath the woolly, white hair, there was a brown-walnut wrinkled face with a potato nose and rheumy eyes that took in all that was happening. The mouth was set in an emotionless line.

Esther finished with her dish and moved on to those by the sink while Caiaphas watched out of the corner of his eye as the figure moved toward the large table in the centre of the room. It glanced round slowly, then picked up a sharp kitchen knife.

Caiaphas took this opportunity to scuttle off. He didn't like being around Solomon.

The old man reached down the side of the table into the vegetable rack that stood there and handled a few onions before selecting one that felt right to the touch. He began to chop with slow deliberate strokes, the clunk of the knife on the chopping board brought a maudlin march beat to the otherwise soundless kitchen and it woke the baby that lay in a cardboard box in a corner of the room. It gurgled and smacked its lips, but did not get the attention of the old man who, finishing with the onions, scooped them into a bowl and picked up his next ingredient.

Esther put her dishes down and picked up the baby while loosening her blouse in one easy movement. She unhooked her bra with a free hand and brought the child up to the surprisingly dark nipple that contrasted sharply with the pale brown skin. Still feeding the child, she moved gracefully across the room and began to fetch spices, meat and vegetables which she placed in front of the old man whose eyes never glanced up at the youthful breasts on display.

'Salt.' The word came strong and clear and Esther moved swiftly to get the condiment for the cook, before returning to polish the clean plates.

The old man continued to work silently with slow deliberate movements, picking up a potato here, placing a carrot with extreme care and neatness on the table. Between each process, he would lean back slightly in his chair, cast his eyes over what lay in front of him, as if deciding what to do next, before leaning forward again to carry out the process he had decided on.

Esther finished feeding and placed the contented child back into the cardboard box, neatened herself up and went to see if the new mistress was in need of anything.

They're laughing at me. Mary sipped at the gin the young girl had brought before disappearing back into the kitchen from where her stifled giggles had soon emanated. Had she not felt that the mirth was directed at her, Mary would have thought that the laugher was warm and infectious, but she didn't even raise a smile, preferring to seek comfort from the glass.

The lodge was really a converted house, set in a forest that grew on the side of the mountain. Further up, near the plateau, the fancy tourist hotel attracted most of the visitors to the area, but those few who liked to get off the beaten track and had stumbled across the rudimentary website that James had set up and then neglected, would come and spend a night or two. Most would go hiking, or perhaps horse riding.

'There are some lovely trails,' James had told her in his numerous emails.

Her room at the back of the house, was comfortable if a little small. The shower had been lukewarm, but refreshing and the afternoon coffee she had taken out on the lawn, a well-cared for square cut out of the wild forest that lay beyond it, was rich and earthy. She had ventured out for a short walk, followed nonchalantly by Rex, the large, dour-faced mastiff that belonged more to the lodge than the lodge's owner. Despite Rex's seeming lack of interest in her wellbeing, Mary felt safer hearing him snuffling in the undergrowth. She was certain that, should she come under attack from man or beast in this hostile land, Rex would be duty bound to protect her. She did not venture too far from the lodge, the unfamiliarity of her surroundings and concern about getting lost, kept her on the path and the walk brief and thankfully, free of attack.

The young woman, Esther if she recalled the name correctly, had seemed kind. Her friendly smile and fussing, one could almost use the word mothering, around Mary, ensuring she was comfortable, had somewhat soothed her and she began to relax as she sipped on her gin. The laughter from the kitchen though was unsettling and when it had stopped abruptly as it had the ensuing silence was even more unnerving, so much so that she nearly jumped when Caiaphas came in, his arms loaded with firewood. The smile on his face did not hold the scorn she expected to see there.

'I will light the fire.'

Mary wondered if he was asking or telling, but he immediately busied himself laying the wood, so she assumed the latter. She watched the young man's back as he set about his task and noticed that, despite his slender appearance, Caiaphas was quite muscular and a ripple ran across the tight t-shirt as he hoisted a pile of wood into the grate and her mind went back to George in front of the fireplace. He had been quite well built back then, but not like Caiaphas.

She wanted to be back there in that small room with her young George when he would light the fire and come and hold her in his arms on their small settee. She had felt so safe and comfortable there. Those were the early days of their marriage, when things, despite the lack of income, were good.

Caiaphas stood up, his movement shattering her reverie.

'It is good?' he asked, nodding at the fire. A cheeky grin bubbled up to his eyes and the thought crossed Mary's mind that he had somehow booby trapped the fire to explode or something because of the look, but she resolved to ignore it and thinking herself foolish, just nodded her thanks.

'Do you need anything else? Another drink?' The smile did not move.

'No. No thank you. I'm fine.' The words came out more curtly than they had left her mind.

He stood for a second, draining the smile, then nodded, almost to himself, his eyes saying, 'No good being friendly here. That's all the thanks you'll get.' But before he could reveal too much of his feelings, he turned and moved off leaving Mary drenched in guilt.

She wanted to call him back, atone for her rudeness, but the apology stuck in her throat, so she swallowed it down with the last mouthful of gin and regretted not having asked for another one.

Warm smells rose up from the stove, but the expression on the old man's face remained cold. Caiaphas avoided his stare and added the remains of the firewood to a small pile in the corner near the aromas and hurried out again, his glance brushing gently against Esther's.

Outside, he moved quickly away from the house and stopped in a small clearing a short distance away. The light had faded and the night sky was strewn with glitter. The air cool, but not uncomfortable.

He dug in his pocket and pulled out a flattened packet of cigarettes, drew one out and lit it. He expelled the first lung full slowly, ridding himself of the anger that had built up inside him. He turned and glared back at the house, the dull light from the hurricane lamps flickered in the windows. He sucked hard on the cigarette again, blew out his rage and kicked at the undergrowth.

The forest hissed and made him turn. In the gloom a strange figure limped, one useless leg sliding through the leaves, trying to catch up with the other. A sucking sound emanated from its mouth and Caiaphas put out his cigarette. He had started too early. Old Man Mawenzi's features filled in the silhouette. He nodded at Caiaphas who returned the greeting and then held out the packet of smokes. The old man took one and stuck it in the side of his mouth, away from the hare lip. Caiaphas lit up for the old man, then for himself and the two men stood silently in the dark, the tips of their cigarettes glowing red dots.

A time passed in silence except for the slight sucking sounds. At length, Caiaphas dropped his cigarette butt onto the path and carefully extinguished it. Old Man Mawenzi took a final drag and threw the butt down where Caiaphas obliged with a stamp and twist of the sole of his shoe. The old man nodded then continued on his shuffle-slide journey.

No words had passed between the two, but a close observer would have seen that this meeting was a regular occurrence. The cigarette was expected, the offer of it was pre-programmed. The relaxed way the men stood silently, neither expecting conversation, the ritual of extinguishing the cigarettes, all this occurred in a kind of rehearsed dance where each move had been finely choreographed.

Caiaphas watched the old man limp away, then slowly turned back to the lodge. The fire of frustration had died in his eyes, perhaps calmed by seeing the troubled old man and being reminded that his woes were nothing compared to the battles his dance partner faced daily.

By the time he returned to the kitchen, his eyes were once again bright with the good humour he showed to the world that lay within those four walls.

'Madam, dinner will be served in five minutes.'

The voice startled Mary from her reading. The light from the lamp wasn't really good enough to see by, but there was nothing else to do. Why hadn't James got the place electrified?

There are solar chargers for things like mobile phones and iPods, his note had said, *but other than that, it's all old school.* He always did like to use the hip language of the youth.

The old man in the darkened doorway did not wait for a reply before turning back into the kitchen. Mary finished the page she was reading, placed the bookmark and tried to finish the gin that she had forgotten that she had already finished, putting the empty glass to her lips and getting a drop when she expected a sip.

'Madam, dinner is served.'

'That was never five minutes,' she murmured under her breath and followed the man whom she guessed from James' email, was Solomon, the cook. He had referred to him as the chef, but her mind did the necessary adjustments, believing her friend to be a little bit delusional.

'You are Solomon?' She felt a need to say something as the old man guided her into a chair at a large dining room table. There was a place set for one with starter and main cutlery as well as a fork and spoon for dessert. She smiled quietly to herself as Solomon confirmed in one, almost grunted word, that yes, he was the one who went by that name, before he returned to the kitchen.

Esther came through immediately and asked if she wanted to have some wine.

'Yes, please.' She smiled warmly, partly because she was feeling a bond with the only other woman in the lodge, and partly from the strange contrast between what she had expected for dinner and what seemed to be occurring.

'All this fuss and ceremony,' she thought as Esther expertly poured a mouthful of wine for her to taste, 'and they are probably going to serve chicken and chips.'

She sniffed the wine, trying to play along, pretending to appreciate its nose and whatever else those wine connoisseurs did, before nodding sagely that this was a good vintage.

Her play was, however, lost on Esther who poured the glass before disappearing.

'Not bad, actually,' Mary thought as she studied the bottle. 'South African. I suppose that is all they can get here.'

Solomon returned with Esther, the latter bearing a plate that she placed neatly in front of Mary.

'Roasted carrots with goats cheese and pomegranate, seasoned with cumin seeds and orange juice,' Solomon informed her. Although accented, his English was excellent and he separated each word to allow the clearness of its meaning to be savoured and digested. His voice was deep, but not gratingly so.

Before Mary could register her surprise, the two servants had already left the room. She poked at the food with a fork before deciding that it was real and, with a disbelieving shake of the head, she began to eat. The flavours were superb. It was not just the contrast of the fruity pomegranate seeds with the tangy cheese and the sturdy undertones of the carrots and cumin that pleased, but also the ingredients tasted fresh and alive.

The wine, which she sipped while she ate, gained appreciation as it wound itself around the taste of the food.

It was with some regret that Mary cleaned off her plate. She would have liked the experience to have lasted longer as, for the first time since landing, she felt, not happy, that would be too strong a word, contented seemed better. The fatigue of travel had all but melted away.

Her disappointment at finishing the starter lasted only a few minutes before Esther returned to clear away, then was back again with a tray laden with dishes.

'That was delicious, Esther,' she smiled at the young girl who nodded as she moved the dishes from the tray to the table then, as if a thought had just struck her, she looked urgently into Mary's eyes.

'Do not say anything to Solomon. He hates compliments,' she whispered and turned quickly to see if the object of her disclosure was standing in the doorway.

He appeared a moment later and Esther scurried off.

'For the main course tonight, we have de-boned chicken drumsticks baked in a white wine sauce and stuffed with lemongrass and herbs. The veg-e-tay-bills,' he stretched the word out and moved his hand from above the chicken dish, 'are rosemary and celeriac mash,' indicating the dish that had mounds of creamed potato piped into gentle twirls like the soft serve ice cream that she and George would have every day at the seaside.

'Green beans,' Solomon's voice moved Mary's eyes to the next dish, 'par-boiled in a light vinegar sauce, then briefly fried with garlic. And cauliflower au gratin.'

He bowed and left a confused Mary still puzzling over Esther's advice and marvelling at the spread of food before her.

She took a minute or two before she could bring herself to disturb the beautifully laid out potato mash, but was soon tucking in with great pleasure.

Dessert was an apricot flan with cashew nuts and homemade custard.

Solomon did not appear again after announcing that delectable dish, but Esther cleared the dishes away and, after checking with Mary what she wanted, brought a French Press of rich smelling coffee.

'It's locally grown,' the young girl said, noticeably more relaxed. Her smile was brighter and she lingered a little bit longer after bringing in the coffee than she had with the earlier courses.

'There is a small farm on the other side of the mountain where they grow it,' she added before cleaning away the remaining dishes on the table.

By now, Mary was feeling mellow. The gin and couple of glasses of wine, combined with the delicious meal, were settling her mind down as she adjusted to her new environment.

'That was sweet of them to prepare a meal like that to welcome me,' she thought.

She was sure that they had been instructed by James to do so, he had always been good at little details like that. Maybe it won't be so bad here after all, although that Solomon character is a bit creepy, and Caiaphas too familiar. Esther was nice, when she came out of her shell.

'Do you need anything else tonight, madam?'

Her thoughts conjured up the young woman.

'No. Thanks very much, Esther. Do I need to lock up or anything like that?'

'No, madam. Caiaphas will come round a bit later and check that everything is locked. You do have the keys anyway if you need them?'

Mary nodded.

'Do you need me to show you how to turn the lamps off?'

'Yes please.'

In the lounge, Esther gave a quick lesson in lighting and extinguishing the lamps. She was just about to take her leave when Mary plucked up the courage.

'Why does Solomon not like compliments?'

The girl stopped and looked round nervously, as if expecting to see the old chef standing there. When satisfied that he was not, she shrugged her shoulders and said, 'I do not know the ways of old men.'

With that she gave a slight bow and wished Mary goodnight before scurrying off into the dark that lay beyond the reach of the dim light. Mary stood watching her go, then picking up the lamp, moved quickly through to the bedroom, shaking her head slightly at the strange phenomenon that was Solomon. Everything about him was disquieting.

THREE

African dreams are different to those dreamt in Europe. African ones come gently on the breeze and settle down to visit you like an old friend. They are not the rushed, designed to thrill or frighten kind of European dreams. They do not hit you with the intensity of those that occur in faster paced societies.

This does not mean that they are any less vivid. In fact, they can be some of the most realistic dreams you can have. They burrow into your spirit and cannot be easily shaken.

Perhaps it is because the continent was the cradle of mankind that ancestors make their way back there, a return to their roots and to come full circle. Here they can roam freely on the open plains, pausing to flit in and out of men's dreams.

Mary did not dream of George. If asked before she went to sleep who would occupy her unconscious mind, she would have guessed her husband. He had been so prominent in her thoughts throughout the day that it seemed obvious that he would get airtime. But he did not come.

The man who did come had kind eyes set in a stern face. He had used his face for business and his eyes for family. Below his eyes an imposing, some might say beak-like, nose protruded from which flowed a dark stream of moustache that waterfalled symmetrically over the edges of his upper lip and threatened to drip down his chin. A pipe was clenched between his teeth and the puff of smoke that emanated from it drenched his clothes in a rich, warm and slightly fruity funk. He wore a tweed jacket, shirt and a tie that was never quite pulled up totally, but never looked sloppy. However, the most remarkable thing about him, was that he was not George.

Mary eased herself slowly out of her sleep and whispered the word 'daddy' before she opened her eyes and blinked, trying to work out where she was. It was still gloomy outside as the sun began to clear away the haze of night. The air was fresh and, from what Mary could tell, quite cool.

As the realisation of her surroundings dawned, so the idea that her father was still alive left with a slightly embarrassed smile for having disturbed her. Mary sighed and sat up in the bed, trying to establish what had brought on the dream of her father, but her contemplation was cut short by a knock at the door, followed by Esther entering, bearing a tray loaded with a teapot, a fine china cup and a selection of tea bags.

'Good morning, madam,' her smile saying only she was privy to the secret of how she knew that Mary was awake. She placed the tray on a small table next to the bed.

'I hope you slept well?'

Mary could not help wondering if James got the same service every morning, and if so, did he get more than a cup of tea?

To hide the blushes that arose from this thought that had taken her by surprise, she turned over to fumble for her glasses and gave a mumbled answer.

'If you need anything else, please call,' Esther said, leaving the room and shutting the door quietly behind her.

For a while Mary lay on her back, staring at nothing in particular. Her sudden thought of James and Esther having 'extracurricular activities' as George used to refer to it, had stirred up strange feelings inside her that did not sit too comfortably. She was not sure if it was the thought itself, or the fact that she had actually thought it that disturbed her the most. She had always been an obedient, if somewhat disinterested partner in that department, finding it more of a chore than a pleasure.

Outside the window, a bird began to chirp and Mary shook off her thoughts and began to pour the tea.

For all there being no electricity, Mary was pleasantly surprised at the warmth of the water in the shower, but was less pleased by the sizeable gecko she had had to chase out of the bathroom before she felt enough at ease to disrobe.

Solar panels and, if the sun don't shine, then Caiaphas will stoke up a fire under the water tank. James seemed to have thought of everything.

The air was still cool when she emerged from her ablutions, but her polo neck jumper kept the warmth of the shower close to her skin. She picked up the tray and started to walk through to the kitchen, but was stopped in the passage by Esther.

'Sorry, Madam, you should have left the tray,' she said, looking away, but still easing Mary of her burden.

'It's no problem,' Mary answered brightly, the effects of the evening meal still lingering in her mood.

Esther nodded with a look that said it was a problem, but Mary was the boss and she was just agreeing to keep the peace.

She turned and moved quickly down the passage, leaving Mary staring after her and taking a second or two before following.

The kitchen door was closed by the time Mary caught up and she hesitated outside, wondering if she dared enter. Would she give further offence to Esther, although she still struggled to see how the simple act of helping someone with their chores should have evoked such a reaction? Or would she be confronted by the moody Solomon, or worse yet, the impudent Caiaphas?

She lifted a confident hand to push the door open, thinking that she was the boss, she shouldn't have to feel like this, but it faltered at the last second and she found Solomon staring into the flat of her palm.

He stood stony faced, waiting for her to regain her composure before announcing in his measured tones that, 'Breakfast will be served on the lawn in five minutes. Could madam please make her way there?'

Once, long ago, when she was still a schoolgirl, the headmistress had ordered her to go and wait in her office for daring to try and enter the staff room without knocking.

The breeze was light and slightly cool, but the sun was strong enough to prevent it being uncomfortable. *It's not too hot up at the lodge*, James had written, *usually quite pleasant. It's only when you have to go into town that you feel the heat.*

Mary tried to relax, sitting at the neat table that had been laid in the middle of the lawn. Clips held the table cloth, a colourful African print, in place and the napkin was weighed down by a dark, heavy (ebony perhaps?) carved elephant.

She was just about to relax and smile at the absurdity of her surroundings when Esther appeared to enquire if she would like tea or coffee and how would she like her eggs and did she want bacon and sausage and tomato and how many slices of toast and please help yourself to fruit salad and cereal. The last comment was accompanied by Esther removing the lace cloth, wind proofed by bright beads sewn into the corners, from the dish that contained a colourful medley of fruit.

Mary watched the retreating figure for a moment, wondering when James would appear and tell her it was all a big joke and that she would not be getting this treatment every day, but a little part of her was saying that this was business as usual and she wasn't sure if she liked this idea.

'We have guests tonight,' Esther was much more relaxed as she brought Mary her morning cup of tea. The lounge was brightly lit by the sun and a deep blue sky hovered beyond the net curtain that covered the large window looking out over the lawn.

Mary put down her copy of *Lady Chatterley's Lover*, wondering briefly if that title held any significance to the young girl.

'Oh, I see. Um...What do I need to do?'

Nothing, James' note had said.

'Well, Mr James likes to be here to greet the guests and show them around.'

'Anything else?' There was nowhere she could go, was there?

'Mr James does like to inspect the room once I have made it up.' But he never finds anything wrong, so you will be wasting your time doing it, the tone seemed to add.

Mary nodded. 'Let me know when the room is ready then.' She reached to pick up her book and Esther turned to commence her duties.

'Esther?' Lady Chatterley could admire the gamekeeper, Mellors, a little longer.

'Yes ma'am?'

Should she ask the question?

'Where did Solomon learn to cook like that?' It didn't sound too condescending did it? It didn't sound like, 'How can an old black man in the middle of Africa have possibly learnt to cook as well as this?' did it? Maybe she should have joined Lady Chatterley in a spot of man watching, rather than be asking impertinent questions.

'He is an old man, he has learnt lots,' Esther replied her face showing no emotion. Then, after waiting a second to see if there were any further questions from the strange white woman, set off to attend to her chores.

'That was not an answer!' Mary screamed silently after her.

She took a moment to recompose herself and then picked up her tea. Thoughts of George were beginning to filter into her mind, so she drank quickly and snatched up her book, hoping to seek refuge there, but the spectre of Clifford Chatterley threatened to bring back unwanted memories. What a stupid book to have brought with. She managed to read a page before putting it down with a sigh and finished her tea. 'The days here are going to be long', she thought.

The kitchen was bright as Esther returned to it. Solomon, having finished his work of cooking, would not be seen again till dinner time and Caiaphas had been dispatched down the mountain for provisions for the evening guests. It was a time that Esther enjoyed, even when Mr James had been around, he never bothered her in the kitchen and, with the young one now, she could at least have a little time with her son before cleaning the breakfast dishes.

She picked him out of his cardboard box crib and lifted him up in the air before bringing him back down to land a playful raspberry on his naked stomach. The child giggled and threw its chubby arms up, begging her to do it again, and Esther repeated the process. It was on the third lift that she realised that she had an audience and turned to the door.

'Don't stop on my account,' was what Mary later wished she had said. The obvious delight the little child took in such a simple pleasure was a salve to her troubled soul, but, 'May I have some more tea, please,' were the words that came out of her mouth instead.

She sat like a wicked step-mother cursing her stupid mouth for not saying the right thing. She didn't even want the tea now, it was poisoned by her stupidity, but she drank despite the taste of resentment bringing a bitter tang to the brew. The clatter of dishes also accused her of denying the child a few more moments of pleasure.

Twice she stood up to go back and apologise, to put things right. But she couldn't bring herself to do so. The discordant dish symphony stopped and shortly afterwards, Esther appeared.

'Does madam want anything else?' The smile on her lips did not reach her eyes and she had swept up the empty tea cup before Mary even had a chance to lift it to save Esther the small task of bending down slightly. The voice accused her of what she was already feeling guilty of.

'Er...no. Thanks...'

'Coooeeee!' A shrill cry diverted her attention to the front door of the lodge where a slim woman in tight fitting jeans and a loose white blouse stood removing a pair of riding gloves.

'You must be Mary.'

Her face was pretty, although her cheeks were flushed from exertion and her nose seemed slightly too red, displaying early signs of a love of the bottle. The mop of silver blonde hair couldn't decide if it was spending too much time in the sun, or merely aging.

'James said I should look in on you. Everything okay?'

Mary glanced briefly at Esther as she disappeared into the kitchen, then at the stranger who seemed more interested in removing her back pack than Mary's answer if she bothered to give one.

'Fine, er, Joyce?'

'Oh, so he did remember to tell you about us. He can be so forgetful sometimes.' Joyce didn't look up from the bag which she was now fumbling to open.

'No. James said that you...'

'...Recharged his battery.' Joyce giggled as she took a laptop out of her bag and handed it over to Mary.

'Well, he never said it quite like that,' Mary said after a pause and before taking the machine.

Uninvited, Joyce threw herself down in Mary's chair, picked up the copy of *Lady Chatterley*, thumbed through a few pages, raised an eyebrow at Mary, then threw the book carelessly aside and said, 'No, I suppose he wouldn't. Our James is frightfully staid,' and then added almost to herself, 'and more's the pity.' Her public schoolgirl accent seemed to become more pronounced as she spoke of James. 'He ought to get the place electrified. There is no reason why he hasn't, you know.'

Mary sat herself down on the large sofa, missing the support-ing arms of the single chair which Joyce was busy wriggling in to till she sat sideways with her riding boot clad legs dangling over the side. She was staring at Mary now, studying her in her unease.

'So, what are you running away from then?'

'I beg your pardon?'

'What are you running away from? All James' women are running away from something.'

'I'm not one of James' women,' Mary protested, wondering who the others were and surprising herself with a slight pang of jealousy.

'Esther! Juice!' Joyce called through to the kitchen then looked back at Mary. 'Nah!' She dismissed Mary's protest with a wave of her hand. 'What is it? Divorce? Unrequited love? Didn't get that promotion?' She watched Mary for a reaction.

'Your old man got caught downloading kiddie porn from the Internet and is busy doing time?' She went on after a pause and started to look less sure of herself, then suddenly sat up, swing-ing her legs on to the floor with a loud clunk.

'Oh my god, you're not pregnant, are you?'

By now Mary had recovered from the onslaught and was beginning to feel angry at this prying. She decided to play along and glance coyly away at the latest suggestion.

Joyce stared at her, not quite sure whether to believe it or not. Mary could almost see the question forming in this inquisitive mind.

'Who's the father then?'

That was not quite what Mary expected, she had thought that there would be some comment about her age. She shook her head to indicate that she would not divulge.

'Let me see. A toy boy? No? Best friend's hubby? No?' The game was back on. 'A one night stand that you met down the pub and who looked ugly next to you in bed the morning after, but you could swear he was dead handsome when you took him home, but you had too much of a headache to really care and didn't think you needed the pill anymore anyway?'

Mary was enjoying the game now and struggled to keep her face blank.

'No? Where is my juice? Esther!' She stood up now and began pacing the room.

'You weren't raped were you,' her eyes begged Mary to nod; that would be a juicy one.

Mary almost considered nodding, but shook her head, hoping the split second hesitation had not been detected, but Joyce was too excited now to notice.

'What then? Esther!' Her voice got shriller each time she yelled the young woman's name. 'Your best friend's son?' It was a desperate and outrageous guess, but Mary decided that this was the one and looked away with, what she hoped, was an expression of shame.

'Oh. My. God.'

Joyce's staccato sentence was accompanied by the crash of a glass of juice on the floor and both women turned to Esther who stood with an empty tray in her hand, staring straight at Mary.

'Esther!' Joyce jumped in before Mary could deny the story. 'Go get another juice, then come and clear up that mess. You can't get the help these days.' She clicked her tongue and shook her head while Esther scurried back to the kitchen.

'Oh my god, Mary. That's...that's...' She shook her head, hoping to catch the word she was looking for, but quickly gave Mary a warning look to indicate that Esther was back with a new drink.

After placing the drink on a carved wooden coaster, Esther left, holding the tray to her breast and giving Mary a sidelong glance.

Joyce grabbed the juice and downed it in a few gulps, then looked at her watch, then at Mary.

'I really must be going,' she was almost at the door, 'but you will have dinner with us tonight.' It wasn't a request.

'I can't, we have guests,' Mary was rising, trying to catch up, trying to blurt out that she wasn't pregnant, but Joyce was bustling out as quickly as she had arrived.

'Oh yes, silly me. The honeymooners. They're out riding at the farm, then heading over to you this evening. Don't worry, I won't say a word.' Joyce misread the panic on Mary's face as she hoisted herself into the saddle of a grey mare that stood docilely round the side of the house. She settled herself, grabbed the reins, then paused.

'You *will* come for dinner tomorrow night. Caiaphas can run you over to the farm.' She smiled, then raced off, presumably to blurt out the false news to Ray, the husband whom James had mentioned in his notes.

Mary stood staring down the path at the fading horse and rider, then plucked up the courage to go back into the house.

The teller's eyes shone brightly while those of the hearer were wide with surprise. Caiaphas shook his head and clicked his tongue as if these actions would somehow change the news he had just heard into something believable.

'With her friend's son? That is not right. She is worse than the others. Are you sure?'

Esther nodded. 'That's what she told Mrs Joyce. I was standing by the door with her juice, listening.' She pointed at the spot where she had dropped the tray.

Caiaphas shook his head again, then unpacked some more of the shopping.

'No wonder Mr James didn't even want to be here. Where is she now?'

'She has gone for a walk.'

'Is it safe for her to be out walking? European women are not as strong as African women. They need lots of rest when they are pregnant. You must let Mama Shiwa know that her services may be required.'

'Don't be silly Caiaphas, she won't want the help of an African woman. She will go to the city when her time comes and have her baby in the clean European hospital there.'

'But you never know,' Caiaphas took a six pack of bottled water out of the box on the work surface and slung it on his shoulder before taking it into the pantry. 'When your time came, we had to run and call Mama Shiwa, you were too busy doing the dishes to even notice your birth pains. I remember Mr James was in such a panic,' his laugh floated back from the small room, slightly muffled by the stores it held. 'That's why he's not here. He doesn't want to have to see child birth again, especially not if it is Mrs Mary, she will...'

He emerged from the little room to see Esther bustling round the sink and he knew that the old man would be in the doorway. He shrugged his shoulders, more to himself, and hurried out the room. So what if Solomon knew. He wouldn't say anything.

The old man moved slowly into the room, took up his usual seat, and surveyed the potential ingredients for dinner. He seemed to take slightly longer than usual to select an item, as if he were changing the menu he had in his head when he walked in. Twice he reached for something, only to lower his hand and consider before picking something else.

Esther kept her back to him, responding only to the demands for ingredients that he would occasionally growl. He seemed to be more abrupt than usual.

The young couple who arrived in the late afternoon had a happy glow about them that Mary tried to take warmth from, but her unhappiness had taken too strong a hold on her. And just to add insult to injury, they were French. Mary had never quite understood why, as an English person, she was required to hate the French. She had not met many and those whom she had were always friendly and not one of them had smelt of onions and garlic. But it had been drummed into her from a young age that the French were horrible and they smelled. This had always made her ill at ease around French people as she couldn't help feeling that this approach was racist. But, being English, she was duty bound to obey this age old tradition. Of course she had never said anything, especially not to George who, despite all his genuine warmth and affection for most humans, seemed to counter balance this goodwill with a particularly vulgar dislike of the French. She wondered how George would feel if he knew that she was fraternising with the enemy, but he was no longer there to pass judgement and she was glad of that at this moment.

She sat in the comfortable chair and watched the young couple on the sofa as they gushed in their stilted accented English about what they had seen. They were comfortable with each other, their bodies seeming to slot together naturally. It had never been like that with her and George. Physical contact had always seemed formal with him, but they had loved in that way. Different strokes, Mary told herself, and she meant it. She could love George without that clingy, touchy, feely love that some couples seemed to thrive on. And perhaps that was why their marriage had lasted longer than most of her friends' had. She had watched Karen and Ben's marriage shrivel up and die as the novelty of the excitement and passion of pawing at each other had slowly rotted and Ben found fresh pawing patches while Karen, who had been Mary's maid of honour two months after she and Ben had tied the knot, was left embittered; a term she believed meant hanging around the kitchen of your pre-marital best friend, drinking her wine and sprouting forth on the evils of men and marriage while your best-friend-in-law would sneak in to make a cup of tea and sneak out again to the sound of 'present company excluded of course.'

He never complained about Karen's visits, or showed any kind of concern that his wife's mind may be poisoned. He believed and trusted in their love, almost to the point of smugness and it was that, rather than the poisoned bile of Karen that rubbed off on Mary, so that she loved her man even more whenever Karen would make her way down the garden path with the hint of a slurring in her goodnight and a slight wobble to her walk. It never crossed Mary's mind that her friend might be turning into an alcoholic, at least not until the night Karen hurled an empty wine bottle across the kitchen, narrowly missing George who had come in to make his late evening brew.

Mary was mortified, Karen embarrassed. But George, he just calmly picked up the pieces of glass, cleared away the mess and made tea for all three of them, then left to return to the crossword that he would struggle over most evenings. The shock of her attack left Karen weepy and bemoaning not having found herself a man like George. Mary walked Karen home that night, mildly amused that her husband had gone from 'boring George' to 'I want one of those' in just under seven years.

Karen's visits became less frequent and more sober. Then she found herself a new Ben and Mary hardly saw her again.

'Ladies and gentlemen, dinner will be served in five minutes.' Solomon broke into her thoughts and she nodded in agreement to something the young Frenchman had been saying.

About two minutes later, Solomon informed them in his official manner that dinner was served and they made their way through to the small dining room. Mary knew what to expect and enjoyed watching the growing delight on the guests' faces as the wine was followed by the starter, then the main. As with the previous evening, each course was presented in detail by Solomon.

'This eez amazing. The meat eez cooked to perfection and so tender. And the flavours, mon amie, are just superb, the way they blend,' the Frenchman gushed and continued to do so till his wife smiled and shrugged.

'You must excuse Jean-Jacques, you see 'e eez a chef at 'is own restaurant in Paris.' The woman leaned over to Mary and half whispered, ''E 'as a Michelin star,' then leaned back again, 'Food eez very close to 'is 'eart.'

'And you could get a job in my restaurant any day, Mary,' Jean-Jacques added.

'Oh, no. I'm not the chef, Solomon, the man who announced dinner. He did all of this.'

Jean-Jacques sat back in his chair. 'Ze old man? It eez amazing. 'E could come and work for me any time.'

The conversation was interrupted by Esther who came in to clear away the dishes. Once she had left the room, Mary turned to her guests.

'You cannot compliment Solomon on his cooking.'

They looked puzzled and she shrugged.

'Apparently he does not like to be complimented,' she kept her voice low, expecting the old man to suddenly appear.

'But why not?'

'I don't know,' Mary paused, then added, 'he is an old man and I do not know the ways of old men.'

She could see that Esther's answer when she had asked the same question, did not really satisfy, but had a strange sort of African mysticism about it that one felt obliged not to question.

The couple nodded, just as Mary had nodded to Esther.

It was during dessert that Jean-Jacques, young love sparkling in his eyes, turned to his wife and said, 'Mon Cherie, when you are pregnant with our first child, I will make you a dinner like we 'ave 'ad tonight, this meal has all ze nutrients a pregnant woman needs. Mary are you okay?'

He reached over to pat her on the back while she spluttered and felt the red wine that she had choked on, start to trickle out her nose.

'He's going to work in Paris.'

'That cannot be,' Caiaphas shook his head.

'I heard the young man say so. He owns a restaurant there.'

Caiaphas shook his head again. 'But he cannot go.'

'Why not? He will make lots of money there. Real money. The young man said.'

'He won't go. He is an old man, too old to go travelling.'

'We'll see,' Esther sounded too confident for her to be wrong, but Caiaphas shrugged, hoping to break the spell of the prophecy. He didn't like the idea. Even if Solomon wasn't his most favourite person, something felt wrong about him being 'stolen' from the lodge.

Old Man Mawenzi was already waiting when he got to their usual spot. He offered the cigarette and then lit up for both of them. For the first time in a long while, he wanted to speak, to break the rules of the dance, but he knew he couldn't. Even if he were allowed to speak, Solomon leaving to go to Europe was not something he would have felt able to express. Old Man Mawenzi, had grown up as Solomon's best friend. Even today, everyone was sure that some of the old chef's wages made their way into Old Man Mawenzi's pocket. If Solomon were to leave, what would happen to Mawenzi? Maybe there would be money coming from Europe but, Caiaphas mused, that would not be enough to compensate for the loss of a friend, not in Old Man Mawenzi's case.

There was a bond, a deep bond, between the two men. It tied them together, tied them to the village and the continent. A bond that, if broken, would cause major consternation to the deformed man who sucked obliviously on his cigarette.

Caiaphas knew that Old Man Mawenzi would eventually hear the news, but he refused to play the role of the media. He looked off at the wavering lights of the house, trying to act casual and as if nothing was wrong. The cigarettes grew shorter till Caiaphas ended the dance and stomped out the two butts before heading back to the house, leaving the old man to shuffle off in his own time.

Mary had sensed, rather than known something was up with George. She liked to tell herself that she had seen the signs and knew that something was coming, but it hadn't really been like that. She was aware of her growing irritation with him and his seemingly shortening temper, till they were almost constantly fighting. She had started to consider divorce, but didn't really know how to go about it, or even how to find a divorce lawyer. She could have asked some of her divorced friends but was too embarrassed to admit there were problems in her 'perfect' marriage. Besides, George handled all that sort of thing. She could hardly go to him and say, 'George, I want you to get me the best divorce lawyer you can find.'

Strangely, the mood swings and tempers were coupled with a heightened sexual appetite. That she definitely *had* noticed. It had increased quite quickly from once every other month to monthly, then weekly to almost daily. He became insatiable. Mary had wondered about the change. Sex was never her favourite marital chore and suddenly she was being asked to perform every night. At least, she had thought, it wasn't another woman that was causing the problems. From what she had read, no man would be able to sustain that pace with more than one woman. She had been devastated when they eventually found out the cause.

Thoughts of those early issues sloshed around in her mind as she deliberately tried not to think that her joke about being pregnant had been overheard and was being taken seriously. She knew she had to nip that story in the bud tomorrow, but preferred the comfort of an old, thought-worn problem than having to cope with thinking about a new one.

She placed the lamp on the bedside table and reached for her book, then paused, remembering a scene she had read. She picked up the lamp and moved into the bathroom where there was a large mirror. There was nowhere to put the lamp so she placed it on the floor near her feet. That threw her face and torso into a spooky shadow, but there was a strange compulsion to go through with her idea now, so she went back to the room and carried the heavy bedside table into the bathroom and placed the lamp on it. This time the light, although not perfect, was much better.

Her hands shook slightly from the exertion of carrying the table, but there was a hint of excitement at what she was about to do, it was a stepping away from the Modest Mary that she knew. She was about to try something that she had never done before and felt her stomach knot and her breath became a little ragged.

The buttons on her blouse resisted her fingers which seemed to have forgotten how to function properly. The hook of her bra was strangely stubborn, but once free of this, she gained in confidence and her slacks came off easily. She hooked her thumbs into her knickers, then suddenly lost courage. What was she expecting to see? Lady Chatterley had not been particularly enamoured with her reflection. Unripe, bitter, meaningless. These had been some of the words D.H. Lawrence had used to describe what that scandalous lady had felt when viewing her naked body.

Mary suddenly felt an anger surge within her. How dare a man like Lawrence presume to know what a woman felt about their own body? How can a body be unripe or bitter? She was certain that she would never use these words to describe her own body. And meaningless? What a stupid word to use. A body must have meaning.

She felt her reflection, which she had refused to look at so far, grow restless. It taunted her to get on with it. She drew in her breath and exhaled loudly while pushing her knickers to the floor, then stepped out of them, and slowly raised her eyes to meet those of the reflection.

A long moment passed as the woman and the reflection stared at each other, studied each other, slowly taking in everything that was on display and trying not to register an emotion until the inspection was complete.

Mary was not sure what she was expecting to see. She knew it would not be one of those slim, sexily tanned bodies with firm breasts that littered the magazine rack of the newsagents back home. She also knew that she was not yet old enough to be beyond it. Pleasant came to mind as she ran her eyes over her body. Yes, there were signs of over ripeness and softening, but she saw nothing that she would describe as bitter or unripe.

Her figure was still pretty good. Slim, but with enough meat to be shapely. Her breasts still held their own and her belly was relatively flat, albeit slightly marred by the stretch marks that her son, Toby, had bequeathed her. This, along with her thighs, contained most of the over-ripeness she saw.

The physical inspection over, she turned to the next search. Was there meaning in her body? 'What does a meaningless body look like?' she asked herself. What had D.H. Lawrence seen in Lady Chatterley's body that made him write that the character would feel that her physical being would have no meaning? Her eyes roamed over the reflection, examining each bit again, but this time with a different slant.

Some areas, like that below her knees, were in darkness due to the uneven light from the lamp, while other areas, despite twisting her neck to try and see, stayed hidden from her view. But she didn't think those bits were relevant to her search.

The cool air rippled across her skin in a wave of goose bumps and she shuddered slightly, preparing to abandon her search in favour of the warmth of her pyjamas and the blankets on the bed. She sighed and turned to pick up the lamp, then she saw it. Not in the reflection, but in the flesh, the part of her body that had meaning.

FOUR

The light trickled slowly into the kitchen. It was a dull morning. A misty rain had engulfed the mountain and given the garden a pale hue. It would clear up later. All the locals knew this, but their lives could not wait for that and they moved on the mountainside, going about their daily business with little to protect them from the elements, save for the odd plastic packet tied to a head.

In the kitchen Caiaphas threw some more wood into the stove, knowing that Solomon would be there soon. Esther was already looking after the white woman so he had time to nurse his guilty conscience. What had made him go and look through the bathroom window last night? Had he just expected to see her brushing her teeth? He could not say now why he had not just walked on home as usual, but the light had attracted him like an insect and he had felt compelled to peep in.

There had been no shame in the woman as she had stood before the mirror and Caiaphas did not believe that his feelings of guilt stemmed from seeing the woman in that state. It was more that he felt that he had been spying on a private ritual, although he could not understand what it was. Rites and rituals held more significance to him than a body, he tried to convince himself.

He would not let the lights attract him again, like they had last night. He had no right to pry into another person's ways.

Esther returned with the tray from the woman's room and a glow of triumph.

'She was in the shower this morning. I was too quick for her today. She could not do my job for me,' she told her child quietly as she removed him from her back and placed him into his box crib.

Caiaphas nodded a brief good morning before moving quickly outside. He was worried that he may blurt out that Mrs Mary did not look pregnant and then have the embarrassment of explaining himself.

He walked round the back of the house to check that the fire under the water tank was still going, his eyes ignoring the small window that lay a few paces on, while his mind, refusing to let the guilt well up, tried to fathom out why the white woman had said she was pregnant when she wasn't. The only conclusion he could reach was that she just wanted to be lazy and make everyone run around her and wait on her every need. As she was a friend of Mr James, that theory held water in his eyes.

The Frenchies had left after breakfast which had been held indoors due to the inclement weather. Mary was not sorry to see the back of them. Not that they had been unpleasant, nor even because they were French, but rather because they were there and needed attention when she would have rather been paying attention to herself and her predicament.

She had dreamed of her father again in another high definition dream and was wondering why her subconscious had suddenly thrown him into her thoughts. She was barely over the pain of missing him.

Far more pressing though, were the thoughts of the upcoming dinner at Joyce's and trying to get the message round to people that she wasn't pregnant. She had been a little shocked at Clifford Chatterley suggesting to his wife that, due to his inabilities, she was free to find someone else to father a child for her. Imagine George saying that to her. She half choked on her coffee at breakfast when that thought hit her and she tried not to let the giggling in her mind bubble out through her mouth. George hadn't shared Clifford's lack of functionality, Toby was proof of this, but somehow, she had never felt that he was emotionally equipped to have children. Neither of them had been really.

What if she had been given George's blessing to go off and find a proper father for the child they had produced? Would Toby

have left home – run away she called it – at such a young age?
Would she have now been able to turn to him when she needed
someone to lean on? Would a proper father have taught her and
Toby how to love? She shuddered slightly at this 'what if'
thought, chiding herself for being unfair on George when she
was just as much to blame. It wasn't that they didn't want to
love their child, it was as if they just never knew how, always
seeming to do the wrong thing at the wrong time.

She was not surprised when, on his eighteenth birthday, Toby
had announced that he was moving out. Hurt, yes, but surprised, no. If only it hadn't been soon after this that George had
started showing his symptoms. She had been left to cope with
this all alone.

Toby's appearance at the funeral had been, she felt, more for
appearances than for support. To show his girlfriend, what was
her name again, that he cared. She'd never felt as alone as she
had, sitting in that front pew.

George's ex-work colleagues, those that had not totally abandoned him during his illness, did no more than offer fake
condolences. She had wanted to scream that it wasn't her fault.
She did not bring the illness upon George. But then it wasn't the
illness they blamed her for.

She thought back to her time in front of the mirror, staring at
herself in all her glory. She expected to feel embarrassed by this
behaviour so strange and unlike her, but she didn't. She felt
strangely satisfied. D.H. Lawrence, the great D.H. Lawrence,
knew nothing about what women felt about their bodies. Hers
was neither unripe not bitter. And it had meaning. Maybe
Lawrence was too busy looking at the wrong parts of the woman's body to see the meaning. Meaning did not necessarily lie in
breasts or between the legs.

'Typical male,' she muttered to herself, 'only thinking of one
thing.'

She looked at her hands again, studying them. Hands have
meaning. She remembered how often she had stared down at
her hands as she had pushed George's wheelchair. It was better
than looking at all those eyes staring at her husband as he sat
slowly losing control of all his muscles. She picked up her book,

slightly smug in the knowledge that she knew more than D.H. Lawrence did.

'I'd better go check on our new boss,' Esther tickled the child's stomach. The kitchen was clear of all breakfast things and the bed linen had been taken off the bed in the guest room. It was no use washing them just yet, at least not till the sun came out.

Mrs Mary was sitting reading again. Caiaphas had said that it was a rude book, but she didn't believe it. Why would a woman want to read about rude things, she only had to spend some time with a man to experience them. Maybe that was it. Maybe Mrs Mary did not have a man to spend time with, so she felt she needed to read about it. But then, if she was pregnant, she must know about being rude. White people were crazy.

'Here madam, let me get that. You don't need to stand up.' Mrs Mary was trying to do her job again. And besides which, she was pregnant, old and white, so she shouldn't be getting up just to move a silly tea cup.

'I'm not pregnant, Esther,' Mrs Mary seemed as surprised at saying this as Esther was at hearing it. She wasn't sure how to react. Admitting she thought Mrs Mary was pregnant would betray her eavesdropping, but saying she didn't think Mrs Mary was pregnant may be construed as saying that she was just naturally helpless. Esther just stood staring.

'I only said that to shock Joyce. She was being so...so bitchy. I just wanted to shut her up. And the way she treated you, well, I was embarrassed to say the least. I am sorry, but I couldn't help myself. What business is it of hers why I am here?' Mary stopped for a second and then started giggling.

'Madam?' Esther was still processing it all.

'You should have seen Joyce's face. It was a picture.'

Esther started to giggle too. She had never liked Mrs Joyce and Mrs Mary was beginning to make sense now.

The giggling bubbled up to full blown laughter as the air between the two women began to melt and they fed off each other's mirth. Each had their own reasons to laugh at the joke at Joyce's expense but neither cared for the other's, all that mattered was that they were united in their dislike of the brash woman from the farm.

It took a while before the laughter died and even then small giggles would still bubble to the surface and the other would echo it. Neither now wanted to face the awkwardness that they knew was coming when it all finally died down.

Esther wanted this feeling of sisterhood to last. She had never got this close to any of the other women that had come to stay with Mr James, but her entire life had been lived as a servant, firstly as a little girl running round helping her mother at Mrs Joyce's farm. Then, when Mr James had come looking for help at the newly set up lodge, she was the perfect age to oblige. Now she slowly quietened her giggles, wondering what would happen next.

Old Man Mawenzi hobbled slowly down the path towards town. It would take him an hour to get there, the others, the younger and more agile, took about 15 minutes. He spoke to himself as he walked, a muttered incomprehensible language that swung back and forth like two sides of a conversation. The remnants of a cigarette, smoked right down to the butt, hung out the corner of his mouth and bounced up and down in time to the beat of the words.

To the casual observer, this was the usual scene that greeted those on the mountain every day, the old man struggling down the hill, in his own world and muttering away. But take a closer look, especially at the eyes. The eyes speak more than the mouth, even an eye that is glassed over. There was trouble in the eyes, they were not happy. Something was not right with the spirit that lay behind them. And listen with a more attuned ear to his 'conversation'. It is more animated than usual, there is fear and anger in the tone, just a hint, but it's there.

Children don't look at the eyes, or listen with finely tuned ears, so they were not to know something was up with Mzee Kichaa, the mad old man, as the kids liked to call him.

Two of the tomatoes hit their target, one on the back of the head, the other, the back of the legs. Two more went flying by. Tomatoes, soft and overripe like parts of Mary's body, yet flung with the bitterness that Lawrence saw in Connie Chatterley's. Young as they were, the kids had already learnt the bitter dislike of deformity that their parents knew so well, but it was still a game to them.

Old Man Mawenzi stopped on the path, but did not turn to face his attackers. If they wanted to continue, they would have to do so as cowards, to his back. Another missile, bitter, overripe and meaningless, hit him in the middle of the back, spreading a dark stain across the dusty torn shirt. Muted laughs rustled in the bushes behind him, then stopped.

He waited for the next shot, but when it did not come, he pulled up his shoulders which had sagged under the attack, and, without looking round, launched himself back into his shuffle-hobble, his private conversation more animated, but his eyes sad.

All was still around the scene of the assault. Then Solomon stepped quietly on to the path and watched as his friend made his way slowly down to town. His face was its usual stony self that gave away nothing. So we must turn to his eyes to read what is going on in the mind. But the eyes said nothing and we cannot be sure if the water on his cheeks had come from the heavens or his eyes.

And what of the children? Those launchers of soggy missiles? What had become of them? As they played by the stream, trying to catch frogs, what did their eyes tell us? There was no remorse in those young eyes, just a false bravado. False because beyond it lay a fear that Mzee Solomon had recognised them and would be talking to their parents. Young eyes cannot hide things the way an old man's can.

'His name is Thomas,' shy pride shone in Esther's face as she watched, somewhat bewildered, as Mrs Mary cradled the child in her arms. For a woman, she did not seem to know how to hold the youngster properly, but the intent was there.

For his part, Thomas lay quietly, his eyes wide, staring intently at the pale, ghostly face that was looking down at him, perhaps wondering what was wrong with this being that made her skin so pink. Or perhaps he was too frightened of this strange apparition to cry out. He bent his neck to find his mother and, seeing her looking on, smiling, he relaxed.

'He's beautiful,' Mary smiled. She felt strangely warm inside. Her anger at Joyce's prying and rudeness towards Esther had been spontaneously replaced with her laughter as she remembered the shocked look she got when she confessed to a false pregnancy. The side effect of her laughing had been a softening in the relationship with Esther and now she had a friend in what she was starting to think of as a hostile environment.

Thomas had played his part in the proceedings, crying out to be fed just as the giggling had died down and they had to make a decision whether to return to the formal relationship they had had to date, or to change things. Mary had been at a loss as to what to say next when Thomas had cried.

'You'd better go,' she said, inclining her head towards the noise.

Thinking she was being dismissed, the humour drained from Esther's eyes and she nodded her servile nod, an inclination of the head toward authority, then had turned and moved quickly to the kitchen. But authority had followed her, melting and morphing from authority into equal.

'Is he hungry?' Mary asked as Esther picked Thomas out of the box.

Esther nodded and instinctively released her breasts to feed.

Mary looked away, embarrassed, then slowly returned her gaze. They were both women for goodness sakes. Without staring, she took in the healthy glow of skin and the ripe fullness of the breasts. Surely Lady Chatterley would have felt better about herself if she had seen a body like that in the mirror. Mary knew she, herself, would love to have seen breasts like those in her reflection last night. Maybe even D.H. Lawrence would have felt differently toward his character had she been blessed with a chest like Esther's.

Perhaps that was Lawrence's problem. Could he have slept with too many women who had bitter, unripe bodies that he no longer knew what a young, beautiful body looked like. Was the milk that flowed from his mother's breasts soured by resentment of him having been born. He must have had some problems in childhood. He was even ashamed of his given names, hiding behind his initials – D.H.

Mary stopped her thought flow on the author. She knew nothing about him and his life. It was all supposition. She did know though, that the milk that had flowed from her breast to Toby had been bitter. She would not be surprised if he started calling himself T.S. Merskine soon.

Enough, she told herself. What is done is done. You cannot dwell on the past. The past is static, it cannot be changed. It may stare at you with judgemental eyes, but you will never change its opinion of you. It has judged you, given you a life sentence to live with forever, and there is no chance of parole. But you can change the now, make tomorrow's past give you a kinder judgement. She held out her arms to hold the sweetmilk fed child.

Caiaphas shot a quick glance over at his passenger. There was something different about her, a sort of glow. Maybe she was pregnant after all. The flat stomach that he had seen through the window last night had said no, but her eyes today told a different story. There was life, and just a hint of mischief there now. He wondered if this thing called jet lag that Mr James always complained of, had caused her to lose her pregnant glow for a while.

He was not looking forward to this evening, having to wait the few hours while Mrs Mary dined with Mr Ray and Mrs Joyce. He had heard stories about what happened at some of those dinners at the farm and, judging from the flushed faces of some of Mr James' lady friends when they returned to the car, as well as the occasional advances they made, he had no reason to disbelieve these rumours.

Yesterday he would have thought Mrs Mary too staid and embittered to be party to the party, but after last night's bathroom behaviour and today's change in mood, he wasn't sure. Maybe that whole thing in the bathroom had been a preparation ritual, something to cast off the spirits of white Europe and embrace the spirit of white Africa. He would never understand the Europeans and even less so, the women of that continent.

He glanced over at Mrs Mary again. She was not exactly the same as the others who had come. He could not quite determine what it was. The others had been more communicative, that was a big difference. Some of them overly so, telling him things about their European lives that he had no right to know, and sometimes barely understood what they were on about. But each one had a story. A failed marriage, a failed career, a dead husband, a dead marriage. He hadn't understood the woman who had said that.

'My marriage is dead.'

People die. Marriage is not a person, how can it die?

The dead marriage had not, however, stopped him slipping back into the lodge and her room the next evening as he was commanded to.

He looked again at Mrs Mary as he turned down the dusty road to the farm, the picture in his mind of her standing naked before the mirror suddenly became clearer and he now felt himself aroused and this, combined with thoughts of Mr James' other women, was having quite a powerful effect on him. He wondered if Mrs Mary would come back to the car with that glow of a freshly sexed woman, or with the hungry look of one wanting to be. He began to hope for the latter.

'Mary's reading *Lady Chatterley's Lover*,' Joyce's tone suggested mockery. Mary studied her plate, not really wanting to look at those around her. There were two other couples apart from Joyce and Ray. One ran a small safari lodge about ten kilometres away while the other were famers. Mary had forgotten their names already, but she had remembered that of the other guest.

'It's like Peter, but with an 'i" Pieter had said in a thick accent, just slightly shortening the first 'e' sound, then rolling the 'r' a little.

'Pieter is here on contract from South Africa. They're building a road somewhere over there,' Joyce waved vaguely, although her voice and gaze at the road man suggested a less vague relationship.

Mary didn't like Pieter. He already seemed drunk when she arrived, was a little loud and opinionated, and kept casting a leery eye over her body. Joyce's mentioning Lady Chatterley was the last thing she wanted with Pieter around.

A little titter went round the table at Joyce's revelation. Mary dared to look up and tried to face the mockery that was clear in their laugh.

'*Lady Chatterley*? I remember reading that as a school boy. There wasn't anything to it,' Pieter said rather loudly. 'Bloody tame really.'

Before Mary could reply and point out the literary merits of D.H. Lawrence, the conversation moved on to discuss *Fifty Shades of Grey* and how titillating that was. It seemed that the table agreed that this was more like the real deal.

Mary had heard of the book and how it had been all the rage. She was aware that it had a racy reputation, but, from what little she had gathered about it, it didn't rank very high as a literary masterpiece.

The meat was a little tough and, as she chewed on it, she found her mind wondering away from the conversation which was getting smuttier by the sentence, and recalled the beautiful food Solomon had prepared over the past two days. She would much rather have been sitting alone back at the lodge, indulging in a fantastic meal than chewing away at a tough steak, listening to adults giggling like naughty teenagers and talking about things that, Mary felt, shouldn't even be practised in a bedroom, let alone be discussed so openly over dinner.

The farmer was describing how he had tied his wife naked to one of the pillars on their veranda, but was interrupted by Joyce, who seemed to want to get one up on them by explaining what Ray could do with a riding crop.

Mary began to feel a little ill with this talk and the meat was drying up in her mouth. She swallowed a mouthful of wine to wash the remains of the meat down and mentally tiptoed away from the conversation again, only to be summonsed back by Joyce.

'How about you, Mary? Did you get up to anything kinky with that toy boy of yours?'

Old Man Mawenzi was pacing in his hobble-shuffle way when Caiaphas got to him and, despite the fact that he was actually doing the old man a favour by sharing his cigarettes, and that the lateness of the dance could not be helped, he still felt that he was in the wrong. But he could not apologise. He could not offer an explanation as to why he was late.

The dance was not smooth, as if they were stepping on each other's toes. The old man puffed viciously on his free fag, blowing angry smoke back at Caiaphas who, for his part, did not have his mind on his dance partner, but was rather eyeing one of the wallflowers a little way off.

He could see the dim glow of Mrs Mary's bathroom light and he wanted to go and peek, to see if she was doing her ritual again. He was still unsure if the flushed face his passenger had had on the trip back from the farm was due to the activities his mind usually conjured up for the parties there. Something was different about Mrs Mary's face. It was more flustered than flushed, and was there a hint of anger?

He drew heavily on his cigarette and glanced at the old man, noting the anger and flustered look in his dance partner's deformed face which was dimly lit by the glowing point of his rapidly diminishing fag. Undoubtedly his lateness was the cause of the old man's ire. Caiaphas had no way of seeing the dark stain on the back of Old Man Mawenzi's shirt, or the dried tomato pits that clung to his hair. Neither did he recall, at that moment, the possibility of Solomon being whisked off to Paris. Both could be equally responsible for the agitation his dance partner displayed but, for the moment, he didn't care. He just wanted the music to end and the dancers to go home. The dim glow from the bathroom still beckoned.

It felt longer than usual, but the cigarettes played out their lives in big angry puffs, smoke sucked in and blown out in quick succession. This was a quick step rather than a slow waltz. The old man threw his butt down and hobbled off while Caiaphas was still taking his last drag. He stared after the rapidly dimming silhouette, then stamped out the two cigarettes. The bathroom light was still glowing.

FIVE

An unease settled on the mountain as her children slept, or tried to sleep. It was like a scratchy blanket that provides you the warmth to sleep, but irritates you enough that you wake up tired from fighting the itch that keeps trying to break your slumber.

The birds in the trees felt this discomfort and they shrank back inside their nests to avoid the disturbance. A stop-start breeze stuttered through the branches of the trees, too ill at ease to blow smoothly. Even the trees themselves, usually so staid and immune to the mood of the mountain, shook in the breeze in a strange macabre way that was slightly off natural.

The mountain could not help herself. She loved those who lived on her slopes and, when strangers came to visit, she could quickly sum up their character and in this newcomer she saw great sadness. This was not overly unusual, she had seen it before in previous guests, one in particular in such great distress that it had ended in disaster. It had taken the mountain a long time to recover from that sorrow.

But as the morning began to throw splashes of pastel hues onto the dark canvas of land, she shuddered ever so slightly as she threw off the unpleasantness of the night before and, ever the optimist, put on her best smile and waited to greet those on her slopes.

Breakfast was out on the lawn and was shared with echoes of disturbed dreams that gurgled in the glass of orange juice, slithered in the crisp, cool watermelon and rasped on the toast. The watchful eye of the statue of Solomon stood guard over the solitary figure at the table, preventing the dreams from stopping in one place for too long. Like irksome flies, they flittered over the table, tasting the fruit, sniffing at the cornflakes and dipping into the sweet jam, ever mindful of the fly swat patiently watched and which could squash them with a look.

Mary ate without tasting, fearful of offending the statue that awaited her command. Her body still tingled from the scrubbing she gave it in the shower last night. She didn't normally shower before going to bed, but had needed to wash off the smut of the dinner conversation and the dirt of the evening's events that stuck to her skin like a layer of sweat and dust. The water had been tepid, cooler than the tears which mingled with the spray from the showerhead.

She thought she had heard movement outside the bathroom window as she dried herself, but, too tired to care, put it down to Rex snuffling around outside. She had no idea where the dog slept at night and had left him to his own devices.

George had been in the starring role of her dreams, or should she say George's wheelchair. It had seemed twice as large as she remembered it and the wheels were stubborn as they laboured to move in the sticky mud of the dream. Those around her tutted at her inability to care for her husband in his infirmity. She recognised some of their faces, Shelia Cobbler, Amanda Hazell and Mrs Tindall. Neighbours and, some she might even have called friends before George got sick. But, as in the dream, they had deserted her, preferring to sit back in judgement rather than help when George's illness became too obvious to hide anymore.

Mary was used to the attitude of those in the dream, it had gone on too long for her not to be, but that never stopped it hurting.

She swallowed the last of her cheese omelette, oblivious to how light it was and its perfect flavouring with finely chopped fried onion and fresh basil. She waited for the statue to become animated and then watched with some relief as her plate was taken at a dignified pace back into the house. She reached for the toast and jam and, in the solitude of the garden, focussed on her dream again.

Pushing the wheelchair, she had felt naked and exposed to the looks of those around her. She dared not look down at her body for fear of seeing that same image she had seen in the bathroom mirror the night before. She wished for a Mrs Bolton equivalent to come push her Clifford Chatterley in the chair. Someone she could pay to take on the yoke of shame that attached her to that infernal chair, but there had been no one in the reality that her dream was trying to recreate.

The marmalade was good and she spread it thickly onto her toast. Homemade? She was not sure, but was not going to ask the dour figure moving slowly across the lawn to return to its statue post. There was, however, something familiar about the precise way Solomon placed one foot in front of the other, as if each step was measured, each footfall contemplated before weight was applied to it. There had been someone in the dream like that, but Solomon was nothing like her father.

Daddy would have helped, if he had still been alive. She knew that. He was the one person she had ever relied on. He had never let her down. George had been very dependable, but he hadn't lifted a finger to help once he got ill. It was a harsh judgement, she knew. If she blamed George for that, then she may as well blame her father for dying on her a year or so before she really needed his help. But she couldn't, that would not be fair. Besides, daddy had not become a burden, he had just died.

Her mother, with whom she had never really been close, had wrapped herself up in her grief when her husband died and shut herself off further from Mary. She came to George's funeral, more because Barry, Mary's brother and obvious favourite of her mother, had felt duty bound to attend. But aside from that, contact with either her mother or Barry never extended beyond an impersonal news update.

Her thoughts were souring the marmalade and she forced herself back to the table and the beautiful garden in which she sat. Just beyond the statue of Solomon, Caiaphas returned his eyes to the weeds he was meant to be pulling out. There was something in the way he had been staring at her that unsettled Mary.

Some of the words were beyond the meagre education she received at the Catholic Mission School, but Esther got the gist of the first few pages of *Lady Chatterley*. She was a little disappointed when she carefully placed the book back on the little table next to Mrs Mary's bed. She had hoped that it would give her some insight into her new friend's world, but there seemed little in what she had read that differed hugely from her own.

She knew of wars from the refugees who occasionally arrived in town and she was familiar with cripples imagining a 'wheeled chair' to be similar to the square bit of wood with four wheels attached, that she had seen a legless man pushing himself about on during a rare visit to the city. She pictured Clifford in her mind as a clone of Mr James, sitting squat on this contraption, plastic bags tied round his hands to protect them as he propelled himself forward.

The motorised bathchair used to propel Clifford around was more of a mystery. There were no baths at the lodge, only showers. At home they used a bucket to sluice themselves down with. The only bath she knew was the cast iron one with ball and claw feet she had seen at the farm when she used to help her mother out there. Clifford was placed into this, wheels replaced the ball and claws and the taps were used to steer the strange contraption. People here would laugh at such a vehicle, that was for sure. But in Europe, it was probably a common sight Esther concluded.

Apart from this strange new concept there had been stories of girls going off into the forest with boys. Esther knew about that. She had been about fifteen, the same age as the girls in Mrs Mary's book, when she had her first adventure in the forest.

There must be more, Esther thought as she replaced the book, aware that her small window of opportunity to read was going to close soon. *Surely it can't just be that they drive around in baths in Europe that makes us so different. I need to read more.* She gently closed the door to Mrs Mary's room and hurried through to the front room. She would have to contend with Solomon's disapproving looks at her not being there to clear away the breakfast dishes and ensure that everything was alright with Mrs Mary. He would not say anything but his look would let her know that she had neglected her duties.

Mrs Mary was just about finished her breakfast. Her toast plate was empty and she was finishing the last of her tea. Solomon's eyes flickered as Esther moved across the lawn and picked up some of the dishes. She felt rebellious. So what if

Solomon gave her the look. What could he do? He never said anything to Mr James, just came in, cooked, did his funny announcing of dinner, then left. What could looks do? Anyway, he was so old he should be driving around in a motorised bath. Esther nearly dropped a plate as she tried not to giggle at the image that popped up in her mind.

In the kitchen she put the dishes into the sink then quickly picked up Thomas and whispered, 'Please don't ever be disrespectful to me, even in your thoughts, the way I have been disrespectful to Mzee Solomon.'

She placed the gurgling child back into his box and turned back to the sink, the dark figure in the doorway causing her a momentary shock. Had he heard her whispering? She wondered as she began to wash the dishes.

It was easier to concentrate on the gardening when Mrs Mary wasn't sitting a few feet away. He was worried for her now. She did not look right. No one scrubbed themselves that hard. As a child, he remembered his mother saying that if he scrubbed himself too much, he would scrub away his black skin and end up as a mzungu, a white man. He knew that was just a silly thing mothers said to their children to stop them wasting soap.

He tugged at a weed and saw again the picture that had greeted his Peeping Tom eyes last night. Was this just another strange white person ritual that Mrs Mary was going through? He couldn't bring himself to believe that it was that simple. She looked in too much distress, all that scrubbing and, he was sure, sobbing. With the water from the shower and the meagre light, he could not tell if there were tears, but the way her frame juddered and the glimpses he got of her face, he could tell she was not happy.

Maybe something horrible had happened to her at the farm. Rape was practically non-existent in the village, but he knew of it. However, he could not believe that Mr Ray and Mrs Joyce would allow such a thing and the thought disturbed him such that he had to hastily replant the flower he had accidentally ripped out of the ground.

He had half thought of lighting the fire under the water tank so that Mrs Mary could have some warmer water, but that would have given him away. Besides, it would never have heated up in time. He could tell that she needed some warmth. Not just the physical warmth of hot water, but a spiritual warmth. Her soul had gone cold. Something, or someone had caused this in her and it wasn't just what had happened at the farm. There was a deeper problem that he had noticed from the moment he had picked her up at the airport. But back then it was just a feeling that all was not well, but now, as he trimmed the grass round the borders of the garden and re-visualised that pale, shivering body in the shower last night, putting aside the feelings of arousal that still burned in him, now he knew, Mrs Mary was suffering from a frozen soul.

After the warmth of the sun on the lawn, the lounge felt a bit chilly and Mary shivered. *Lady Chatterley* did not appeal at the moment and she was at a bit of a loss as to what to do so she fired up the laptop and, following James' detailed instructions, managed to get Internet connection.

'It's 3G, all done through phone signals or something like that,' the note explained.

There was an email from Barry hoping she was settling in at the lodge and that everything was okay. Mum was doing well, although her rheumatism had been playing up a bit. The doctor was also a little concerned about her blood pressure. There were various other bits about mother's health which Mary skimmed over then wrote a brief reply letting her brother know that she was having a lovely time, the people were friendly and the lodge was stunning. She wished mum a speedy recovery from her ailments and hit the send button.

In a mirror email, James hoped all was going well at the lodge. He put in a cheeky query asking Mary if she was enjoying Solomon's cooking, then gave an update on his mother's health. The chemo had gone well and the doctor was 'cautiously optimistic' although it was still too early to tell if there would be any real hope. There was an undertone of sadness in his email. It was unusually downbeat for James and, reading it through a second time, Mary felt her heart go out to him. Growing up next door to them, Mary had spent more time at their place than at her own and James had been more of a brother to her than

Barry ever had. James' mother would often say that the two of them would get married when they grew up, but as usual with those predictions, that never happened.

Mary did wonder sometimes if James still held a torch for her. It was little things that made her think this. He had not come to the wedding when she had married George, but sent apologies – rather late in the day – citing a business trip to Switzerland as an excuse. She could not swear to it, but as she and George had emerged from the church, she thought she caught a glimpse of James standing in the park opposite. The photographer had made her turn her head just then and by the time she turned back, there was no sign of the figure.

There had been a spate of unsuitable girlfriends then that he had clung to and pawed at whenever she met him. At one party that they both attended, James had a very attractive woman on his arm who laughed too loudly at his jokes and made almost too much of a show of affection towards him. It shocked Mary when she overheard another guest comment that he wondered how much James was paying her.

When Toby was born, James had suddenly upped and left to go travelling. A few postcards and letters arrived from around the world till eventually the note came that he had fallen in love with a lodge in a place called Kilimbati and had bought it. Mary had had to look Kilimbati up on a map.

Letters from James had been sporadic for a while as the postal system in Africa was slow, but with the growth of the internet, contact was re-established and became more regular. When she informed him of George's illness, the tone of his emails changed. They became even more regular and very supportive. Mary wondered if she could have made it through everything if it hadn't been for James' virtual support. But now, as she fired off a reply, a thought struck her which she did not like and quickly dismissed, not because it was not without merit, but because emotionally right now, she couldn't afford it to be right.

The children saw Mzee Solomon this time before they could launch their attack on their hobbling target. He stood a little off the path in the forest, barely visible to anyone heading down to town. His eyes watched the path and the youngsters as they moved into position. Then, as one of them noticed him and sounded the alarm, they moved off nonchalantly with no hint of mischief showing.

Solomon watched them go, then stood waiting till Mawenzi came into view before stepping onto the path. The harelip prevented the beggar from smiling, but he could not hide his joy at seeing his friend. The good eye lit up, his shoulders, normally drooping, straightened and his limp became less pronounced as if the presence of his friend had brought a temporary healing.

They shook hands, a few dirty banknotes miraculously transferring themselves from one hand to the other and quickly disappeared into the pocket of the ragged trousers. They spoke in low voices, not conspiratorially, but rather the old chef seemed to console his friend. There were numerous pauses as the old men would stare off into the distance, as if waiting for the next sentence to arrive. There was no rush for the conversation to be over. It had its course to run and it would do so in its own time. No man could force the pace at which things needed to be said. Nodding also played a part. It was said, 'yes, I hear what you are saying. I will digest it and then offer a reply.'

When news had been exchanged and the conversation was satisfied that it had finished the task at hand, the two men parted, one limping happily down the mountain, a burden removed from his shoulders; the other stared after him for a long while with solemn, unchanging features, then he eventually turned and walked slowly back up the slope. Unlike his cripple friend, Solomon's gait was not happy. He had seen something in his friend that left him thoughtful, some may even say sad. But the mysteriousness that clung to the old chef wafted off after him, leaving no clues as to what was disturbing him.

The path fell silent as the gentle footsteps of the men faded. A slight breeze played in the branches of the trees, breaking the quiet for a moment before it died away. The silence took control of the scene for a minute then a rustling in the undergrowth decided it wanted the limelight. A young wild rabbit emerged from the rustling and stood for a moment at the side of the path. It sniffed at the remnants of the conversation that had just taken place, sifting out the joys and fears in the echoes of the words that remained. Then, deciding that it didn't like what it smelt, turned and headed back the way it had come. The silence returned and covered the remnants of what had been said.

Esther slapped the sheets on the washboard and then rubbed at them. The sun was warm on her back and Thomas, lying on a blanket nearby, gurgled contentedly.

Mrs Mary had said too much this morning. Esther found it difficult to listen to her go on and on about Mrs Joyce and what a terrible person she was. It was not that Esther disagreed with Mrs Mary, Mrs Joyce was not a nice person, but what if word got back to her that Esther had agreed with all Mrs Mary had said. Her mother still worked for Mrs Joyce and she did not want to jeopardise that, but at the same time she could not endanger her own job by telling Mrs Mary to stop talking like she was. Something must have happened at the farm last night for her to be so upset, but it was unfair of Mrs Mary to put her in the middle like that.

Even waking Thomas to try and distract Mrs Mary hadn't helped, and Thomas had not been best pleased by the interruption to his sleep. She put the sheet down in the tub and moved over to her son, her guilt at trying to use him to placate Mrs Mary filled her with remorse and she played with him for a while to ease her conscience. Perhaps her mother would be able to shed some light on what had happened to cause Mrs Mary to be so upset, she thought.

Thomas had long forgotten his disturbed sleep, and welcomed the attention, giggling and writhing in pleasure at being tickled.

It was the sound of an approaching horse that drew Esther from her play and she was hard at work slapping the sheets when Joyce pulled up. She braced herself for the sharp words from her mother's boss, slowly dropped the sheet back into the tub and turned to face the visitor.

'Is Mrs Mary in?' The voice was not what she expected, the question was not what she expected. It was only the rider that matched her expectations.

'No, madam. She has gone out for a walk.'

Why had Mrs Joyce asked if Mrs Mary was in? She never asked, she usually just barged into the house demanding a drink and making herself at home. This was a different Mrs Joyce. She looked bothered and embarrassed. Esther's reply seemed to throw her and she looked around as if hoping that Mary would suddenly appear.

'Um, I see. Well could you please let her know that I...er... popped by. Thank you.'

She turned her horse and dug her heels into its flanks before Esther had a chance to assure her that the message would be passed on.

Thomas was still staring after the sound of the horse when Esther composed herself enough to look back at him.

'Please? Thank You? Something is very wrong with Mrs Joyce. She has never said those words to me before,' Esther told her son.

Rex stopped on the path and sniffed. He could smell the remnants of a conversation that had been stomped into the ground by careless feet, but that did not interest him. He did, however, raise a lazy head to indicate to the new person at the lodge that there was left over human news here if she was interested, but having done his duty, he ambled off in the direction of a fading rabbit scent. He was too old to give chase these days, but felt duty bound to the memory of his younger self to at least give the appearance of being interested.

Mary stopped on the path where Rex had left it, undecided whether to head further down, to wait for the dog's return, or to follow him into the forest. Instead of making her feel better, her rant to Esther after breakfast had just made her anger and disgust resurface and a walk seemed the only solution. Her bond with Esther had been formed over a mutual dislike of Joyce, so it felt natural to vent when Esther had brought her morning tea through, but now she felt she may have gone a bit too far. The question about James had been quickly forgotten, buried under a pile of emotional leftovers from last night's dinner.

'Rex!' she called without too much conviction.

The dog raised its head to acknowledge having heard its name, then continued to follow the rabbit scent.

Mary waited a moment, kicking at the dusty path, unaware that she was further shattering the earlier conversation remnants.

'Rex!' She shouted again, this time with a little more urgency.

The forest absorbed her cry and spat a silence back at her. It wasn't in the mood to be disturbed.

Mary waited a little longer, then stepped off the path, heading in the direction in which the dog had disappeared. She was feeling reckless, rebellious, kicking back at life when it was kicking her. She strode with some purpose through the soft carpet of dead undergrowth till the forest seemed to close in behind her.

The final echo of the earlier conversation between the two old men had died away so that not even the forest could hear it, but the approach of hoof beats now took its attention. The horse slowed in response to a tug on the reins and the rider looked round before urging her mount on.

Caiaphas started with the large lounge window. It would then not look too suspicious when he came to wash the small bathroom one. It was probably a few weeks too early for them to be washed, but he didn't think anyone would really notice. He would do both inside and out this time, allowing him a good view into the bathroom when evening came.

A barman serving up this psychological cocktail would measure out two parts voyeur to one part concerned citizen, shaken to show up the violence of the emotions, and then just a twist of romantic added for flavour.

Mrs Joyce had acted strangely when he had bumped into her on the path, almost as if she was aware that he knew that something strange had happened at the farm last night. She had been evasive rather than abrasive and this had tipped the proportions in the cocktail to include concerned citizen.

He was not sure how, but he believed that the little window to the bathroom would hold the solution. Somehow, something he would see through there would give him the answer. It was there that he had found the question, so surely it would provide the answer too.

The other windows got a quick going over with the sponge and cloths, but the little one at the back of the house was cleaned with great care and attention, digging the cloth right into the corners to clean away long forgotten dirt there.

Once done, he stood back to admire his handiwork. Now all he hoped for was that Old Man Mawenzi would not be late. He had a date for after the dance.

'She's not back yet.'

There wasn't panic in Esther's voice, it had not yet made the trip from her eyes.

Caiaphas nodded. They had had this problem before with one or two of Mr James' women. It was too early to panic, but a little bit of concern would not go amiss.

'And the dog?'

'No, the dog is still out too.'

Neither of them ever referred to Rex by name, unless in the presence of a white person. Animals don't have names.

'Mrs Mary should be okay then if the dog is still with her.'

They had had this exact same conversation before, but Esther could not help noticing that Caiaphas was not as convinced, or perhaps one could say that he was more concerned than before, but he was trying not to show it.

'If she is not back for tea, then we will go and look,' he said, 'I must go get some firewood. I will keep an eye out for her.' He turned and left, not looking Esther in the eye before departing. Neither of them wanted to mention Mrs Judith.

She was the only one of Mrs James' women who had not left in a better condition than she came. Mrs Joyce was right when she said that all Mr James' women were running away from something. The lodge had become a sort of haven for troubled souls, mostly women, but that was more about James' character than the lodge's. He had a large network of women friends in Europe and every time something dramatic happened in their lives, an email of support would go out, followed a respectable time later by a 'why don't you come stay here for a bit' missive. He was a persuasive man and made the chance of getting away from all the hustle and bustle of a European life sound just what was needed. Invariably the slower pace of life, the beauty of the surroundings and the warm blue skies that greeted these refugees of modern life held wonderful healing properties and his guests would head home invigorated and ready to face all that Europe had to throw at them. But Mrs Judith had been the one failure, the one whose condition had not been improved by the sun and the scenery.

Caiaphas moved quickly along the main path. When he reached the top he hesitated, then peered over the edge of the cliff into the ravine below, the sight of Mrs Judith's broken and bloodied body that lay on the rocks below, springing up in his mind. He pushed the thought away, telling himself that Mrs Mary was not like that. She was a stronger woman despite her strange bathroom behaviour. But the reassurances he gave his mind were not strong enough, he still had to look, just to make sure.

It was warmer down in the town. The breeze that kept the mountainside cool was blocked off and at times it bordered on stifling. A pebbledash layer of sweat stood out on Old Man Mawenzi's brow as he hobbled between the vehicles that lined the sides of the streets. Occasionally someone would give him a coin or two for his begging efforts, but mostly he was ignored. The few white people in town took less notice of him than his fellow countrymen, but that never stopped him trying his luck. He had learnt that a refusal by a white person to give some small change ended up with him getting a bit extra from sympathetic blacks. He could almost taste the disgust at the whites in their donations. They have so much and yet they share nothing, the coins would say.

Old Man Mawenzi did not care what his coins said, only how much they said, so he would always try extra hard and be extra stubborn when begging from a white, especially one who obstinately refused to give.

He knew the regular whites in town and when he saw the one who they said was from South Africa, the one who was the boss on the road works over there somewhere, he hobbled as quickly as he could towards the man without looking too obvious. He was a good one to beg from because not only would he refuse, but he would usually tell Old Man Mawenzi to 'bugger off' in a

loud voice. Donations from the locals who witnessed the rudeness of this white man were invariably rich pickings.

He adopted his begging face and held out a palm, his other
hand supporting the begging one at the wrist. His voice took on
an extra slurring and he raised a pitiful eye to his mark and
waited for the rebuke. The road man was in his car and driving
off before Mawenzi closed his hand round the five thousand
shilling note. He had hoped to make a few hundred from those
around him after the white man refused, but instead the white
man had reached for his wallet and handed over the note
without a word.

Old Man Mawenzi had not even thanked him, such was his
surprise. He pocketed the money and glanced round at those
near him. Without the fuss from the white man, no one was
taking any notice of him and he sighed. He was so used to
getting his money from rejection fallout that he felt cheated this
time.

He had not looked at the white South African's face. He never
really looked at the white people properly. They all looked the
same and had a distain of him and his deformation, as if he had
been responsible for his hideous lip, as if it was his fault that
one leg had been stretched longer than the other as he had been
pulled from the womb. He never mattered to the white people
who came to town, and so they never mattered to him.

Had he been one to study faces and been bothered to take heed
of messages there, he would have seen something in the road
man's face that would not have made sense, a distractedness
that went beyond the hangover, some might even have said
there was an air of guilt about the man. Perhaps the uncharac-
teristic donation to Old Man Mawenzi was a manifestation of
this. Others would argue that the man was in fact still drunk
and handing over such a sum to the beggar was a judgemental
error caused by alcohol weakened facilities. A few wobbles in
the trajectory of his receding 4x4 seemed to uphold the latter
theory, but no one could fully dismiss the guilt theory.

The view from the clearing was just stunning. Kilimbati with
its violet jacaranda lined main road looked picturesque in the
slight haze below. Around it, the red-brown sand contrasted

with the green fields of the coffee farm and stretched to the horizon giving the land a mint chocolate flavour. A few small hills broke up the plain.

Mary stood on the large flat rock outcrop that made up the clearing and breathed hungrily at the clean air and immaculate scenery. All the tension and anger in her body forgotten as her senses overdosed on the beauty of her surroundings.

There was still no sign of Rex and she was not sure if she could find her way back to the path, but those thoughts were stashed away for when the potent hit the view was giving her had died down. In that moment, she knew that if she were ever to find peace within herself over what had happened with George, she would find it at this spot. There was a feeling about the place that told her this; it was as if the place had a pulse of life throbbing in it.

There had to be a path or something that led to the clearing, or was it a little island in a sea of forest with no navigable routes to its shores. That was a question for later, Mary decided, finding a rock to sit down on. A small gecko that had been basking in the sun nearby scuttled off, indignant that its morning ritual had been disturbed. It liked this spot because those bulky humans never came here. It eyed Mary from its crevice and eventually decided that this large creature meant it no harm so moved slowly back out into the sun, all the time watching for a change in the human's demeanour. And it was changing, but our friendly lizard had nothing to fear, the human was mellowing. The events of last night were being processed and the sting of anger was slowly being drawn out by the warm sun. The light breeze played its part, gently blowing away the strange looks she had got from Caiaphas this morning. There had been something quite sexual and predatory in his stare. Could he be a Mellors for her? Unlike Lady Chatterley, she felt no real attraction to the grounds man at the lodge, but still wondered if she could ever find a Mellors out here in Africa, one that she would feel that forbidden attraction to, the way Lady Chatterley had to Mellors? And if she did, what would George's ghost in the role of Clifford Chatterley say? She lay back and closed her eyes.

The first time Toby visited his father after the illness set in, Mary could have cried. Her son could barely conceal his disgust. A kind of hatred seemed to well up in his eyes and escape in a poisonous cloud from the sneer that contorted his lips. It was not for herself that Mary choked up when she saw the expression, but for George. He was still in possession of his facilities, just not his muscles and body and he would undoubtedly have seen and understood their son's expression.

Toby had recovered from his initial shock and disguised his emotions quickly. But the damage, for Mary, had been done. She cursed herself for not having been a better mother, someone who could have instilled enough love in her son so that he would care about the plight of his father. Did he not understand that his father was slowly dying? There was no known cure. He would continue to shrivel up until there was nothing left of him. Why couldn't he see that and at least act as if he cared even if he didn't.

Toby had refused point blank to go out with them when she suggested a walk. She had thought that pushing his father's wheelchair may somehow give them a better bond, maybe Toby would get to appreciate that, despite his condition, there was still a remnant of his father in there somewhere.

Instead he had just commented roughly, 'I don't want to be seen in public with that!'

Mary was unsure whether the 'that' he spoke of was the wheelchair, or George. To push away the abhorrence that was threatening to consume her, she focused on the wheelchair, seeing it as a 'that'. But despite all her best efforts, some of the 'that-ness' rubbed off on poor George. He was in too close proximity to the chair to avoid the fall out and Mary had struggled while taking George for a walk later that day after Toby had made a hasty retreat. People were looking. They had always done so, but it now seemed to her as if the looks were saying, 'how can you bear to be seen in public with that.' Their definition of 'that' was certainly not the wheelchair.

She had deposited George in the lounge on their return and spent a good half an hour in the bathroom sobbing. Pity, self-pity and anger sloshed around inside her. Anger at herself for her feelings and anger at George for causing these feelings,

even if it wasn't really his fault. Eventually she took a big
breath, washed her face and went to see how the growing 'that'
in the lounge was doing. Toby's poisoned view had planted the
seed of disgust in her mind and she felt the rot in her relationship set in then.

Rex re-joined her as she made her way home, snuffling his way
out of the undergrowth with a look on his face as if to say he had
been with her all the time. He zigzagged up the path, padding
ahead a little to sniff at a small pile of rotten tomatoes, some left
over indignation and a cluster of childish fright discarded by the
kids as they ran off. He did not, however, stop to tell Mary what
it was he smelt. He also did not concern himself with the
strange auras that clung to the new woman at the lodge. All he
bothered with was that he did not smell the despair he had in
that other woman before watching her jump off the cliff.

Occasionally he would recall that scent and remember the
woman, tears streaming down her face as she had stood for an
age at the edge, trying to work up the courage to take that step
forward. He had known she would jump. She was drenched in a
funk of despair, but there was enough of a hint of the will to do
it that he had detected in her smells.

Realising what she was about to do, he had busied himself
rooting around in the bushes a little way off. He didn't want to
distract her from her chosen course. When he heard her disappearing scream he had padded slowly back to the spot and
peered over the ledge at the body on the rocks below. He waited,
just to make sure that it was all over, then slowly turned and
made his way home.

It wasn't too long after his return to the lodge that things got
hectic, the strong smell of panic assaulting his nostrils as he lay,
twitching occasionally in the warm sunlight on the veranda.
People left and his ears picked up their vague shouts from the
mountainside.

'Judith! Judith!'

He contemplated showing them where to look, but the sun
was nice and warm and the cries far enough off not to disturb
him. His dreams that afternoon were pleasant, but cut short by
the fuss the people made.

'Why all the commotion?' he would have asked if he could speak. 'It's just a dead person.'

'We were all a bit too drunk and it was all talk. We've never done anything like what we said,' Joyce's apology was stirring up Mary's anger again and she longed for the solitude of her clearing.

'I guess Pieter just couldn't control himself. I'm really sorry it happened.'

Mary nodded slowly, outwardly accepting the apology, but inwardly questioning why it was Joyce and not Pieter who was the one there apologising for the way he had groped at her at the dinner table, pulling her blouse open for all the guests to see. Yes, he had been very drunk, but Mary had never felt so violated as she stormed out. It had taken large quantities of self-control to not show any of her anger and upset to Caiaphas in the car on the way home. She did not want his sympathy.

Pieter did not equate with any character in *Lady Chatterley*. Perhaps he was sort of an anti-Michaelis, that wishy-washy character with whom Connie had had a doomed relationship early in her married life. Lawrence described him as a 'curious and very gentle lover', but 'detached'. And the lovemaking meant nothing to Connie. It was a sort of platonic sex that they had going. But where Michaelis had been 'curious and gentle', Pieter had been lewd and rough. Mary could almost feel the pinch of his claw-like hands on her breasts as Joyce stumbled over the apology. This was only slightly sweetened by the memory of the slap she had given that obnoxious South African.

'You really must come over again for dinner. I won't invite Pieter.' Joyce added the exclusion almost reluctantly in response to the face Mary pulled. She was slowly returning to her brash self and Mary regretted being so forthcoming with her forgiving appearance.

'Maybe,' was all she could muster in response as a loud 'Noooooo!' raged in her head.

Joyce nodded, pondered, then yelled, 'Esther! Where's my juice?!'

'Caiaphas is up to something. He has been acting very strange lately,' Esther whispered to Thomas. 'What do you think?'

Thomas gurgled a thank you for having his stomach tickled, but did not venture to speculate on what Caiaphas could possibly be plotting.

'He has cleaned all the windows when he did not need to.'

There was another tickle and gurgle.

'At least Mrs Joyce is back to normal. I think that maybe she dropped her rudeness in the forest this morning, then found it later on. It is a good thing the birds did not find it first, we do not want the birds to be rude, now do we?'

Thomas clapped his hands to indicate that he agreed.

'Mrs Mary seems better though. She was so cross this morning, but I don't know why. Maybe it was the way Caiaphas was looking at her. Did you see him this morning?'

Thomas went quiet, lying back and staring at her so that she knew that she needed to return to work.

Solomon moved slowly to his seat, rested his hands on the surface and gathered his thoughts. Then in a slow, deliberate movement, reached down into the vegetable rack.

Esther busied herself at the sink, but kept a watchful eye on the old man, awaiting any commands that may be fired from his lips. It took her a little while to realise that all was not right with him. He seemed distracted, lacking the usual confidence that he displayed. This was unusual and disturbing. Solomon, for as long as she could remember, even from when she had been a little girl, was always Solomon – quiet, serious, stern, focused and unchanging. Every movement he made seemed deliberate and pre-meditated, but this evening, he seemed to be operating on automatic. Movements and decisions were being carried out by long-bred custom, rather than a re-evaluation of each chore. Even his commands for ingredients to be fetched were like ritualistic chants, memorised and regurgitated for the occasion.

But Esther obeyed each command as she had always done. Just because his orders were not issued in his usual tone gave her no excuse to ignore them.

'What could be worrying the old man?' she wondered. The last time she had seen him like this, his brother had died not long after his mood had started. She placed the thyme in front of the old man and turned back to the sink.

'Madam. Dinner will be served in five minutes.'

Mary was beginning to enjoy the formality of the evening meal. In a strange way she found herself building up an affection for the solemn chef's announcement. His seemingly impenetrable facade and stoic mannerisms had started to endear him to her. Perhaps, she thought, he is an inspiration as to how to cope with the barrage of abuse that life threw at you. Instead of getting all worked up and worrying about silly little things like a drunken man's groping, just get on with life.

She put the marker back into her book exactly where she had taken it out. Connie Chatterley had not got up to any further shenanigans this afternoon as Mary had sat staring at the page, stewing in the anger that had been re-ignited by Joyce's supposed apology.

She had wanted to have a word with Esther to try and apologise for her fellow white person's behaviour, but worried that the vehemence she felt would only stoke the fires rather than extinguish, so she sat pretending to read as thoughts whizzed and banged in her head. Even the interruption of the evening drink did not bring solace, but the calm measured manner of Solomon seemed to rub off on her and she absorbed as much as she could of the dignity that wafted in the room as he departed.

'Tonight for starter, we have an avocado, mango and walnut salad with a light chilli and lime dressing, topped with roasted sesame seeds.'

George had loved avocado, Mary thought, a sadness creeping over her as she swallowed a mouthful of wine before picking up her fork. Suddenly she wished he was here with her, he would have enjoyed the food here. James often invited them to come and stay, but they never seemed to find the time. Well, that was really Mary's excuse, but she had felt it would have been awkward if they had managed to get to the lodge. James was not over her and it would have been difficult to cope with him trying to pretend that he was, yet still giving off vibes that he wasn't. One small compensation of George becoming ill was that James had ceased with his invites and Mary was relieved of the burden of making excuses.

She wondered now, how George would have coped if they had ever managed to holiday here. Undoubtedly, he would have

been George, not noticing, or pretending not to notice, any
subtle hint at unextinguished flames coming from James. He
would possibly have even befriended Joyce and her crowd,
fitting in neatly with their 'colonial master' ways without taking any of the taint of it on himself.

And he would have loved the food. He had always enjoyed
good cooking and Solomon's was the best she had ever had.

The warmth of the memory cooled suddenly as she remembered sitting, spoon-feeding George his food, his face taking no
joy in eating, the way it used to. The disease had robbed him not
only of his mobility, but also his ability to enjoy.

This began to sour her own enjoyment of her starter. She
thought of Solomon and his calm, unflustered ways and was
soon able to concentrate on the gentle bite of the chilli and the
sting of lime that were vying with the creaminess of the avocado
and the sweetness of the mango for her taste buds' attention.
Memories were not good things, not when they were the ones
she had. She sipped her wine and finished the last few mouthfuls of the starter.

'For the main course, we have tender braised lamb in an
apricot and garlic sauce. We have some wild rice, seasoned with
cumin. The veg-e-tay-bills are minted new peas, and carrots in
an orange and ginger sauce.'

Mary closed her eyes once the old chef left the room, took in a
deep breath, put aside the nagging little thought that, despite
its excellence, tonight's dinner was not quite up to the standard
of previous meals, and renewed her efforts to pursue the stoi-
cism of Solomon.

Caiaphas was pleased to see Old Man Mawenzi waiting for him
as he approached their usual spot. He offered the cigarette and
it was taken as usual, without a word. His hand shook slightly
as he lit up for his partner. The anticipation of looking through
the bathroom window was exciting and arousing him. He wondered what rituals the white woman might perform for him
tonight, that is if she performed at all.

He dragged slowly on his cigarette, looking at, but not seeing
the old man who stood opposite him, only focusing momentarily

when the old man coughed then spat, but quickly let the glaze return to his eyes and Mary's naked body to his mind.

The dance ended quietly as it always did. Only the scrunch of Caiaphas' feet could be heard as he snuffed the last light of life from the cigarettes on the ground and the two men departed, one shuffling a little slower than usual and stopping to cough and spit again. The other strode off with a purpose, not looking back at his friend.

Silence slipped stealthily through the undergrowth and covered the crumpled remains of the dance props and then slid over the old man's expectorant which, had it bothered to examine it, was flecked with blood. But no one looks at spit.

SIX

Dreams swarmed on the dark mountain slopes, skittish dreams, heavy with meaning and dripping with the experiences of the day, the week, the lifetime, dreams hungry to find a fertile subconscious in which to lay their eggs. The mountain stood silent and majestic in the soft African night like a large tree, letting the dreams flit in and out of her nooks and crevices as they searched for a place to nest.

One dream held a ghostly white figure, vague scents of feminine sex coruscating in its aura. The figure danced and teased the dreamer who tried in vain to grasp the elusive promise.

Elsewhere, a small child sat in a bath tub, cowering under a whip that flayed mercilessly, each crack shouting out a harsh cry of 'Juice! Juice! Juice!' The dreamer tried, but could not rescue the child. Each crack of the whip seeming to cause the bath to hop a step further away.

An alcohol deadened subconscious played host to a dream that would have made D.H. Lawrence blush, the dreamer grunting lewdly in his sleep.

Another dreamer heard the call of his ancestors. They appeared on the periphery of the dream, dark shapes moving fluidly in murky outlines. They offered cigarettes that would melt as soon as the fingers of the dreamer clawed at them.

Then there was the dream that was more a feeling than a dream. There were no people or characters to populate it. No voices or sounds inhabited it, but the dreamer knew who the feelings were and what they meant. A sense of impending loss hung over the dream, lightly seasoned with the sharpness of chilli and the bitterness of lime.

Another dream hovered outside a subconscious, hesitating, wondering if it should enter that nest of bitchiness. It was a good dream, one that would allow the dreamer a deep peaceful sleep, allow them to wake refreshed. It flittered around the potential home, then decided to leave, feeling that perhaps the next night it might find a better place.

One subconscious frustrated the dreams. It was turning on and off as the dreamer tossed and turned, dozing then waking then dozing again. The dreamer teased the dreams, inviting them in, only to shoo them away till they were so jumbled.

At last, dawn began to dust off the dark of the night. The dreams fell away from the mountain as subconsciouses faded into daily lives. The mountain smiled and yawned gently as those in her care rose from their beds.

Lady Chatterley was a half-virgin. Esther replaced the book in its place.

'How can a woman be a half-virgin?' she thought. From what she had read the previous day, Mrs Connie had been to the forest and experienced the 'sex thrill'. Esther had liked that phrase as she read it – sex thrill. It summed up rather well what she had first experienced in the forest and occasionally now when time permitted, she experienced it with her husband.

She hurried through the house, aware that her neglect of duties would not go unnoticed. A job can be half done, but a virgin? This concept still puzzled her. Perhaps European women were built differently and needed to have more than a sex thrill in order to lose their virginity fully. Or maybe it was the number of sex thrills they needed. How many sex thrills would a woman need to no longer consider herself a virgin? She thought she was no longer one after her time in the forest, but now she was not sure anymore. Was she only a half-virgin herself without knowing it? Or was she maybe an eighty per cent virgin?

The kitchen felt warm and welcoming and Esther was more sure of herself. She was a full, one hundred per cent house maid, no half measures here. And she was not, she hoped, anything like those old, dried up ones who failed to welcome Mr Clifford and Mrs Connie to Wragby. Mr James had taught her how to welcome people to the lodge and had even commented once that she was very good at it.

Aside from the half-virgin comment, the other thing that puzzled Esther in what she had read was this lack of welcome and also why Europeans would choose to live in a place as horrible as Wragby sounded. Europe was supposed to be full of money. If they could motorise their bathtubs, why couldn't they live somewhere nice, with nice people who would welcome them home? She would never understand the whites.

Having spent time reading, she could not stop to check that Thomas was okay, but moved quickly to the front lawn to clear away the breakfast dishes. Mrs Mary smiled kindly at her as she did, and although the watchful eye of Solomon prevented any conversation, Esther did notice how tired she looked. Mr James' women usually looked a lot better after a few days at the lodge. Their pasty European faces would brighten and their smiles would become warmer. But Mrs Mary looked worse than when she arrived. Esther hurried back to the kitchen, needing to catch up the time lost to reading and trying hard not to think of Mrs Judith.

He didn't go near the front lawn. He was angry with Mrs Mary for not appearing in the bathroom as usual last night. A quick brush of the teeth in her pyjamas did not, in Caiaphas' eyes, count as an appearance, not after the shows of the previous two nights. He knew it was wrong to blame Mrs Mary for his frustration, but having built himself up so much for his evening thrill, he felt he needed to vent against someone.

'She will just have to do without seeing me this morning,' he muttered, as if the strange white woman would be devastated by his non-appearance on the lawn.

He rearranged the fire wood near the water tank for a third time. His dream had not helped, that teasing promise that pushed his relationship with Mrs Mary further into a sexual realm and away from caring about her wellbeing. He recalled, with some pain, the hardness he had woken up with this morning and groaned quietly as it threatened to resurface.

Why had Mrs Mary not appeared for him in the bathroom last night? He began to wonder if perhaps he had given himself away by washing the windows. Had she noticed how clean they were and now felt too exposed to perform one of her rituals? He considered rubbing some dirt onto the windows to return the dustiness to them, but knew that wouldn't work.

He picked up a log and moved it to another part of the pile, stared at it for a long time, then picked it up and put it back in its original place.

'You are being foolish,' he told himself and his stirred loins. 'Just because she did nothing last night doesn't mean she won't be back to normal this evening. Maybe she was just too tired and needed to go straight to bed.' He would try again tonight.

Having resolved this, he felt a bit better and moved the log again, then stood back to admire his handiwork.

'There you are Caiaphas. Why are you not in the front doing the garden? You need to go into town for some things. We have got guests tonight.'

He glanced over at Esther who stood holding Thomas against a naked breast, the young child happily sucking at the milk on offer.

'Okay,' he said, returning his gaze to the pile of wood which he adjusted once more just for good measure, then followed a few steps behind Esther to the kitchen. He picked up the list of supplies that were needed, casting his eye briefly over Solomon's tidy print, then moved towards the door.

'Oh, Mrs Mary wants to go into town with you,' Esther called after him.

He stopped and looked back, trying to disguise the alarm that had jumped to his face.

'Why? Why does she want to come with me?' The silent question screamed in his mind while his head nodded and a mumbled, 'Okay,' fell from his lips.

The air warmed slowly as the car descended the mountain and Mary closed her eyes, letting the breeze, which had been quite nippy at first, cool her as the temperature rose. She was still not sure why she had asked to come into town with Caiaphas, she would only get in his way. It was really a need to get away from the lodge for a bit that drove her, and she hadn't fancied the solitude of the clearing. It was while eating breakfast that she recalled James' reference to a small coffee shop in town.

It's run by a batty old Swedish woman called Annika. Her husband died while they were out here on safari and she never went home. The coffee is okay and she makes a pretty good ginger cookie, but it's not much. We like to support her, a bit like a charity. She's got no one else.

Another one of 'James' women'? Mary wondered as she recalled the note.

Caiaphas dropped her in front of the shop promising, rather sullenly Mary thought, to return in two hours to collect her. She stood for a moment at the bottom of a small set of faded red stairs that led up to the building's veranda. Small walls curled away from the steps on either side and terminated in square brick pots, each containing rather sad looking bushes. The shop was in a converted colonial house, the façade of which was a dusty white. The veranda skulked under the peak of a slightly rusty, corrugated iron cap. A table covered in a faded African print in a corner of the veranda and was held up by two attendant, rickety wooden chairs which offered a view of the street. A small vase sporting a wilted material flower tried hard to liven up the scene. A second, more desolate table came in to view as she ascended the stairs and moved through the wooden front door. The little room inside boasted a ceiling fan, the last turn it had witnessed was the turn of the century. The three tables scattered round the gloomy room appeared marginally more capable of standing on their own four feet than their outside sibling. A small counter mooched at the back of the room, a solitary plate containing five biscuits on a bed of doyleys and protected by a glass cake cover sat crying out for company.

Mary sniffed at the air, feeling more depressed about the inside of the shop than the veranda, but not keen to spend time in either space. She turned to leave, but was summonsed back by a sing-song voice.

'Hello dearie, table for one?'

The speaker was a stereotypical Nordic woman – blonde, blue eyes, tanned skin. The smile that touched the lips paled by a light lip-gloss, lacked reality but at the same time appeared genuine and warm.

Mary nodded, despite her gut instinct to leave the establishment.

'Inside or on the veranda?' There was just a hint of accent in her otherwise perfect English. 'The veranda is better, slightly cooler, my dear,' she added, guiding Mary out the door and giving her no choice in the matter.

The chair was surprisingly sturdy in stark contrast to its appearance and a light breeze caught the scent of the jacaranda in the road. The relief the breeze brought and the soothing balm of the fragrant smells gave the setting a more pleasant appeal and Mary smiled at her hostess as she was handed a small menu. It was an A5 page with faded and peeling laminate and contained three items:

Tea	1,000 shillings
Coffee	1,000 shillings
Biscuit	1,500 shillings

Mary began to laugh, then looked up to see Annika standing, note pad and pen at the ready to take her order. She turned her laugh into a cough, perused the menu again as if trying to decide what she wanted, then ordered coffee and a biscuit. Annika studiously wrote the order down, before disappearing inside.

Locals, made their way up and down the main road, going about their business. A man in a torn shirt and tatty sandals pushed a wooden cart laden with large yellow plastic bottles up the road. Liquid, water perhaps, sloshed inside the bottles. Perspiration dotted the top of his head like a pimply rash and his skinny arms belied the strength he obviously needed to push his load.

Two young women carried large bags on their heads, their necks taut and slightly strained, yet they seemed to be floating on gently swaying hips.

'People seem happy,' Mary thought, then corrected herself, 'maybe not happy, but content.' There did not appear to be the judging of others that she had felt so acutely back home. Of course, it could all be a cultural difference that prevented her from recognising the signs of snobbery in the black people who walked these streets. 'Maybe,' Mary thought, 'they sneer in a different way to the Shelia Cobblers, Sarah Slaters and Amanda Hazells of this world.'

Her thoughts went back to England, to the days before she had decided to come out here. How dare those women judge her? They had no idea what she went through with George. Unless you had experienced it, you could never understand. She had never been unfaithful to George and yet they saw fit to alienate her. If she, like Lady Chatterley, had run off with...she searched her mind to find an equivalent of Mellors in the village back home, but failing to find one finished her thought rather lamely with...a lowlife, what would they have done. Thinking back to Karen and her divorce, she could not recall anyone being as cold towards her friend as they had been to her. The pall of death seemed to bring a stigma to one that even fooling around outside of marriage could not.

'There you go, dearie.'

A tanned arm moved in front of her vision to place a mug of coffee and a plate with a solitary biscuit on it, in front of her.

Mary looked up at the Swedish woman, remembering that she too was widowed, and tried to see if the pall of death still clung to her.

Caiaphas opened his new packet of cigarettes and gave one to Old Man Mawenzi who sat on a low wall just near to the car. The shopping was complete but it was still too early to go pick up Mrs Mary and, spotting his dance partner, he had called him over, waving the cigarette box as bait. This was an out of hours meeting, so the normal rules wouldn't apply and he could chat to the his friend to help pass the time.

The old man dragged on the cigarette, coughed and spat into the grass in the graveyard that lay behind the wall he was on. The grey-white tombstones lay in neat rows and the grass around them was well kept. Caiaphas had heard that this was a European graveyard from the war, but he didn't know which war. A man from two villages over had the job of keeping it clean and occasionally Caiaphas had seen some white people in there looking at the graves and taking pictures, but this all meant nothing to him. These people were long dead, why would you want to take a picture of their grave stone?

'How is everyone at the lodge?' the old man slurred through his harelip and sucked in his spit.

'All is fine there,' Caiaphas lied. It was not good manners to tell the old man of his problems with Solomon, whom he hated for the way he watched everyone and would always appear at inopportune moments. Nor could he mention his growing anger towards Esther who now seemed to be checking up on him these days, as if she were Solomon's spy, and of course he could not mention the frustration the white woman was causing him on the sexual front.

'That is good,' Old Man Mawenzi said and lifted the cigarette to his mouth again, his good eye following it and the strange squint that resulted, unnerved Caiaphas a little. He began to wish that he hadn't caught his dance partner's attention.

'I have heard that my friend Solomon is going to leave us, that he is going to be a cook in Paris.' The good eye now concentrated on Caiaphas.

'That is just talk,' he replied, hoping that he sounded convincing. 'You know how white people are, they come here and promise you everything, but never keep those promises. It was like that. The white man from Paris just said that Solomon should go work for him, but he never meant it.'

The old man nodded, took in a lungful of smoke, held it for a few seconds then, as he blew it out of his nose and mouth, he began to laugh. It was not a pleasant sound, sort of a sucking hyena laugh. Caiaphas smiled, unsure of what was so funny.

The laugh dissolved into a coughing fit which went on long enough to cause Caiaphas to reach for the alarm bells, then petered out just in time with a final spasm and another phlegmy missile launched at the long dead soldiers.

The old man sucked in a lungful of air, steadied himself, took a soothing drag on his cigarette then slowly blew the smoke out before he spoke.

'Solomon will not leave us. He will not go to Paris, or London, or even Dar es Salaam. He was born in Kilimbati and, like me, he will die in Kilimbati.'

Caiaphas was not sure if he was prophesying, stating a fact, or pre-ordaining this event, but he nodded his agreement anyway.

They sat in silence for a bit and watched the young girls walk by with their balanced loads, then both heads turned to watch the swaying buttocks move slowly on. The old man sighed then turned his head back to see Samuel pushing his cart of water up the road.

'You're looking very smart today,' Old Man Mawenzi called to him.

The labouring man grunted and lowered the cart, waiting for it to steady itself before he answered, 'I am taking this water to my mother-in-law. I have to look smart.'

The old man hooted with laughter, 'You will never be smart enough for your mother-in-law.'

Samuel laughed and nodded. 'You are right, Mzee. She would have preferred it if her daughter had married Caiaphas here.'

They looked over at Caiaphas, but he was staring down the road towards the mad woman's coffee shop.

A few things puzzled Esther about the bit of Mrs Mary's book she had read after doing the breakfast dishes and before she had to go and make up the guest room. Firstly, there had been all that talk by the men at Mr Clifford's house. They had said that sex was a form of communication. The only thing she thought sex communicated was that a man was horny. It had never spoken to her in any way other than that this was what men wanted. Did sex say other things in Europe, or was it just that, for men, it spoke? Maybe that rhythmic slapping of his flesh against hers sent out a message like the drums of old that

bore the news across the land. If so, then her husband never had
a lot to say when he 'spoke'.

Esther put those thoughts aside, assuming that for the whites
this meant something different and turned her attention to the
next strange occurrence in the book. Mr Clifford, whom she had
worked out, could not 'communicate', had told Mrs Connie that
she should try and have a son by another man. At the Catholic
school she had attended, it had been made very clear to her that
sex outside of marriage was a sin reserved for the cardinals in
Europe. She had not read that Mr Clifford was a cardinal, let
alone a priest, so how was it that he was allowed to tell his wife
that she could sin like that?

Perhaps she had misunderstood the sisters at school because
Mrs Connie had only taken a couple of pages to try to obey her
husband when she had slept with Michaelis. However, this had
sparked a crisis, well he had had his crisis first and then had to
grit his teeth till Mrs Connie had hers. It was odd that these
whites could have a crisis while 'communicating'. From overheard conversations between Mr James and Mrs Joyce, most of
the women who came to stay at the lodge did so because of a
crisis.

As she straightened the sheet on the guest bed, her thoughts
turned to Mrs Mary. She knew that her husband had died
recently so who was she 'communicating' with to have a crisis?
Suddenly she stopped her bed making and her hand flew up to
her mouth as if trying to prevent a thought that had just
jumped into her mind from escaping through her lips.

'No!' she thought, 'it cannot be him.'

'You're the woman looking after the lodge for James,' Annika
said, lowering herself into the chair opposite Mary. It was a
statement and Mary was unsure if she wanted this uninvited
conversation, but felt a little relaxed by her surroundings and
was curious about how the death of this woman's husband had
affected her, so she nodded, half in agreement with Annika's
statement and half in agreement to her sitting down at the table.

'How are things there? You settling in okay?'

For a mad woman, she seemed quite normal and friendly.

'It's taking a bit of adjusting, but I think I'm beginning to get the hang of things up there,' she gave a half shrug, 'still adjusting to not having electricity, but James seems to have thought of everything.'

Annika smiled and nodded. 'He is a good man, James. He is my best customer here. Drink your coffee, dearie, it will get cold.'

Mary took a sip of the coffee and nibbled on the biscuit. Both were surprisingly good.

'So, do you think I am mad?'

Mary half choked on her mouthful of coffee and began to fumble around for some words.

'Go on,' Annika urged gently, 'be completely honest and don't be all British and coy with me. Tell me what you really think. We Scandinavians are used to being blunt.'

'I...um...well...' Mary took a deep breath. 'I...I can't just throw off my British-ness like that,' she blurted out.

'So you do think I am mad then?'

'No, I mean yes, I don't...I mean. Hang on. Let's start again.' Mary writhed slightly, but noticing that her host was smiling at her, she forced herself to calm down and then said, 'I've only just met you. I don't know if you are mad or not. You seem pretty sane talking to me now.'

Annika's smile bubbled over into laughter. It was a pleasant sound. 'I'm sorry. It was unfair of me to ask you such a question. I am sure that James told you I was mad. And probably Joyce too, I assume you've met Joyce?'

Mary nodded, 'Joyce never said anything about you.'

'Not? I am surprised. She usually gossips about everyone. I am sure James said I was mad. No?'

Mary looked away. She was not used to this sort of bluntness, but she still replied rather quietly, 'He called you batty.'

Annika chuckled. 'Batty? I like that. More coffee? On the house this one.'

Mary started to shake her head.

'Oh, don't give me that. You British. Too polite. Have some more coffee and don't worry about me. I am well looked after by the life insurance that my husband had and my krona go a long way here.'

Mary gave a resigned nod, feeling a little unsure of herself at the mention of Annika's late husband. It was, after all, what had apparently driven her batty. But, as she waited for her host to get the pot of coffee and to pour the refill, she thought, 'Sod it. I am a widow too and probably called worse things than batty by those horrible women back home. I am no better than them if I carry on avoiding the elephant in the room. I like Annika. I like her directness.'

Once the coffee had been topped up, a new cookie put on the plate and Annika had sorted some out for herself, she sat down again.

'Er, how did your husband die?' Mary asked before Annika could say anything and as her new-found courage floundered slightly, she added, 'if you don't mind me asking.'

'Of course I don't mind,' Annika smiled. 'We were on a safari, on a boat on one of those lakes,' she gestured vaguely. 'We disturbed a hippo who up-ended us and Nils was the unfortunate one that the hippo chose to bite. The rest of us made to the shore safely, but poor Nils...well at least he didn't suffer very long, he was gone within a minute.'

'I'm sorry,' Mary said as Annika stared out at the road.

'Thank you. You are very kind.' Annika took Mary's hand in hers and patted it gently, then drew in a deep breath, sat up straight and said, 'But that was all a long time ago.'

'How long?'

'Ten years.'

'Do you still miss him?' Mary knew the answer.

'Every day.'

It was Mary's turn to stare out at the street as memories of George bubbled up in her mind, memories of good times.

'Does it ever get any easier?' she asked. A small tear started its slow journey down her cheek.

'For starters we have wild mushrooms marinated in a balsamic and parsley vinaigrette and served in a filo pastry shell.'

The guests were boring. An Austrian couple who sat very politely hardly talking.

'It must be the language barrier,' Mary thought after a fifth attempt at conversation faded away into the gloom of the room.

They had arrived soon after her return from town and she had had no time to freshen up.

The couple, a good few years older than Mary, had hardly settled before they decided to go out for a walk, leaving Mary to try and marshal thoughts that she did not want to be with. To distract herself she sought out her copy of *Lady Chatterley* which, she could have sworn she left on the small dressing table in the room, but which she found on the little bedside one.

Connie was having more fun than she was. Connie was getting up to all sorts of mischief with Mellors while all she was doing was mulling around a small corner of Africa feeling decidedly lonely. Her encounter with Annika had helped, and Esther was becoming better company, but the chat at the coffee shop that morning had starkly reminded her of the gap left in her life by George's departure and she found herself hating him for deserting her.

She hated him for the pain he had caused. Never during his life had he been the bringer of such feelings. She had occasionally been annoyed with him and sometimes even angry. But generally they had a good married life. He was too gentle a man to cause her too much upset. But now he was gone and that hurt so much that she hated him. She also hated herself for hating him. He could no more have stopped his disease than she could have.

It was only the return of the Austrian couple that prevented her tears flowing for a second time that day and she hurriedly packed Connie, Clifford and Mellors off to her bedroom before returning to the lounge to play cheerful hostess to the dour guests.

'Dinner should liven them up,' she thought, 'Solomon's cooking has got to produce some conversation.'

Only the clink of the cutlery on the plates disturbed the incessant chirping of the crickets as they ate. All the husband managed as they stood to go off to bed was, 'Very good, thank you.' He nodded at the table then bowed and mumbled a 'Good night.'

No matter how hard he willed it, Caiaphas could not get Mary to remove her pyjamas. In fact, he could not even get her to linger in the bathroom. She was gone within a minute of him peering through the window, having caught her spitting out her toothpaste. He cursed Old Man Mawenzi despite knowing that even if his dance partner had been on time and not dawdled over his cigarette, he would not have missed anything. Mawenzi seemed to be slower than usual in all his movements.

Caiaphas stood staring at the dim light that filtered through the bathroom door from the bedroom. Maybe she would return to the bathroom for one of her rituals; it was clutching at straws.

He stepped up closer to the window, straining his neck to see if he could get a glimpse of Mrs Mary, but the angles would not allow it. Suddenly, he stepped back in shock, his head turning wildly to locate the source of the sound he had heard.

Rex ambled past, ignoring him and lifted his leg next to the carefully stacked pile of wood. It was Caiaphas' cue to leave and he moved off quietly, muttering indignant curses at Mrs Mary and the dog, the latter only once he was far enough away from the animal.

A pair of old rheumy eyes watched from the dark of the forest.

SEVEN

A breeze wiggled its way around the trees as it slid slowly toward the lodge. As it moved it gained momentum and picked up dust and smells on its way. Sweet and tangy undergrowth offered up its scent to the breeze as it lay decaying on the forest floor. Squirrels, rabbits and birds gave generously to the olfactory brew and, if you were to breathe deeply, you would catch a hint of the previous day's coffee that was roasted at the farm miles away, but whose odour had made the long journey up the side of the mountain, carried on the back of the travelling wind.

The breeze slipped in through the small bedroom window that Mary liked to leave open, and deposited its load of smells on the bed, the occupant of which turned over to face the window and sighed. She lay still for a moment, then resigning herself to another sleepless night, stood up, lit the lamp and shuffled through to the bathroom.

As she moved to return to the bed, she caught a glimpse of herself in the mirror and stopped. The memory of the time spent staring at her naked reflection came bubbling up. Her first instinct was to repeat the process, to study herself again in all her glory, but she knew she did not need to undress this time.

Holding the lamp up, she looked at her face, the dark eyes made darker by the shadows her brow cast over them, the slight wrinkling of the skin around the eyes, the neat, slightly up-turned nose and the mouth set in a sort of Mona Lisa pout.

Her eyes moved in a slow circle, taking in her features. There had been something in Annika's face, a sort of peace, an accept-ance of her fate that Mary now hankered after. It was difficult to say what exactly it was that she had seen, but she knew she would recognise it again. There was no sign of it in her face. She had a long way to go yet before she could be truly at peace with what had happened with George. One thought that did pass through her mind as she searched her face for the slightest hint of this, was what Annika had said. 'Everyday,' was her response to the question, 'Do you still miss him?' It was not said with regret or sadness, more with a hint of pride, as if she were saying that her attachment to her husband was so strong that even death could not conquer their love. There was something in the 'batty' woman's voice that said to her, 'hold on tight to the good memories, they are the ones that will see you through.'

The wind rattled the bathroom window slightly and took her attention away from her reflection, but in that split second before she looked away, and so brief it was that she didn't see it, her eyes smiled.

Esther watched Caiaphas as he watched Mrs Mary. 'Surely Mrs Mary was not "communicating" with him,' she thought, but there was still a nagging voice that said one could not put it past him. There had been stories of him and some of Mr James' women. She had not believed the stories back then, but looking at him now, the way he was eyeing out Mrs Mary, she felt there could have been some merit in these rumours.

Despite the temptation to read more of Mrs Mary's book, Esther did not feel she could get away with being late for breakfast duties again, especially as there were guests to look after. She glanced across at the elderly couple. They were strange people. Normally guests chattered away at dinner and breakfast, telling tales of their travels. But these two hardly spoke a word. She could see that Mrs Mary was struggling with them and she felt a bit sorry for her.

'More tea, sir?' She moved to the table to perform her duties and also to help Mrs Mary out.

'No, thank you.' The man put his hand over his cup as if Esther would not understand the word 'no' nor the shake of his head.

'May I take your plates?' She asked in her best English as Mr James had taught her.

The man nodded on both his and his wife's behalf. Esther shot a sympathetic look at Mrs Mary before clearing the dishes away and got a 'thank you' look in return.

By the time she returned to the table to clear away the rest of the dishes, the guests were gone and Mrs Mary sat alone, a topped up cup of tea in front of her. She smiled and shook her head, communicating her frustration with the guests, but fearful of vocalising it.

She looks a little happier today, Esther thought as she picked up the honey pot and salt cellar and glanced across at Caiaphas. He was still looking at Mrs Mary in a strange way, sort of lust and anger mixed together. Esther could understand the two emotions separately, but the combined effect was puzzling till she looked back at Mrs Mary who seemed oblivious of the attention she was getting.

Esther half chuckled. 'He has been used and then cast aside,' she told herself. 'Typical man. He has had his "crisis" and now he must grit his teeth till Mrs Mary has hers.'

Solomon was still in the kitchen when Caiaphas came back with the wood for the evening. He paused for a second, a little surprised to see that the old man was still there after breakfast and sitting at the work surface. But refusing to let the man's presence affect him, he moved quickly to stack the logs neatly next to the oven. Out the corner of his eye, he saw that Solomon was watching him closely and he fumbled in his task, quietly cursing himself for showing this weakness. He picked up the fallen logs and restored them to the pile, then stood up, wanting to leave the kitchen and the watchful eye of the old man. He did not like the way he was being scrutinised.

'Sometimes we see things,' Solomon's voice was grave, but yet there was no sign of anger or judgement in it, 'things that we should not see. This is never good for the soul.'

He nodded to indicate that he was finished, then shuffled out of the kitchen without waiting for a response from Caiaphas.

It was warm in the clearing. The colourful gecko scurried for safety while Mary found a comfortable spot to sit. She had brought *Lady Chatterley* with her, but the book waited patiently in her bag while Mary settled herself, then breathed in the clean, fresh air and surveyed the view.

'It's so beautiful up here, don't you think?'

George did not answer, but she persisted.

'I love the colours, the browns and greens, then you get the splash of purple of the jacarandas in the town,' she pointed and George, still rather hazy and translucent in her memory, nodded.

'And the sky. You'd never see a sky like this back in England. It's so deep blue and it does seem bigger.'

'Yes.' George's voice was faint and distant, but the details of his face were beginning to sharpen.

Mary surveyed the scene for a while, content just to be with George.

'Wasn't dinner last night wonderful?'

George wavered, but still nodded.

'Who would have thought that one would find such brilliant chef out here in the middle of nowhere? James knows how to keep a secret, doesn't he?'

At the mention of James' name, George disappeared. Mary looked round, but could not conjure him up again. She stared out at the scene before her and a tear rolled down her cheek.

'She is not here. She has gone out for a walk, sir.'

Esther did not like the man who stood at the door of the lodge. His eyes moved too much, never settling on one thing for long, never meeting her own and spending too much time looking at her chest. He spoke to her as if she were a child, as if it was her fault that Mrs Mary had gone out.

'She is probably having a secret meeting in the forest with Caiaphas.' The thought kept well away from her lips.

She had not seen this white man before and was more than a little disconcerted with his appearance at the lodge. Maybe he was someone Mrs Mary had met in town yesterday, but Caiaphas had not said anything.

The man studied his feet for a bit, then cleared his throat.

'Please could you tell her that Pieter called. Thank you.'

As he turned to leave, Esther caught a whiff of alcohol. It was not strong enough to say that he had just been drinking, but rather it was part of an aura that clung to the man.

'Maybe this is why Caiaphas is so angry with Mrs Mary. She has found someone of her own colour and dumped him,' Esther told Thomas who stared up from the cardboard box at his mother. She lifted him out and bounced him round the kitchen much to his delight.

Mr Pieter could not have been gone five minutes before Mrs Joyce arrived. Esther served her juice in the lounge as instructed, then left to fetch the laptop for Mrs Joyce to take back to the farm to recharge.

'Is Mrs Mary really pregnant?' Joyce asked on her return. Esther nearly dropped the computer.

'I don't know anything about that, ma'am.' She moved towards the safety of the kitchen.

'Come on Esther, I know you overheard us the other day. You heard her say she was pregnant by her friend's son, didn't you?'

Esther paused, but did not turn round.

'Well?'

'I do not know, ma'am. I did hear her say she was, but I do not know if she is or not.' She kept her back to Mrs Joyce as she answered, then began to move to the kitchen again.

'I see. You know, your mother is getting a bit old. Maybe I need to start looking for someone to replace her. Do you know of anyone good who can come and work for me?' Esther turned sharply. 'Ah, now tell me, is Mrs Mary pregnant or not?'

Esther shook her head slowly.

'No, ma'am.'

'Then why did she say she was?'

'I don't know, ma'am.'

Joyce studied her for a bit, then nodded and muttered, 'the bitch,' or at least, that's what Esther thought she said.

At the word 'bitch', Rex, who had been dozing on the floor next to the couch on which Joyce sat, lifted his head, looked round, then put his head back on his paws with a loud sigh. Esther struggled not to giggle at this.

'Do not mention this conversation to Mrs Mary now, you understand?'

Esther nodded obediently, understanding the implied threat in Mrs Joyce's look. She accompanied the white woman to her horse, helped her to mount and watched her race off without a word of farewell.

'Bitch,' she muttered under her breath, but didn't feel any better.

Did he know? Had he seen?

Caiaphas sucked strongly on his cigarette, held the smoke in his lungs for as long as he could endure, then blew it out in a low, whistling cloud. He sat on the edge of the cliff, his legs dangling over the side and looked down at the ravine below. There was thankfully, no battered body down there today. Maybe it would be better if Mrs Mary went that same way as Mrs Judith, he thought. It would relieve him of his frustration.

He did not want to admit it, but he knew that Solomon was right. Nothing good would come from his spying on Mrs Mary in her bathroom. He remembered the time one of Mr James' women had lured him to her bed. She had used him and then discarded him. But Mrs Mary was not like that one. She did strange things in her bathroom but, if he was honest with himself, there were no signs that she would seek his services in that way.

A light breeze came up and played with the smoke he exhaled. He watched as it dissipated, feeling all hopes dissolve too. Mrs

Judith's body again as he stared down into the ravine and a slow anger arose in him. Life was not going to get the better of him the way it had with her. He was not going to give in. Life was not going to make him jump, he was too strong for that.

'I don't care,' he told the breeze and blew some more smoke defiantly, daring the wind to play with it. 'I don't care what the old man says, I will carry on.'

She had gone to the clearing hoping that the beauty of the spot would soothe her and for a moment it had, but when George had disappeared from her mind, her spirits sank. She had tried to direct her thoughts back to him, but when that failed, she tried to think of James and if she had in any way given George the impression that there was something, other than a brotherly love, between them. George knew they were close, but surely he had understood that it had been sibling love. Well at least from her side. She could not be sure of James' feelings, but surely they were irrelevant. What James felt about her meant nothing if she did not love him back in that way.

Would she not have deserted George when he fell ill? Packed him off to a care home and only visited occasionally while forging a new life with James on the side? No. She had been truly faithful to her husband until death did them part. Enduring all those looks and whisperings that she knew were going on about her in the village. But she had not abandoned him.

Why had he left her now when she was trying to connect? Why could he not offer her that little comfort she craved at the moment? Anger began to brew inside her. She had stood by him through everything. Everything. And yet he could not be there for her now when she needed him, all because of some petty and unfounded jealousy. She felt betrayed.

Why had she given in to him when he had asked, no, pleaded with her. He was being selfish, thinking only of his own comfort. What about her comfort? Did he ever stop to think about what he was asking and the effect it would have on her?

She stood and brushed the dust from her skirt, as if exorcising herself of the memory of him. If he was going to be like that, then she would just let him go. She snatched at her bag and started to head back home, slowing her pace only when she stumbled slightly over the rocks. Despite everything she had just thought, she knew that she would not, could not, abandon George. This was just a little tiff. Anger is part of the grieving process, a small voice told her.

Esther was disappointed when she cleaned Mrs Mary's room. The naughty book was not there. She had hoped to get a good chunk of reading done while Mrs Mary was out, but the white woman must have taken it with her.

How can she read and walk, Esther wondered. She will trip and fall. But it is not my place to tell her that. She will learn the hard way.

She straightened the duvet and swept the floor, then began to dust the little bedside table. Suddenly she stopped, stepped back and eyed the table suspiciously. Mrs Mary had moved it. Not very far, but it had been moved. Why would she do that? Had she perhaps dropped something under it?

Esther clicked her tongue and shook her head. This was a mystery. She continued with her cleaning humming quietly to herself. In the bathroom, she poured bleach into the toilet as Mr James had told her to do, then mopped the floor of the shower and neatly rearranged the soap and Mrs Mary's shampoo and bottles of cream. She returned to the toilet and gave it a perfunctory clean with the brush, flushed it, then moved on to wipe the basin.

Picking up the broom, she began to sweep, then stopped and stared at the floor. There were marks near the window, as if something had been dragged there. She put the brush down and studied the floor for a moment, then went back into the bedroom and picked up the bedside table.

The drag marks matched the feet of the table. So this was what was happening. Mrs Mary was using the table to climb out the window to meet with Caiaphas. They would then go experience the 'sex thrill' and he would have his 'crisis' and Caiaphas would then have to grit his teeth till Mrs Mary had hers. It was all clear to Esther now.

She sat down on the bed, taking in this new-found fact. In the book, she suddenly remembered, Mrs Connie's world had fallen apart after the 'sex thrill' with Mr Michaelis. He had been cross that he had had to grit his teeth. Esther pictured Caiaphas gritting his teeth, waiting for Mrs Mary to have her crisis, then telling her off for making him wait. It was hard to imagine Caiaphas telling off one of Mr James' women. Surely he would just have gritted his teeth and not said anything afterwards. Despite this thought, Esther could not help worrying that Mrs Mary's world would be falling apart. Then she remembered Mrs Judith and caught her breath.

After Mary left the clearing, it fell silent. The last echoes of the stones scrunching under her feet and her sharp intake of breath, almost a sob, dissolved slowly to become one with the air. The clearing seemed to breathe a small sigh of relief and, after a suitable time, the gecko stuck its head out of its hole. It looked round, checking that the human had gone, checked the skies to ensure no dangerous birds were circling, then moved cautiously out into the sun.

The breeze, as if no longer needed to cool the person who had been sitting there, folded itself up and found a tree at the edge of the clearing to rest under. The warmth of the sun spread itself slowly over the rocks like a table cloth. The low buzz of an unseen fly tiptoed across it.

A figure moved quietly from behind a tree into the clearing. The breeze glanced up, smiled and settled back. The buzzing intensified slightly while the warmth ran in and out between its feet. The gecko nodded a greeting as the figure came to a standstill at the spot where Mary had been sitting. Other than this, his progress did not disturb the tranquillity of the place.

The figure nodded back at the gecko, dark rheumy eyes slowly surveyed the scene, then it sniffed the air carefully, as if some olfactory trace of Mrs Mary's thoughts still floated there. It stood for a long time, eyes slightly closed against the bright sun. At length, it nodded to itself, bid the gecko farewell, and left.

'Mrs Joyce was here.'

Mary pulled a face and Esther started to giggle, then stopped suddenly.

'What did she want?' Mary asked taking the tea off the tray and placing it on the table next to her.

'Only to recharge the computer.' Esther did to not want to look at her properly.

'I see.' *I wonder what's up with her, she's not telling me everything. I can do without this at the moment.* 'Anything else?' Mary ventured, hoping that perhaps Esther would open up.

'Oh, a Mr Pieter came.'

Mary wished that she had not just taken a sip of tea.

'What did he want here?' she spluttered through her coughing.

'He did not say, only to tell you that he came,' Esther watched the white woman struggle with clearing the mis-swallowed tea, concern etched on her face.

'Does ma'am want some water?' she asked.

'No,' Mary coughed again, then added a stronger, 'No. Thanks. I'm alright.'

She took a deep breath and wiped away a cough induced tear from her eye. She smiled at Esther, 'I'm fine, thanks.'

Esther paused, uncertain if Mrs Mary really was okay, then moved off to the kitchen.

What the hell did Pieter want? It was too late for him to apologise for his behaviour and besides which, hadn't he sent Joyce over to do so on his behalf?

She sipped slowly at her tea, letting it soothe the irritation that it had caused earlier. There was too much happening and she didn't want to face any of it. She had come here to get away from all her problems back home, but seemed to have picked up a fresh set. George had followed her here. She had hoped to leave him and everything attached to him, back in England but, she supposed, that had been wishful thinking.

The accusing looks she got from her neighbours after George had died came flooding back as she stared at her cup of tea. They would mutter to each other in the supermarkets and on the high street, quickly parting and moving off without even acknowledging her as she approached. They wanted her to feel guilty, but she refused to give in. The guilt she felt was not because they wanted her to feel it; it was she that demanded it of herself.

Toby, in his one brief visit after George's death had watched her every move with an accusing look. What right did he have to accuse her, she had silently screamed as she made him a sandwich. He never gave a damn about his father, especially during his illness, so how dare he accuse her?

She gripped her tea cup tighter, trying to suck the waning warmth from it, wanting something, anything to remind her that she was not a cold person, but instead of getting warmth from the cup, she just felt that it was taking on her coldness. She wanted to drop it, or better still, hurl it across the room. She lifted it, as if to throw it, but the kitchen door opened and Solomon came through.

On seeing her, he pulled himself up to attention, his heels clicking slightly, and gave a small bow.

'Good evening, madam,' he intoned, his face giving no indication that he realised what she was about to do. 'Please excuse my intrusion, but I do need to pick some herbs for dinner.'

He moved towards the window ledge where there were a number of pot plants containing green shoots. He paused halfway across the room, glanced up at Mary who had frozen with the cup in launch mode.

'May I take that, madam?' he asked and before she could answer, or move, he had gently pried her fingers from the cup and moved back to the kitchen.

Mary sat back in her chair, glad to be rid of the cold cup, then slowly rubbed her hand where Solomon had touched her. It had been gentle, but more importantly, it had felt warm.

'Thank you, Caiaphas.'

Her voice sounded the kindest it had been since she first arrived at the lodge. There was a warmth to it that made him feel she was talking *to* him and not *at* him. He nodded and looked back at the fire he had just got going. He wanted to look at her, to study her, but lacked the courage. It was almost as if she were standing naked as she had done in her bathroom, but this time she could see him and he could now not look.

'Is there anything else you need, Mrs Mary?' he managed to ask.

'No, I'm fine, thank you.'

He shot a glance over at her. She sat on the sofa with her legs tucked up under her. An elbow rested on the armrest and took some of her weight as she leaned on it. In her hand, looking like an afterthought, was a glass of gin. Her head was lowered and studied the book on her lap. The glow from the hurricane lamp gave her hair a slight orange halo. She wore dark slacks and a white polo neck sweater.

Although her voice had spoken to him, she was not looking at him. He took the moment to study her form as she sat there looking somewhat angelic. He knew he could not take too long over this, so tried his best to imprint the picture on his mind, but he was too slow as she looked up, becoming aware of his stare. He moved quickly to turn round and poke at the fire, fumbling with the stick he was using to do so. He could feel her eyes on his back, he could sense the confusion there as she tried to fathom out why he had been staring at her.

He poked at the fire again, nearly causing the carefully built pile of logs to collapse and hastily withdrew the stick before he caused it to go out. He had to leave the room and do so with his dignity still intact, but was not sure how he could. Should he acknowledge her before he left, or just get up and walk off without even glancing at her?

The longer he left it, the worse it would be.

He straightened, made to turn round, then looked back at the fire, then started to move off, then paused and glanced back at the fire, then risked a glance at her, then fled.

'For our starter tonight, we have ass-pa-ra-gus with cheese and herbs, wrapped in smoked bacon with a basil and vinegar dressing.'

Solomon waited a second to let his words marinade in their own deliciousness, then moved off. Mary stared at her plate, letting the delicate aromas assail her nostrils. She still felt the warmth of his touch on her hand when she had frozen mid cup throw. The last time a touch had felt like that was when her father had welcomed her into the house for dinner one cold evening, shortly before he died. It was the dinner and the warmth of the welcome that she remembered now, and this gave her confidence to try and summons George up again. She would apologise to him for mentioning James and they could enjoy this wonderful dinner together. The candles on the table cast a romantic glow on the scene and she raised her glass slightly to her husband and then began to eat.

The flavours caressed her palate and she smiled at George's face, the way his eyes seemed to close slightly as he savoured his food. She knew she could not talk to him, Esther and Solomon would hear her, but she reached out in her mind and took his hand, and for a few seconds, everything was perfect.

'The main course this evening is oryx steak in a red wine and garlic sauce, sweet potato chips, pumpkin, slightly sweetened and flavoured with cinnamon and steamed cabbage with aniseed.'

George's eyes lit up.

The old chef gave a small bow and began to shuffle back to the kitchen.

'Solomon.'

'Yes, ma'am?'

Mary hesitated, a little unsure if she should say anything, Esther's warning about complimenting the old man rattled in the back of her mind, but, she needed to say this.

'Thank you.' It was not for the food.

Solomon nodded slowly and then smiled. It was the first time Mary had seen him smile.

'A pleasure, ma'am.'

His eyes said that he knew the 'thanks' was not for the food. He continued into the kitchen.

Old Man Mawenzi's cough was worse. Caiaphas eyed his silhouette in the darkness of the forest. The small red dot of cigarette end bounced in time to the hacking in the man's lungs. Caiaphas wanted to help, to ask if everything was okay, but this was the dance. There were rules that he could not break, so he sucked quietly on his own cigarette, helplessly watching his dance partner stumbling.

His mind was still playing with the idea of breaking other rules tonight and part of him was annoyed at the coughing. It was only slowing things down.

There was a throaty grunt and he could almost feel the phlegm rising in the old man before he heard him spit. At least that stopped the coughing for a bit and his partner was back in step, dragging on his smoke.

He could now let his mind wander to the bathroom window again. Would he be rewarded tonight? He would have to make sure that Solomon wasn't spying on his spying, but felt sure that the old chef wouldn't be there. He had said his piece and would expect to be obeyed. Caiaphas was confident that his viewing would not be watched.

Old Man Mawenzi coughed again and Caiaphas held his breath, waiting for the accompanying clatter of a fit, but it was a solitary cough that seemed to have got separated from the earlier herd that passed through. It came quickly as if running to catch up.

The red dot moved up to the old man's lips, glowed brighter, then eased down to his side.

Not long now, Caiaphas thought, as long as he doesn't start coughing again.

One-two-three, one-two-three. The dance moved quickly now that they were in step again.

Caiaphas stamped out the glowing butts and watched as the old man hobbled away, stopping to cough some more, then disappeared quietly into the night. Caiaphas moved quickly and quietly to his post, checking round to make sure that Solomon wasn't to be seen, although, in the dark, he would have been lucky to spot him.

The light from the bathroom window grew stronger as he got near. Perfect timing, he thought.

Connie Chatterley had stood before the mirror in all her glory and studied her body. She had not been best pleased with what she saw. Mary had done so a few nights ago and had found meaning in her hands, hands that had pushed George in his wheelchair as his own hands had become useless appendages to his wasting body.

Tonight, Mary was not looking for meaning in her body. She was giving herself to George again, like she had on their wedding night. Yes, her body had changed since then. Her body had shrunk within its skin, leaving it slightly loose. Her breasts no longer rode so high on her chest and her hips were wider, thanks to Toby. But tonight she was to be the blushing bride again, giving the ultimate physical gift she could.

She watched the reflection slowly undress, removing each item of clothing with precise movements, its eyes constantly staring back at her, as if mesmerised. Then it stood naked before her and...and what? She shuddered as the cool air made itself known.

The warm glow that dinner had brought as she imagined George being there with her, enjoying the good food, that was all imagined. This was reality. She was standing naked in front of a mirror in the bathroom of a lodge somewhere in the middle of Africa and George was not there. He would never be there again. And she was cold once more.

The fantasy had sprung a leak and all the warmth it had brought was suddenly draining out of the body very quickly. She watched the reflection as it seemed to shrivel up, almost implode, and sink slowly to the floor. She heard the reflection sob as her image faded from view.

How could she go on without George? When he had been well, he had been her rock, always there whenever she needed him. And when he was ill, he had been her purpose in life. Caring for him had got her out of bed every morning. Then he had left her, just as this evening's fantasy had, and this left her empty, a hollowness gnawing at her guts.

She clutched at her stomach as the pain of these thoughts hit and gave a low moan.

'Why? Why? Why?' she sobbed and drew her knees up, hugging them in her arms.

EIGHT

The darkness of the mountain was intense. It closed around everything, painting it a solid, impenetrable black. The moon was in shadow and the sun was frolicking on the other side of the world, so darkness had the mountainside to itself.

Only a small light dared to stand up to the dark as it flickered out through a small window, but it was losing its nerve as the enormity of its task was becoming apparent. It had tried, valiantly to protect the prone figure on the floor from the writhing black tentacles of the monster that covered the mountain, but now it stumbled, coughed, spluttered and gave up.

A pair of eyes stared in through a window, unsure eyes that now lost the object of their stare to the blackness that descended. They blinked and tried to adjust while behind them, a mind worked hard. Another pair of eyes watched the space where the watcher had been absorbed into the darkness, unable to determine what they were up to.

The darkness swirled tighter round the eyes, throwing up sprites and spirits that flickered and flashed, distorting anything that the eyes tried to focus on. Neither set of eyes moved, fearful of making a sound that would disturb the blackness.

Then a low moan, like a sob, squeezed its way out into the dark. It came muted, as it journeyed through the molasses of the night. There was a fumbling, then a *thwack* and a *woosh* and a tiny light melted onto the dark window. It dimmed slightly, grew in strength, settled for a moment, then dimmed again. The eyes at the window moved off into the night and the forest. The second set of eyes waited for a while, then followed the first set.

'Morning, Mary.'

The greeting was slightly icy and Mary could not quite understand why.

Joyce sat down at the breakfast table without being invited to do so. Mary had wondered why they always set out an extra chair on days when there were no guests at the lodge, but now she understood. Joyce would occasionally pop in unannounced for breakfast with James.

'Esther! Bowl!'

Esther was already halfway across the lawn with the bowl. She placed it in front of Joyce.

'Does ma'am want eggs this morning?' she asked politely.

'Of course, Esther. You know I always have eggs.' She shook her head at Mary and clicked her tongue.

'You just can't get the staff these days, she said, loud enough for the retreating Esther to hear.

Mary shifted uncomfortably in her chair.

'I've got the laptop, fully charged,' Joyce ladled some fruit salad into the bowl Esther had brought, then sprinkled some sugar over it. She picked up the jug of orange juice, looked round, sighed and half whispered, 'glass,' then put the jug down. 'Esther! Glass!' she screeched.

Mary's eyes itched from lack of sleep. The night had not been a good one. When she had sunk to the floor, she had felt like an alcoholic, overindulging on her misery. Then, as she had lain there, her mind imagined that she was a suicide, her wrists slit and her life slowly bubbling out on to the floor. Despite the coldness of the room, she had stayed there, slowly dying with no one to come and save her.

It was only when the wick of the lamp had burnt too short and gone out, and the darkness enveloped her, that she had momentarily felt frightened, as if the darkness had actually brought the death she had been conjuring up in her mind.

Later, the bedclothes had slowly warmed her body, but not her soul. She felt the burning cold of abandonment that froze all her emotions, except the hurt of it all. When she had finally dozed off, her dreams were plagued with guilt. Eyes watched her wherever she went, judgemental eyes that accused her, shamed her. The last thing she needed this morning was Joyce.

But her visitor was oblivious to her condition. She ate nosily and heartily, slurping coffee, sucking fried eggs and smacking her lips. She spoke all the time too, but nothing of consequence. The weather, the laptop, have you heard from James?

Mary responded politely to the questions and added to the conversation without interest. She concentrated on her own breakfast, trying to enjoy the pancakes and maple syrup, but it was impossible with that woman at the table. She seemed to sour the syrup and turn the pancakes dry. She wanted Joyce to leave.

Out of the corner of her eye, she noticed the statue of Solomon, standing, waiting to serve. His whole demeanour betrayed no emotion. You could not tell if he despised this crass white woman who treated Esther like dirt, or if he was, as his face seemed to say, completely neutral about it all.

Mary remembered his touch as he had taken the teacup from her. Surely he could not have such a caring and gentle touch like that and yet be unmoved by Joyce's behaviour. He hid it, if there was an 'it' to hide, remarkably well. Esther showed her emotions much more so. Not to Joyce's face, but one could see in her body language and the occasional grimace she managed when Joyce was not looking. How did Solomon manage to remain so stoic amongst all this, Mary wondered.

The statue sprang to life. Her glance had summoned him, even though she had not meant to. He reached the table, realised that he had not really been called so, without missing a beat, he filled Mary's empty coffee cup. As he did so, she looked up at him. With the slightest movement of his eyes he let on that she was being watched. Mary turned to Joyce and caught a venomous look that quickly scurried over to the toast rack as soon as it was discovered.

'That toast is burnt,' was Joyce's cover story.

Something funny was going on. First Solomon's behaviour last night – smiling at Mrs Mary. Solomon never smiled at anyone. Then there was Caiaphas' visit to the back of the house which had not resulted in the liaison she thought would happen.

Esther had been sure she would see Mrs Mary being helped through the bathroom window by Caiaphas so that they could have their fun, but the window had not even been opened. He had just stood staring in. But something had happened inside. Something that had disturbed him. He had seemed anxious just before the light went out and relieved when it came back on. What had Mrs Mary been doing to evoke these reactions?

All this intrigue had made her forget about the rude book and she pondered these events as she went about the breakfast routine.

Then Mrs Joyce had arrived. Esther tried to hover round the table as much as she could to see if there would be any accusations made about the pregnancy claims, but she kept getting sent off to the kitchen.

'Esther! Juice!'

'Esther! Toast!'

'Esther! More butter!'

Why couldn't that stupid woman work out all that she wanted and then give her a list of things to bring, not send her back to the kitchen every time she brought something back. It was, she suspected, her punishment for being complicit in Mrs Mary's deceit.

It was not my fault, she thought as she returned to the table with the mustard. What business is it of mine if Mr James' women want to lie to each other? I cannot tell Mrs Mary to be honest to Mrs Joyce. And how was I to know that Mrs Joyce would be so upset?

She placed the mustard next to Mrs Joyce and stood back, awaiting the next command. Mrs Joyce ignored the mustard and chewed noisily on a slice of toast and marmalade. The conversation between the two white women had shrivelled up and, other than the noise of Joyce eating, a silence fell on the garden. Esther stood ready, waiting for the question to come. She could see it in Mrs Joyce's face, she was building up to saying something.

'You know, Mary,' the rude woman swallowed the last of her toast, 'you don't look very pregnant.'

Rex was being a nuisance. He got in a mood sometimes and did everything in his power to disrupt the target of his mischief.

Maybe he smells my guilt, Caiaphas thought as he came round the corner of the house, the bucket full of scraps destined for Mr James' compost heap just missed Rex's nose. He gave a low growl and glared at Caiaphas.

'You shouldn't get in the way, Rex,' Caiaphas said, his voice trying to placate the ruffled hound, but betrayed his nervous state. He and Rex never got on. They tolerated each other, Caiaphas accepting the dog as something Mr James wanted to have around and Rex obeying the unspoken command from James – don't bite the staff.

But James wasn't around at the moment and this worried Caiaphas.

'Good boy,' he tried to get the tone right, the way Mr James always said it, 'Good boy, Rex.'

He backed away slowly, not taking his eyes off the slightly bared fangs that Rex was displaying.

'Damn dog,' he grumbled as he returned back round the side of the lodge, his still full bucket of scraps nearly smashing the kneecap of Esther who was coming in the opposite direction.

'Sorry, sister,' he mumbled and tried to move round her, but she continued to stand in his way, hands on her hips.

'Sister?'

She stared back at him, her teeth slightly bared and there seemed to be a low growl coming from her.

'Sister?' he asked again, 'What is the matter?'

He looked round for an escape route, but was hemmed in by a hedge on one side and the lodge wall on the other. Now he had an angry dog behind him and a growling bitch in front of him.

'What were you doing last night?' Esther spoke in a low voice despite using Swahili.

'Last night? I...I...I was sleeping. Why do you want to know? Did you want me?' he grinned lewdly, hoping this would distract Esther from asking further questions.

'Want to be with you? You are a funny man, Caiaphas,' her voice held no humour.

'Come on, baby, you know you can't resist me,' he reached out to grab her waist, but she flicked at his wrist with the dish towel that she was carrying and he withdrew his hand quickly.

'What were you doing last night?' She asked again.

He did not need this. He didn't have to answer to her.

'That is none of your business,' he pushed her aside, almost sending her into the hedge, and was gone before she could recover.

'You must stop it,' she shouted after him, 'you will get caught one day.'

Mary let the breeze calm her as she drove the 4x4 down the mountain. Apart from the long, bumpy driveway, the road was tarred all the way. She didn't need Caiaphas to take her everywhere, she was big enough to look after herself, thank you very much.

The road took a sharp, almost u-bend and she suddenly realised with a shock that she was travelling too fast for this descent. The tyres screeched a bit as she narrowly missed going over the side and plunging down the steep ravine.

'Damn that Joyce,' she muttered and forced herself to slow down. 'This is her fault. Anyway,' she continued after taking the next corner slowly, 'what right does she have being upset? She's so bloody rude, poking her nose into everyone's business like she does.'

The next corner was a little too fast again.

'She was so eager for a little bit of gossip, so eager to have some juicy titbit about James' latest woman, but she didn't care how that woman might be feeling. Vulture!'

The phrase 'James' women' also riled her, but she didn't want to admit that.

The wheels squealed a protest at the speed the corner was taken.

'I should have denied it, continued with the silly charade. Why did I give her the satisfaction of being right? Stupid bitch!'

The car narrowly avoided a woman walking up the road with a bucket balanced on her head. The head turned quickly to watch the car disappear, but the bucket wasn't interested and remained firmly in place.

'Well, now she knows that I'm not pregnant, so what? What difference does it make? She can go running back to her little group of perverts and tell them all that I'm a liar, a prude or whatever, I don't care.'

She slowed for a particularly sharp bend, then the car picked up speed as the road sloped steeply downwards.

'And then she had the nerve to ask me what my problem was. Well, you silly cow, my problem is that you are a rude, insensitive bitch who has no respect for her fellow human beings. The way she speaks to Esther is beyond rude. And what business is it of hers what problems any of the people who come to stay with James have. These are personal issues. If you're so starved of silly gossip and such like, why don't you go live in a village in England? I can recommend a good one where you would fit in, one full of whisperers and gawkers and holier-than-thous.'

The car was travelling at quite a rate now as there was a long straight stretch down the side of the mountain.

'I'm a grieving widow for goodness' sakes. Has she no compassion? She just wants something, anything to prove that she's better off than those around her. Well, she's not. She's bloody not. She never had twenty wonderful years of marriage to George. She would never be lucky enough to have someone like George as a husband.'

Mary's eyes began to mist over as the thought of George hit her. The car raced towards another bend.

The rude book helped to take her mind off what happened at breakfast as well as Caiaphas and his strange behaviour, but it had not been easy reading. Firstly, she had read about a man who did not like women. Well, he did like women, the man had said, but he couldn't love them and it seemed that his reason was that water should not be as wet as it is. What a strange thing to say. How can water not be wet? Also, how can a man only like a woman, but not be interested in the 'sex game'?

She had heard of homosexuals, the evil of their existence had been explained in detail during her time at the Catholic school, but she had never known one herself. She could only surmise that men, by being this way, were what caused all the problems that Mr James' women had, except maybe for them being pregnant. Having thought that, she realised that Mrs Mary was actually the closest they had had to a pregnancy from any of the visitors.

Connie, in the book, had been forlorn after the man had told her he liked women, but could never love them. Europeans made things so complicated, she thought. A man likes a woman, they get on with things, they have their sex thrills and don't worry about gritting their teeth. Why do they have to worry about 'like' and 'love'? Doesn't that just confuse everything? And even if a man likes another man, can't they just get on and do whatever it is a man in love with a man would do? Apart from not being sure what two men in love with each other would do, she was also not sure if they would both need to grit their teeth.

Fortunately, the bit about 'like' and 'love' was short and then the story began to make a bit more sense. A little girl was upset because her father had killed a cat saying that it was a poacher. Esther remembered the first time she had seen her mother kill a chicken by wringing its neck. She had been upset, but it wasn't long before she was doing the job herself.

'It won't be long,' she told the girl in the story, 'before you will be killing the poacher cats yourself, do not worry.'

She read on. This Connie woman was not happy and it seemed to revolve around sex and having babies. She was still trying to decide which of her husband's friends she could have a baby with, but was finding that none of them were right. And then she had seen that man, the cat killer, and he was bathing. Now she seemed to be interested in a man again. But how could she want this man? She was a boss and he was a servant.

'It would be like me and Mr James,' Esther thought, 'or...,' she stopped reading, '...or Caiaphas and Mrs Mary.'

Despite nothing happening outside the bathroom window last night, it could just be that Mrs Mary was interested in Caiaphas. But she could not have seen him bathing. Esther stopped her thoughts again...but maybe *he* had seen *her* bathing.

The clearing was quiet. There was a slight breeze and the gecko sat enjoying the sun, the warmth of which heated the rocks and pulsed back into the air. Scents wafted in from the forest and surfed on the waves the heat created.

An old man stood as a statue in the middle of the clearing, his face showed no emotion and his rheumy eyes betrayed nothing of what was going on in his mind, but the heat, the gecko and the forest scents knew what was going on. The man was consulting with nature, he was discerning what the sun thought, getting ideas from the breeze and hearing the opinions of the gecko.

He stood for a long time, then nodded slowly and bowed slightly before he moved noiselessly into the forest.

The gecko shook its head and the breeze agreed. They were not disagreeing with what the old man had decided, it was rather a sad gesture, a showing of pity for the person central to the problem. The forest scents, which had soured slightly while the old man was consulting, remained so for a short period of respect for the problem, then sweetened at the prospect of a solution.

The gecko picked up on the change in the scent and nodded. They must remain positive and do what they could to help. Nature did not want a repeat of what had happened a while back. It had been left as bruised as that body that had been brought up from the ravine. The hurt and pain of that person had seeped into the ground like poison. Nature had taken a long time to recover from that death.

'Are you alright, dearie?'

Mary sat down heavily in the chair on the veranda. It creaked ominously, then settled.

'Yes. No. I'm fine now. But...'

'I'll get you some coffee.'

The Swedish woman disappeared inside the shop and Mary watched her hands shaking. It was as if she were someone else watching those hands from somewhere far away. They were not her hands.

Slowly, she floated back into herself and gripped her hands together to stop them from shaking. They felt cold to each other. Mary gulped in a lung full of the warm air, the jacaranda scent almost cloying.

'There you go, dearie,' Annika placed a cup in front of her along with a biscuit. 'Now, tell me what happened.'

She settled herself in the chair opposite and cocked her head to one side, a calming smile playing on her lips.

Mary sighed and stared out at the street. Her hand clasped the coffee mug, pulling warmth from it despite the heat of the day.

'It's nothing,' she said at length, but her eyes did not meet Annika's, rather they watched the town go about its daily business. Annika did not reply.

'Really. It was nothing, just a stupid...' Mary was getting annoyed. She could feel Annika's silence slowly pulling at the story, coaxing it out of her. It was like a tug of war as she tried to hold on to it, to keep it private, but the silence was strong.

'Okay,' she said at last and looked at Annika now, daring her to be anything but sympathetic. 'I nearly had an accident coming down the mountain.' There, she had said it.

Annika nodded, but still did not speak. There was more story to come out.

'I was travelling too fast and couldn't take the bend properly.'

Still Annika was silent.

'I was lucky,' Mary admitted after a bit. She took a sip of coffee, letting the bitterness of it shudder through her body. She felt better after the caffeine hit.

'You know the bend by the reservoir? Well, it was that one. I skidded off the road onto the gravel, that bit where there is a sort of stopping point for people to get a view of the lake. Fortunately the gravel slowed me down quickly or I would have been in the lake.'

There, she had said it, told everything. She sat back in her chair and looked at Annika.

'You were thinking of him, weren't you?' Annika spoke softly, kindly.

Mary dropped her gaze to the plate and her biscuit.

'Yes.' It was a barely audible whisper. She felt Annika's hand on hers as she fought back the tears. She felt so silly, she had nearly killed herself. Annika patted her hand.

'Don't worry. You're okay now. And it's perfectly natural. Everyone does silly things when they lose a loved one. We cry, we deny, we get angry, we ask the "what if" questions, we get upset and worry about silly things. It's natural what you are going through, but hang in there and you'll get through it.'

Mary sniffed as a tear began to make its way down her cheek.

'Let me tell you what I did after my Nils was killed by that hippo. I went for a walk in the middle of a game park. I booked a safari and acted normal, but then slipped out of the lodge when we returned there for lunch. Had a whole lot of people in a panic.'

Mary looked up.

'There had been a pride of lions spotted near the lodge earlier that day, so everyone was running around like mad trying to find me.'

'What happened?' Mary couldn't help the alarm creeping into her voice.

'Nothing. I went and sat under a tree and waited for the lions to come and get me.'

George, the speeding 4x4 and sharp bends were forgotten.

'And?'

'Well, I hadn't been sitting too long before I felt something stinging my bottom.'

'What was it?'

'Red ants. Boy those things can bite. I jumped up like a jack-in-the-box, ran back to the lodge and dived straight into the pool with all my clothes on.'

'What did the people say?' The grin that had grown on Annika's face was beginning to spread to Mary's.

'Nothing.'

'Nothing?'

'There was no one there. They were all out looking for me. So, I sneaked into my room, changed, put some bite cream on my backside and when they all got back I was sitting by the pool with a drink in my hand that I had stolen from the bar. I told them I had gone to my room and had been listening to some music with headphones on, so I didn't hear them knock.'

Mary began to giggle.

'They were not impressed,' Annika smiled, sat back and joined Mary in her laughter.

'It's alright to have moments,' Annika said as they began to settle again.

'Thank You,' Mary smiled and sniffed, then stiffened slightly as she noticed the humour drain from her companion.

'Er...Mary?' The voice was familiar. Mary turned and saw Pieter standing at the bottom of the stairs.

The garden was looking good. The lawn had been cut, the flower beds weeded, and the bushes trimmed back.

Why had she taken the car? It is my job to drive. Caiaphas cast his eye over the garden, seeing if there was anything else he could do to take his mind off Mrs Mary and her disturbing behaviour in the bathroom last night.

What had she been up to? There was something wrong, but what? He was torn now between the voyeuristic delights of the bathroom window and a concern for the wellbeing of the white woman. On top of this, both Solomon and Esther were now aware of his evening activities. Even Rex seemed to sense that what he had been doing was wrong.

But what if Mrs Mary really had a problem, something like what Mrs Judith had? What could he do to stop Mrs Mary following that other poor woman down into the ravine? Who could he confide in and how could he explain himself and his behaviour?

No, he could not say anything to anyone. All he could do is keep as close an eye on Mrs Mary as possible. He would have to forgo the bathroom window routine for a bit because his work colleagues would be keeping an eye on him, but, he thought, that seems to be when she needs to be watched the most.

He looked round the garden again, seeing if there was anything that he had missed, but it all looked neat and tidy as Mr James liked it.

Esther put Thomas back into his box and covered up her breasts. He would be asleep soon and she could get on with her tasks now that he was fed. There were more guests coming, so she got out the clean bedclothes and began making up the room. She was a little behind schedule so worked quickly.

The thought of Caiaphas watching Mrs Mary bathing and did he 'like' her or 'love' her and did Mrs Mary 'like' or 'love' him, still swirled around in her head. This was a complicated issue. She decided to push that thought out of her mind for the moment and spend some time thinking about the scene at breakfast this morning.

She had felt sorry for Mrs Mary who was obviously uncomfortable with Mrs Joyce being there and all the questions she was asking. She could see the way Mrs Mary had not talked, but only answered Mrs Joyce with a 'yes' or a 'no'. Mrs Joyce was doing all the talking.

When the pregnancy was mentioned, which Esther was sure it would be, she expected Mrs Mary to glare at her and half turned to go back inside to avoid the anger she was sure she would be the target of. But Mrs Mary had not flinched.

'And what makes you say that?' she had challenged Mrs Joyce.

'Well...I'm just saying,' the reply had put Mrs Joyce off her
stride a little, 'that you don't look pregnant, that's all. No need
to get all uptight.'

'I'm not uptight, I'm just upset. That's all.' Mrs Mary's voice
was calm, but a knot tightened in Esther's stomach. *Was she
upset with me because I told Mrs Joyce that she wasn't pregnant?* She thought.

Mrs Joyce didn't speak for a bit, then eventually said, 'Upset,
but not pregnant.'

'No.' Mrs Mary almost whispered it.

Mrs Joyce sat back, looking very pleased with herself.

Thankfully, Esther thought, *she did not look at me. That
would have made Mrs Mary think I had told her everything.*

'So what is it then? If you're not pregnant, it must be something else.'

Esther had expected that to be the end of the conversation,
but Mrs Joyce wanted more. Instead of more conversation, all
she got was Mrs Mary hurriedly jumping up, knocking her
coffee over and running into her room.

Mrs Joyce hadn't expected that, Esther could see, but was
more surprised by the flicker of concern that crossed Solomon's
face. He seemed almost about to walk off to see if Mrs Mary was
alright, but stopped himself and resumed his statue pose.

The horrid white woman took a sip of her coffee, a nasty smile
on her face. If her mother's job hadn't depended on Esther
behaving herself, something would have accidently spilt on Mrs
Joyce's lap to rid her of that evil grin.

Esther smiled to herself now as she checked that there was
soap in the guest bathroom. It would have been funny to see the
change in Mrs Joyce's demeanour if she had had the courage to
do that. But she had not and the smile drained away as her
mother and the security of her job came back to her mind.

At least Mrs Joyce had left soon afterwards. She would be
back again, that was a given as she was needed to recharge the
laptop battery. Esther helped her onto her horse without a
word, not even a thanks, being spoken.

'Now there goes a lady that a man could not even like, let
alone love,' she muttered to herself as she watched the horse

and rider disappear. The next problem was the question of whether she should go and see if Mrs Mary was okay or not.

'What do you want Pieter?' Annika's voice was terse.

'Just a word with Mary, if I may,' he was already at the top of the stairs.

Mary nodded to Annika to say that it was alright. He didn't look drunk so it was unlikely that he would be doing any groping.

Annika gestured for him to get a chair from the other table.

'Would you mind, Annika, if I spoke with Mary alone?' He held a broad brim felt hat in his hands and nervously fed the rim from one hand to the other. He was a rugged looking man. His facial hair was more than stubble but less than a beard. His face, red from the sun and a long term relationship with the bottle, was flat and uninteresting. It looked as if it had been sculptured from volcanic rock by a bad artist. Grey flecked black hair, combed neatly in a side parting covered the rock face.

Annika sighed and stood up, 'You want a coffee?'

'No. Thanks, Annika.' He pulled the chair out from the other table and sat down without drawing it closer to Mary as Annika disappeared inside.

Mary began to feel a bit uncomfortable as he lifted his eyes to her. They were like little slits in pink dough, pinpoints of black glimmering from the centre.

He waited until he was sure that Annika was properly inside, then began. His voice was uncertain and he kept his eyes lowered.

'I just wanted to apologise to you myself for my behaviour the other night. I have been on site for the last few days so haven't been able to see you myself. I did ask Joyce to convey my apologies,' he looked up to ask the question.

'Yes,' Mary said, bristling slightly at the mention of Joyce, 'she came.'

'I got a bit drunk and with all that crazy talk I got carried away. You see, I've spent a long time away from home and, well, I miss my wife and, you know,' he paused and played with his hat some more. 'You know what I mean. I miss my creature comforts. I get a bit, well, lonely, you know and, well, you reminded me of my wife, you look a lot like her. I was feeling vulnerable and all. It's no fun being here on your own. I didn't mean to offend you. Please accept my apologies.'

He looked at her again, waiting for her reply.

It's no fun being here all on your own. These words stung Mary, but she did not want to spend more time in this man's company. The easiest would be to grant him his forgiveness and dismiss him.

'That's okay Pieter. I accept your apology. We're all human.' She spoke as kindly as her irritation would let her and hoped she sounded genuine.

He smiled, almost kindly, although to Mary it did seem a little artificial.

'Thank you, Mary. I would like to make it up to you. Could I buy you lunch? Tomorrow maybe? I've not got to go out to the site and the Nyala Hotel, you know the one at the plateau at the top, they do very nice food.

This time he sounded sincere and despite herself, Mary paused, then regretted it. This gave the impressions that she was actually considering it.

'Please, I will be most grateful if you would accept.'

Well, she *was* considering it. Partly because the comment about 'being here all on your own' had touched a nerve and partly it was giving her an excuse to go up to the Nyala. According to James, there were some spectacular views from up there.

'Okay,' she said. What harm could it do?

Lunch at the lodge was usually a simple affair, unless there were guests who had pre-arranged it. If that happened then Solomon would appear and perform his magic. Otherwise, Esther would usually prepare something light for James, a sandwich or a salad or, if he was particularly hungry, a tuna pasta. During the colder months, when it did get quite chilly up the mountain, she would heat up a tin of soup for him.

Mary like the informality and the lightness of the lunch, given the wonderful cuisine she could look forward to in the evening. But she did not feel too hungry when she got back from town, and she told Esther she only wanted a small salad. She sat out on the small veranda at the front of the lodge. There were a few

sun-bleached, but comfortable chairs which guests would sometimes sit in while having their sundowners.

The anxious gnawing at her gut prevented her from tasting
the food. Why had she said 'yes' to that horrid man?

'Well, because he sounded too sincere and you fell for it,' her
non-self-pitying-self replied.

She shoved a large piece of lettuce into her mouth as if to try
and shut that inner voice up.

'I should have known better.'

'Yes, you should have. Just because you're grieving, doesn't
mean you've lost your senses.'

A chunk of tomato and cucumber also had no effect on the voice.

'Someone who gets drunk and leery like that is very seldom a
nice person. *In vino veritas* they say. You see their real self...'

More lettuce, slowly chewed.

'...when they are drunk. If they are horrid when they're
drunk, they will be horrid when sober.'

A little salad dressing escaped from her mouth and began to
dribble down her chin. She had stuffed too much in and quickly
leaned forward over the plate to avoid messing on her clothes.

'I suppose he told you how lonely he was and that he was
missing his wife and he's not usually drunk at all?' Annika had
asked after Pieter had moved off down the road, whistling
tunelessly.

Mary had nodded.

'And then asked you out to dinner?'

Mary shook her head.

'No, not dinner. Lunch? At the Nyala?' Annika pulled a face.
'He and Martin, the man who runs the Nyala, are as thick as
thieves. He'll have organised a room for the afternoon. I hope
you turned him down.'

A whole cherry tomato, a fat slice of cucumber and a chunk of
goats cheese filled her mouth as her mind replayed the conversation at the coffee shop. She didn't want any judgemental
comments coming from her brain's peanut gallery.

'Of course I did,' she had given a slightly disdainful guffaw at
the idea while her heart dropped onto her guts and it had
weighed heavy on them ever since then.

'You are staring, Caiaphas. You should be less obvious about these things.' Esther spoke in Swahili. They were out of earshot for Mrs Mary to hear, but she was taking no chances.

'It's not like that,' he rested his chin on the handle of the rake. 'Look. She does not even notice us. We are looking straight at her and she does not see anything. She is attacking her food as if it had insulted her. There is something not right with Mrs Mary.'

Esther cast a glance over at the woman on the veranda. She did seem to be in another world and was treating the salad brutally.

'Maybe she is just *forlorn*.' She used the English word 'forlorn' in the middle of the Swahili.

'*Forlorn?*' He took a moment to recall the meaning of the word. 'Of course she is *forlorn*, anyone can see that. She looks *forlorn*, she acts *forlorn*, everything about her is *forlorn*.' The English word bobbed on a sea of Swahili.

'Yes Caiaphas, she is *forlorn*. But whose fault is that?' Esther gave him a knowing look.

'Whose fault? I don't know. She is a European woman. European women are often *forlorn*. You have seen them all come and stay here and they are often *forlorn*. Maybe it is Europe's fault. Maybe Europe makes people *forlorn*.' He shrugged his shoulders. 'How can I know what makes her *forlorn*.'

Esther gave a dismissive laugh. 'I think that you know why she is *forlorn*. You may have to *grit your teeth* until Mrs Mary has had her *crisis*' and that has made her *forlorn*. It is not Europe, it is you.'

The English 'grit your teeth' and 'crisis' flared up against their Swahili backdrop.

'*Grit my teeth? Crisis?* What are you talking about. I have done nothing with my teeth.' He stared at her as if she were mad.

'Don't waste my time Caiaphas. We have guests tonight and I must go and sort things out. But you must let Mrs Mary have her *crisis* and not *grit your teeth*. Maybe then she will not be *forlorn*.' Esther turned and marched back towards the kitchen.

Caiaphas stared after her and even when she had disappeared inside, he kept staring. At length he shook his head and began raking again.

'Forlorn. Grit my teeth. Crisis,' he muttered, 'that woman has gone mad.'

The guests were a recently retired English couple, thankfully. Mary did not feel like she could clamber over a language barrier this evening. The conversation over evening drinks was pleasant, if not a little dull. They discussed England and Africa, the weather back home, the weather here and how they had stumbled across the lodge.

'Quite by accident, really,' Alan said, and Lucy had nodded her agreement and they were off again, explaining web links and talking about Trip Advisor which Mary eventually worked out was a kind of website where people put travel tips and reviews of hotels and lodges and suchlike. There were also forums where one could ask for advice on where to stay and what to do. But none of this was relevant as they had not come across the lodge through the Internet. Rather they had met a lovely Swiss couple at the game park they had just come from.

'They were very taken by this place and I can see why,' Lucy enthused. 'It has such an African feel to it.' She gestured round at the zebra skin rug on the floor, the bright batiks on the walls and the vast array of carvings that littered the veranda.

'And it's cosier than the hotels we've stayed in this trip,' Alan added.

And cheaper, Mary thought as she tried to suppress the image of Pieter that the word 'hotels' had returned to her thoughts.

'Yes, well James has worked to make it a little bit different, a sort of getaway on your getaway, he calls it,' she tried to emulate the enthusiasm James showed for the place.

'He's not here then, James?' Alan asked.

'No. He's back in England looking after his mum. She's not well.'

'Oh, sorry to hear that. Is he your husband?'

No one likes to talk of death or dying, Mary thought, noticing how quickly Alan had added his question.

'Oh, no. James and I are old friends. We were neighbours growing up. His mother always said we'd get married, but things never worked out that way. He was more like a brother than husband material.'

'Often the case. Kids grow up like brother and sister and the parents expect them to marry, but they seldom do. I presume you grew up and met someone else then?'

'No.' Mary was a little shocked at how easily that came out. 'Well, I mean I did grow up, but I never found Mr Right.' Why was she saying this?

'Why don't you hook up with this James character then?' Lucy said.

'Lucy!' Alan chided her mildly, then turned to Mary. 'She's impossible. Always wants to marry everyone off. It is quite possible that Mary here is completely okay being single. Marriage is not for everyone.'

'I was just saying,' Lucy smiled sweetly at Mary as if to say, *Men! They just don't understand us women. Of course, we all want to be married.*

Mary smiled back, hoping it would placate both of them. She would rather have burst into tears, especially as the guilt of denying George was beginning to hit home.

'Ladies and gentlemen,' Solomon's voice to the rescue, 'Dinner will be served in five minutes.'

'Ah, dinner.' Alan was glad of the intrusion as well. 'You know that was the one thing that Swiss couple were not so enthusiastic about. They thought the food was a little ordinary, but then they moaned about it where we were last night and we thought it was fine, so I'm sure it'll be lovely.'

'For the starter tonight, we have dried apricot wrapped in bacon, with sweet chilli sauce.' Solomon placed a plate in front of Lucy and moved slowly round the table to put one with extreme precision in front of Alan. He served Mary last, bowed slightly and left the room.

In the kitchen, he put the final touches to the main course in his solemn and unflappable manner. Smells erupted from pots and danced in the air. The plop! plop! plop! of a gently boiling pot played a duet with the brrrr of vegetables bouncing around in water. He sniffed at a dish.

'Parsley!' he commanded, and Esther scurried to get the herb, while he stirred a pot slowly.

Esther placed the herb next to him and then busied herself preparing the dishes for the food to go in. Solomon began to gently tear the parsley to place as décor on top of the food, then paused.

'Esther,' he said.

She nearly dropped the dish she was wiping. He had never addressed her by name before.

'Yes, babu.' She called him grandfather, a respectful title.

'You spend the days with madam. Do you think that she is unhappy?'

'I...er...she does seem a little...forlorn.'

Solomon nodded slowly. 'Yes. Forlorn. That is a good word.' He stirred the food once more, then said, 'It is ready. Dishes.'

Esther brought the dishes and he transferred the food from the cooking pots into them.

'The main course tonight is rabbit, cooked in a white wine and garlic sauce. We have a lemon rice, flavoured with spices and onion, braised red and white cabbage seasoned with cumin and roasted carrots in a honey and almond glaze.' He took his leave of the room and retreated back to the kitchen to prepare the soufflé dessert. Through the door, the guests' voices could be heard singing the praises of the food, but he did not listen.

'Milk,' he commanded Esther.

It had been a pleasant evening. Alan and Lucy were good company and Mary had quietly slipped her wedding ring off her finger as they moved from the veranda inside. Just in case. She still felt guilty at lying about her marriage, but, she thought, it had left the evening uncluttered by death. They would have shrunk away from her if they had known that she was freshly widowed.

As she got ready for bed, she took the ring out of her pocket and contemplated it for a bit, recalling the day when George had first put it on her finger. That glance across the park where she was sure she had seen James came back to her too, James who couldn't make the wedding because he had to be in Switzerland on urgent business.

Could it possibly be that he felt something for her. She found it strange that after all these years, he might think that there could be anything between them other than the love that siblings have for one another.

She brushed her teeth and slipped into bed. The light was too dim to read by, so she turned the wick of the lamp down till it went out, then lay on her back and stared at the ceiling.

Why don't you hook up with this James character? Lucy's words came back to her.

Well, she asked herself, *why don't you?*

It felt odd this thought, yet there was a degree of comfort in it. She got on well with him, she always had. But getting on well and 'hooking up' were two very different things. Besides, she told herself, it is too soon and she began to feel guilty again. These thoughts were another betrayal of George. Twice in one night. Once more, she thought, and I'll be hearing a cock crow. To prevent a biblical betrayal, she closed her eyes, forced her mind into neutral and coasted off to sleep.

There was no dance that night. Caiaphas waited, but his dance partner stood him up. This was unusual. He would make enquiries in the morning. Ghosts of the hacking cough of the previous night floated in the dark, haunting him as he began to contemplate whether to dance solo, or call it a night.

He could not go to the bathroom window, but his thoughts flittered around the dim light that would be coming from there, like insects around a lamp. They were busy thoughts, hell bent on trying to establish the secret behind the light. If you could just climb into the light, then all will be revealed.

But that is never the case for the insects who tried to penetrate the core of the mystery of the light. They get burned.

He recoiled slightly from the thought, as if the heat had scalded him and he flittered gently round the subject for a bit. But the light kept attracting him, flirting with him and he flew closer again.

NINE

Life. That strange and mystical thing that slowly starts to crumble and erode from the moment it is given to us. Each second, each minute that passes brings everyone closer to the end of the journey through this thing we call life.

Death. That strange and mystical full stop that ends life. It is the one ultimate inevitability that we all face, as unavoidable as it is unwanted. It is always locked in battle with life – a life and death struggle – but it will always win.

Two things in life are certain, we say, death and taxes. Perhaps we could even add that taxes are more certain as we know when we have to pay them, how much we have to pay and what the consequences are if we don't. But death. It can creep up on one at any time, it can come in a variety of different ways and there are no consequences if you don't die because there is no option not to.

Death and taxes, the brother and sister of certainty. But try and explain the certainty of taxes to a deformed beggar lying on a worn mattress in a lonely, run down hut in a remote part of Africa.

The last remnants of life were crumbling away. A life eroded by age, hardship and cigarettes. Each cough another milestone passed en route to death. Each rasping breath another one ticked off his allotted number.

Death was hovering close on the mountain, but it was not ready to strike just yet.

The new day strolled nonchalantly into Mary's room and wished her a cheery good morning. And it felt good, Mary thought as she stretched. The night had been restful and uncluttered by dreams.

'Good morning, ma'am.' Esther put the tea tray down and opened the curtains.

'Good morning, Esther. It looks like a lovely day.' Mary watched the sun stream into the room and smiled.

'Yes, I think it will be hot today,' Esther replied and stared at Mary, almost to the point that it became uncomfortable, then left hurriedly, mumbling something about guests.

Mary gave herself a little more time in bed, luxuriating in the good mood she had woken up in. The last few days had been tough and, she sort of knew, that the feeling would be a temporary hiatus in the difficult times of her grieving, so she had to make the most of her 'up' time before she hit another 'down' patch.

The front lawn looked lovely. Caiaphas had done a great job of it yesterday and she made a mental note to remember to comment about this to him.

Alan and Lucy were up – she had heard the shower going – but not yet ready for breakfast, so she ignored the table set in the middle of the lawn and wandered alongside the flower beds, admiring the blooms on display. Esther came out with some more things for the table and they smiled at each other before the young woman disappeared back inside.

A butterfly settled on a yellow flower and slowly fanned its wings. Mary stood still, admiring its colours and wishing she had brought her camera out with her.

'Good morning, madam. Did you sleep well?'

She turned, a little surprised at the question. She usually only got the greeting from the old man.

'Good morning, Solomon. Yes, I did, thank you.'

'That is good madam,' his lips didn't form one, but his face seemed to radiate a smile.

'It's a beautiful morning, isn't it?' Mary thought she would take advantage of this softer side of Solomon.

'Yes, madam. It should be a very good day.' His face smiled again and then the stoniness returned as Alan and Lucy emerged from the house, throwing 'good mornings' and 'lovely days' into the fresh, sweet air.

'I love this coffee,' Alan said pouring himself and Lucy a cup. 'Can we buy it anywhere?'

'You can get it at the general store. I don't know if you noticed it before you came up yesterday. It's just as you turn off onto the mountain road. But, I believe you can also do a tour of the farm where they grow it. There's a leaflet inside about it, looks rather interesting. I haven't had a chance to get there myself, but you may want to try it if you're not in too much of a rush.'

'Sounds lovely,' Lucy said, 'why not love? We should have enough time to do that and get to the next game lodge.'

Alan spooned some fruit salad into a bowl and nodded. 'Great idea. I've always wanted to see how coffee is processed. Can't start my day without a cup of it, so I should really understand where it comes from shouldn't I?'

He handed the fruit salad bowl to Lucy who started to dish some for herself. She suddenly stopped with the spoon in mid-air. 'Why don't you come with us, Mary? If you've never been, here's a good opportunity. You can call it research for future guests.'

'That's a good idea, 'Alan agreed.

'You know what? I think I will join you. For research of course if James asks,' she winked at Lucy.

'Great, that's settled then,' Lucy continued dishing.

'Oh no. I can't.' The goodness suddenly drained out of Mary's morning. 'I'm supposed to be meeting someone for lunch and I'll never get back in time.' Her stomach knotted as she remembered her appointment with Pieter and a feeling of dread engulfed her.

'That's a pity,' Lucy stuck out her bottom lip in a mock sulk.

The knot returned to her stomach as she saw Alan and Lucy off. They did faff a lot, but finally loaded everything into their hired car and moved slowly off down the dirt track that served as a driveway. They had been a good distraction from thinking about the pending lunch meeting. In fact, they had been a good distraction from all her problems and as she turned to go back inside, she found herself wishing they could have stayed another night.

There was an email from James, one from her brother Barry and strangely, one from Toby which she decided to open first.

Hey mum. Hey? That was modern speak. She didn't like it, it was too much like *hey you,* an insolent and disrespectful greeting. She would have been okay with *Hi mum* and could only hope to be addressed as *dear*, but all she got was '*Hey.*'

Hey mum. I checked on your place like you asked, and someone had dug up your rose bed. They left the plants lying on the lawn. Just thought I'd let you know. Toby.

No *kind regards* or *best wishes*. No *love froms*, just *Toby*. That hurt her more than the vandalism. She had endured worse than that when George was gone and refused to even conjure up an image of the damage. She would move, she decided. When she returned to England, she would start looking for somewhere to start a new life.

Barry gave an update on their mother's rheumatism and blood pressure. The former was still playing up, the latter was down. All was well there and, despite them never having been that close, signed off *Love Barry*.

James did not have good news. The doctors thought it was only a matter of time for his mother. They were doing everything they could to ensure that she was comfortable – in other words, preparing her for death. Mary was saddened by the news, but rather hoped that things would not linger. She knew first-hand what a lingering disease in a loved one with only one possible outcome felt like.

After the update on his mother, James asked, 'And what have you been doing to upset the neighbours?' She could almost imagine him saying that to her, a slight glint in his eyes as if he knew exactly what the neighbours had been doing to upset Mary. That Joyce was impossible!

She wrote a quick reply to *Dear Toby*, thanking him for the update and hoped that Eric – the village simpleton and gardener to most – would clear up the mess. She signed off *with love.*

To Barry she commiserated with mum over the rheumatism, expressed delight at the lowered blood pressure, enthused at how lovely Africa was and signed off as *Your Sister*.

James was a little more complicated. She wanted to say the right words to support him at this difficult time, but it all felt so impersonal as she sat in front of the screen. She was also acutely aware of using up battery power. The less she used the longer the time before she had to rely on Joyce to get it recharged.

Why don't you hook up with this James character?

It was no use. She logged off the laptop to preserve the battery and tried to hand write a response that she could type up quickly once done.

'What would you like for lunch today, ma'am?' Esther appeared with the mid-morning cup of tea.

'Oh. Um. No. I won't need anything. I am going out for lunch.' She tried not to look flustered about the thought of the lunch date.

'Very good,' Esther left, and Mary could hear her talking to Thomas in the kitchen.

Dear James, she wrote on the fifth clean page. How could she begin to write to James about coping with his mother's illness and the sense of hopelessness he would no doubt be feeling. She tried to search her mind for any pearls of wisdom she had been given when George was in his last days, but nothing came.

Those that did still communicate with her, those that had not been frightened away by the cloud of death that hung over the house, they had been supportive, but useless. Their sympathetic eyes had all said, *oh you poor thing.* No one had ventured to go, *oh you poor thing, but here's what you need to do...*

Perhaps, Mary thought as she stared at the new page, there is no answer. There is nothing I can say or do that will be of any use.

She sat back and closed her eyes, trying to conjure up any good moments during George's illness while simultaneously holding at arm's length the hurt, pain and feeling of uselessness that had assailed her then. It struck her that there was another feeling that she had not really considered and that was the lack of support she had had. The neighbours had all but shunned her and Toby was useless. Barry had been sympathetic but miles away. What she had needed most was someone she could have talked to, someone who could have taken her mind off the situation, even if it was just for an hour or so over a cup of tea. But she had had no one.

Being at the lodge, she could not very well pop round to James for a cuppa and a natter, but, she decided, she could send an email that said very little about his mum, just enough to show that she cared, but then spend more time on other issues. He has so much of his mum's condition on a daily basis, a change of thought would do him good.

Having resolved this, the words flowed quickly and soon she had filled up three pages of news, including a slight moan about Joyce and some kind words about Annika, all written in her neat, small handwriting. She suddenly realised with a start that she had very little time to prepare for lunch and put the pages down next to her bedside table and hurriedly set about getting ready. The knot in her stomach tightened as she brushed her hair. She wanted to look nice, for the hotel, not Pieter, she didn't want to encourage him, but how to get the balance right? She was just putting on a little lipstick when she heard a car pulling up outside.

Esther has been superb. She is taking very good care of me.

Esther read the sentence a third time, pride rising in her. Mrs Mary had told her this before, but to see it in writing, especially in a letter to Mr James, somehow made it official.

The page and a bit about Mrs Joyce didn't quite describe how bad things were, but they painted a fair picture. It was obvious that Mrs Mary didn't like that horrid white woman, but Esther could see that she didn't want to say too much, especially as Mr James seemed to have no problems with Mrs Joyce.

There was a bit about Solomon and how wonderful his cooking was. Mrs Mary had even written down all the things he had cooked the last few days. There was nothing though that would explain why the old man seemed concerned about her.

Caiaphas has been very helpful too, lighting the fire in the evening and he had made a great job of the garden. However, he does seem to be giving me some strange looks, but I just grit my teeth and carry on. Not sure what that is all about, but other than that, we have not had any crisis to speak if.

Esther nearly dropped the letter. So it was Mrs Mary who was gritting her teeth, not Caiaphas. And she had not had a crisis. No wonder she seemed so upset all the time. Maybe this Mr Pieter will sort her out with a proper crisis, Esther thought.

Pieter was obviously well known at the Nyala Hotel. The staff all greeted him by name although, Mary noticed, none of them gave a warm smile, rather they were polite hospitality industry smiles that said, I am only doing this because the text book said I must.

The air was a little cooler right up at the top, but it was still pleasant enough to sit on the patio and admire the views. The surrounding land shimmered in a heat haze blanket. Browns and greens intertwined all the way to the horizon, an untamed landscape full of mystery and secrets. Beyond the patio was a stretch of green lawn, neatly trimmed, which marked the boundary between man maintained and nature maintained as the rocks and some low scrub started where the grass left off. The rocks sloped gently for a few yards, then disappeared over the precipice.

A few small monkeys foraged amongst the bushes in the rocks, keeping a constant eye on the patio for any unattended plates.

'Bleddy nuisance they are,' Pieter said, pointing at the primates. 'They'll steal anything.' His coarse accent flattened his words. He was dressed in long khaki trousers and a light cotton shirt.

'It's lovely up here,' Mary said gesturing at the view and not wishing to get into a discussion about the monkeys which she thought were cute.

'Hmmm.' Her companion grunted. 'Go to the edge there, you can get a better view.' He seemed more interested in finding a waiter, but they were alone for the moment, having been deserted by the hotel staff after they were shown through to the patio.

Mary edged towards the rocks, keeping an eye on the monkeys who, in turn, watched her closely.

'They won't bite,' Pieter called after her, then took a few steps towards them and shouted, 'Shoo! Bugger off!' and waved his arms. The monkeys scampered away to safety and eyed him, but he had returned to his mission.

'You want a drink?' he asked as Mary took another step closer to the edge.

'Yes. A glass of wine please.'

She peered over the side.

'Red or white?'

'Red, please.' The cliff was not quite as sheer as what it appeared from further back, but Mary didn't want to venture any closer to the edge.

They were on the other side of the mountain from Kilimbati, so she could not see the town.

'Ah, finally. Why do you buggers always disappear when we want to order?' Pieter's voice floated on the breeze to her and she turned to see who he was talking to. A young waiter stood smiling politely at Pieter, his face showed none of the anger that he should surely be feeling at the rudeness of the man.

Suddenly Mary wanted to just jump off the side and glide through the air back to the lodge. This man would be no better sober than what he was drunk. She pictured herself swooping bird-like through the air, the freedom from earth and all its unpleasantness flowing through her veins. She could go where she wanted to and not have to answer to anyone. Despite losing George, and having come here, she was still tethered to her life back in England. There was the village, the house and her garden and, she supposed, Toby. She owed none of them anything and they only held bitterness for her, but their tentacles seemed to stretch across the world and strangle her as she stood at this dizzy height. If she could only take that step forward and fly.

'Careful,' Pieter grabbed her wrist roughly and brought her back to earth with a bump. She realised with a slight shock how far she had been leaning over the edge.

'Thank you,' she managed as she felt her knees go weak.

He grinned at her, his mouth a lascivious slot in the rock face of his stubble.

'Come,' he half led, half pulled her back to the patio. 'Our drinks are here.'

They sat at a table near the grass where a glass of wine stood opposite a large beer bottle and an empty glass. Pieter poured his drink and lifted it in a toast.

'Cheers,' he said and without waiting for Mary to lift her glass, downed half of his.

'Ah!' he smacked his lips while Mary managed a sip of her wine. It wasn't a very good one.

'So,' he said at length, 'what brings you out to Africa?'

'James asked me to look after the lodge for him. He's back in England, his mother is not well.'

'James?'

'You don't know James? He owns the lodge where I am staying.'

'Oh, I've never met him. Spose I should of, I've been in this godforsaken place long enough. But that bleddy road keeps me busy.'

Mary sipped her wine and wondered if she should ask about road building, but could not face having to hear the answer.

'Joyce told me you are pregnant.' He looked at her now as if he was imagining her in the act of being impregnated.

'No, I'm not. That was a misunderstanding.' She felt her cheeks redden.

'Oh,' he sounded disappointed. 'She said that it was the son of your friend,' he grinned again.

'A joke. I was only joking with Joyce but she didn't realise. She took me seriously.' Mary grabbed her wine and gulped a mouthful.

'Oh,' he said again and looked her up and down as if trying to decide whether she would be naughty enough to sleep with the son of one of her friends. He downed the remnants of his beer and gestured for the waiter to bring another without seeing if Mary was in need of a top up.

'What you want to eat? The food here is okay. The steaks are nice and they also do curries, but they don't have an Indian chef, so they're not that great. It's hard to find decent food in this place.'

'Is there a menu?' she asked.

A flash of irritation crossed his face, then he smiled, 'I'll get one,' he said and deserted her, returning a minute later with a half empty glass of beer and a menu which he dropped in front of her before sitting down heavily and finishing off his beer.

That's two beers he's had to my two sips of wine, Mary thought.

'Told you that the steaks were nice,' he said as if he was annoyed that she was taking her time to choose.

'Okay, I'll have one,' she forced a smile. This was a big mistake, she should not have agreed to come.

'Great.' And he was off again, unable to wait for the waiter to come back. This time he took longer and when he returned he had a tumbler of whiskey in his hand and possibly another two inside him if his eyes were anything to go by.

'So, like I said, I get a bit lonely here without my wife,' his words were a little slurred now. 'It's nice to have a bit of company with the weaker sex every now and then.' He cast a leery eye over her and she instinctively drew her cardigan closed, feeling as if her breasts were on display. The image of her naked body that she had studied in the mirror the other night popping into her mind, but this time, the reflection could not look her in the eye.

'What do you say to us skipping lunch and getting a room?' He sat back, a stupid grin on his face.

Mary choked on the wine she was trying to hide behind.

'I think I had better go now,' she said rising. She had no idea how she would get back to the lodge, but she was not going to be going with him.

'No. Stay.' He grabbed her wrist and pulled her down. 'I'm bleddy buying you lunch, so the least you can do is give a guy a little bit of comfort.'

'Let go of me,' Mary wriggled, but his grip was strong.

He glared at her, but then seeing the waiter approaching, he smiled and let her go.

'Have another drink,' he said, accepting a new one for himself from the waiter.

Mary shook her head.

'Come on, man. It'll lighten you up a bit. You're too bleddy uptight. Oi!' he called the retreating waiter back, 'where you going, you stupid bugger? Bring the lady a whiskey.'

'No thanks,' Mary told the waiter and he stood confused, not sure who to obey.

'Yes, bring a whiskey and hurry up. You buggers are useless. Never bleddy do as you're told.'

This was just like he was at Joyce's the other night, but Mary was scared. There did not seem to be any whites around to help her and the black waiter looked too scared to stand up for her if she needed help. She sat quite still while the waiter disappeared and Pieter gulped down his new drink.

'Now, I think I deserve a little in return for buying you lunch, don't you?' His voice was polite, but Mary could sense the threat in the undertone.

He smiled now as if nothing had happened.

'Did I tell you how much you look like my wife?' he asked.

Mary nodded and shrank further into her chair. He was a mad man, she thought as the roughness of earlier seemed to melt away and he sat eyeing her in an almost pleasant way and passed complimentary comments.

The waiter took an age, but eventually returned with a fresh round of drinks.

'Cheers,' Pieter said, grabbing a glass from the tray and downing it. The waiter placed Mary's in front of her and began to retreat.

'Oi!' Pieter's voice flared up again, causing the monkeys to scatter and the waiter hesitated. 'Doan worry with the food now. I'm not hungry anymore, just get us a room key. Any room.' He ran his eyes up and down Mary's body while the waiter stared blankly at him.

'Get me a bleddy room key now!' he roared.

Mary looked round frantically for something, anything to get away from this insane man who was running hot and cold. Then she saw her chance. He was still staring after the waiter, so she reached for the car keys that lay on the table, but he was too quick, grabbing her wrist and pinning it down.

With her free hand, she fumbled desperately for the whiskey glass and flung the contents into his face, the glass slipping through her fingers and following its contents in a slow motion arc that ended in a collision with his bushy eyebrow.

Mary, freed from his grip, did not wait to see what damage the may have done. She flung the car keys as far away as she could and started running.

His dance partner lay on a mattress in the corner of the dark room. He looked withdrawn, curled up in the foetal position, eyes fluttering open occasionally. A plastic mug of water stood on the floor next to the mattress. At intervals a word or two would escape from his lips and would be followed by a hacking cough that rattled, not only the old man's lungs, but also Caiaphas' nerves.

He didn't really want to be there, not because of the impending death, but because his mind was elsewhere.

Despite the warnings from Esther and Solomon, he could not keep away from the bathroom window last night. But he had not got the show he had hoped for. The irritation at the lack of nudity was offset by the fact that Mrs Mary had actually looked happier than any of his previous evening's viewings. She had been humming to herself as she brushed her teeth, a cheerful tune that was just audible through the window. It was the inconsistency that now concerned Caiaphas. She was either distressed, or cheerful. No one should have those extremes.

Then there was that man who had come to take Mrs Mary to lunch. A South African, from what he had heard in town, not a nice man. He was rude to people and, rumour had it, that he raped one of the house girls who was looking after him. He did not think that this white man would rape Mrs Mary, she was white too, and did not have a job to lose if she reported him. But it still concerned Caiaphas that she had gone off with such a man. No good would come of this.

Old Man Mawenzi coughed again and held out a feeble hand. Caiaphas helped him lift his head and sip some water.

'It is good of you to come,' the old man's voice was weak and more slurred than usual. Talking was an effort. He smiled up at Caiaphas as best as the limitations of his lip would allow. Caiaphas nodded, not wanting to draw the man into further conversation which he could clearly see was not easy. The water revived the old man somewhat and he struggled to sit. Caiaphas helped to prop him up against the rough wall where he sat with his eyes closed, breathing heavily.

His breathing slowed and Caiaphas thought he may have fallen asleep, but he suddenly opened his eyes and brought two fingers to his lips and sucked.

Caiaphas took out his cigarettes and put one in the cleft of the hare lip, then lit up, causing a fresh coughing bout, but this didn't stop the old man from enjoying his vice.

If I could just get away from here, Caiaphas thought, *I could go and check on Mrs Mary to see if she was okay.*

He could do it surreptitiously as if he were visiting his friend who worked up at the Nyala. He would be able to check on her, but, if she saw him, make it seem like this was one of his normal visits. But he could not leave Mawenzi, not until Solomon got back and he was not due for another hour.

The cigarette was just about finished when Caiaphas heard the chef's slow footsteps outside. He stepped into the room, stood at the door for a few seconds, allowing his eyes to adjust to the gloom, then nodded at Caiaphas to indicate that his watch was over and that he was free to go.

He walked quickly along the path back to the lodge. He would take the 4x4. Mrs Mary wouldn't know that he wasn't supposed to use it for private visits but, just in case, he would park it round the back of the hotel so she wouldn't see it. Hopefully Esther would not be at the lodge, she would be suspicious and probably try and stop him from taking the car, especially if he told her the real reason why he wanted it.

Mary crouched in the undergrowth, the violence of her heart-beat scared her. Surely Pieter could hear it too. And her breathing. The altitude made the air thinner and she wanted to take in large mouthfuls to ease the aching in her lungs, but she had to satisfy herself with controlled grabbing bursts. Her legs shook underneath her and she steadied herself against a tree.

She could hear the curses thrashing through the forest as Pieter stumbled drunkenly in pursuit. He was close and she tensed up.

Why didn't I just take his keys and use his car to escape, she thought. She would have been long gone by now. But, as she steadied her nerves, she had a vision of her fumbling with the door and being yanked back by his brutish hands. No, this was the course of action. As long as he didn't find her here, she could wait till he gave up, then make her way down this small bit of forest to the road and then on home.

She heard him getting closer, crashing his way roughly through the trees. She sucked in a large lungful of air and waited.

'Mary!' He yelled. 'Mary! I'm sorry. Please come back.' He stumbled into view and stopped. Mary peered through the leaves at him. The side of his face was covered in blood from where the glass had cut his eyebrow. 'Mary! Come back. I'm really sorry. It's not safe out here.' He yelled and, despite his drunken state, he did look contrite. Mary studied him and began to wonder. Had the shock of being hit by the glass sobered him up enough for him to be genuinely sorry?

'Come on, Mary. I'll take you home if you want. I'm really sorry, man.' He stretched out a hand to steady himself against a tree, then rubbed his wound and winced slightly.

Mary watched him. His body seemed to sag slightly, then he eased himself down onto the ground, leaning his back up against a tree.

'I'm just so bloody lonely,' he muttered to himself. 'Just bloody lonely. Can't she see that. I just wanted some comfort. Someone to hold. I wouldn't have harmed her.' He gave a sob and shook his head. 'That bleddy road. Why did I get this job in the middle of nowhere?'

He wiped his face with the back of his hand, oblivious to the blood.

'She is such a nice woman. But I had to go and fuck it up. Why do I always mess things up?'

His head sank and he sat still like this for a while, looking so forlorn that Mary found herself beginning to feel sorry for him. He seemed genuine in his remorse. A kind of motherly instinct began to rise in her as the seconds ticked by and Pieter didn't move, other than to shake his head and sigh.

Maybe, she thought, maybe if I just talked gently to him, he will be okay and take me home and we can forget this whole episode. He did appear to be susceptible to some kind words. She began to stand up, but just as she did, he lifted his head and growled, 'Fucking bitch! How dare she treat me like that? I'm going to find her and teach her a bleddy lesson.' He pushed himself up, his face screwed up in hate as he began to move further down the slope away from her. Mary held her breath until she could not hear him anymore, then very slowly started to head back up to the hotel. Maybe she could find his keys and get out of here.

Her legs were unsteady as she picked her way up towards the hotel, not too sure if she was going in the right direction, but either way, she should reach the hotel or the road up to it. She stumbled on.

Esther was also worried about Mrs Mary and did not object to his taking the car.

'There is something not right with that man that came. I could see it in his face,' she said as she walked Caiaphas round to the vehicle. She did not get into town much, so probably had not heard the stories about the man and Caiaphas thought it best at the moment to keep those from her.

He jumped in behind the wheel and moved off quickly, still not sure what he would say if Mrs Mary saw him up at the hotel. As he neared the peak, a figure came stumbling out of the forest on the side of the road, right in front of the car. He slammed on brakes, stopping inches away from the man whose face was bloodied and whose eyes burned with a rage. He was swearing and gesticulating and, before Caiaphas had time to settle his nerves, was sitting next to him in the car, demanding to be taken up to the hotel.

What was he doing on the road like that and why was he bleeding? Caiaphas put the car and his brain into gear. He could not disobey this white man, especially not when he was so angry. And where was Mrs Mary? He eased the car round the final bend and pulled into the hotel parking area. He could not now drive round to the back as he had hoped, this Mr Pieter would want to be dropped here.

The man grunted as the car stopped and climbed out without a further word. He staggered towards the hotel entrance, then was gone. Caiaphas edged the car back, then drove along the bumpy track down the side of the hotel to where the safari drivers parked their vehicles after dropping their charges off at the entrance. He would find his friend and see if he knew what was happening and where Mrs Mary might be.

He parked and headed into the back entrance of the hotel. There was no one around, so he walked quietly towards the bar and dining room where his friend was usually on duty. The room was deserted, but through the large patio doors, he saw him out on the grass beyond the patio and heard Mr Pieter's gruff voice shouting at him to 'Bleddy well find those car keys, you useless bugger. You saw where that bitch threw them. Now hurry up.'

Caiaphas paused. No sense in two of them being bossed around, he thought and turned and headed back to the car, wondering what to do next. As he walked out the door, he saw some movement in the bushes a little way off, but dismissed it as monkeys and headed towards the vehicle when suddenly he heard his name being called in a whispered shout.

'Caiaphas. Oh thank God, Caiaphas, wait.'

She was in his arms before he even knew that he had opened them to receive her. He could feel the warmth of her body pressed up against him and could smell the sweetness of her thick European hair. He felt the trembling, but worried that it was he himself that was shaking.

'Where is he? We must get out of here,' she lifted her head and then he saw the fear in her eyes.

'He is looking for his car keys, madam.'

'Quick. We must go.' She was suddenly aware of their embrace and pulled away, not looking at him as she commanded him to get in the car and drive.

Bewildered, he obeyed, despite his mind still trying to process the emotions stoked up by the physical contact he had had with her. He risked a glance across at his passenger as they began to wind their way down the hill towards the lodge. She sat watching the road, her face taut and while he knew he could not ask any questions, he thought that he may know some of the answers.

Two quick gin and tonics later, Mary was no longer outwardly shaking. Inside, her gut still churned and her mind stumbled as the events of the afternoon ran and re-ran through her head at breakneck speed. Her ears remained sharp for the sound of a car pulling up, expecting Pieter to still try his luck at the lodge. Would Caiaphas protect her if he did come? She wondered.

Esther hovered at the kitchen door, not quite sure what to do. This irritated Mary, but she could not dismiss her young friend. Her presence, although useless as a defence against the drunk South African, did give her a slight sense of security. Should she let Esther know what had happened? She was too embarrassed by it all to say anything. She had been stupid to accept the invite up to the hotel. She should have seen through his fake apologies.

'Are you alright, madam?' Esther's voice was soft, almost too scared to come out.

Mary managed a smile.

'I will be. Perhaps I should go and lie down for a bit.'

'What happened?'

Mary was hoping that the question, no matter how timidly asked, would not come up. But now that it had, she felt glad to be able to talk to someone about it.

'He got drunk. Very quickly.' And suddenly the whole story tumbled out of her and the more she told, the more acutely she missed George. She just wanted to be held in his sensible arms and feel the fear and disgust being drawn out of her.

Despair and emptiness began to trickle feed into her as each detail of her torrid afternoon came out, as if these new feelings were needed to fill the void the vacating story left. But the story had to be told. It was as if she had no control over it. It had to come out of her, how she had thrown the glass at him, how she had hidden from him in the forest, then made her way back to the hotel.

'That was when I saw Caiaphas...' She stopped abruptly as the warm, strong and safe embrace of the lodge's handyman came back to her in a rush of sweaty, musky smells and strong, rippling muscles. She recalled suddenly the gentle and caring way he had held her, almost as one would a lover. She caught her breath, then, remembering Esther, she went on.

'Caiaphas rescued me. If he hadn't been there, I don't know what I would have done.'

The sound of a car moving up the long drive halted her flow again and she froze. The warmth and security of Caiaphas' arms evaporating in an instant.

'I'll go and see,' Esther said, sensing the potential problem.

Mary did not want to be left alone, but had no choice. Her eyes darted round the room, searching for something she could use as a weapon should it come to that.

'It is only Caiaphas,' Esther's voice preceded her into the room.

Mary hadn't heard him leave after he had brought her back to the lodge. The noise of the car had awoken the shakes and she concentrated on calming them out of her system.

The last shudders left her as a grim-faced Caiaphas appeared at the kitchen door. He seemed almost unwilling to cross the threshold into the room.

'What is it, Caiaphas? Come in.' She hid the last vestiges of the fear the sound of the car had awakened and forced the memories of the embrace to duck down behind her calm facade.

'That man is dead.' He could only take a couple of steps into the room.

'Dead?' Mary gasped. 'How?'

'He drove his car off the road and down the side of the cliff. The police and ambulance are coming, but he is dead.' Caiaphas looked down at the floor, unable to keep her gaze. Mary stared at him, trying to force the relief that she was safe now out of her mind. Pieter was someone's husband. She knew what it was like to lose a husband. She *must* feel sorry for this widow she did not know, otherwise she would rejoice too much in the death of the man and, no matter how bad he was, that would not be right.

'He was very drunk, Mrs Mary, and he went too fast. You cannot drive fast on these roads,' Caiaphas explained further as if he felt it necessary to make excuses for Pieter's bad behaviour that had cost him his life.

Mary nodded, her mind shocked and numbed.

'Thank you, Caiaphas,' she said, then added, 'and thank you for rescuing me earlier.'

He smiled a serious smile, then nodded as if confirming something to himself.

'Hakuna matata, no problems, Mrs Mary,' he said and took his leave.

'For the starter tonight, we have a coconut milk and noodle soup, seasoned with thyme and lime juice,' Solomon placed the dish in front of Mary and stepped back. Mary nodded her thanks and reached for the soup spoon.

'How are you feeling, madam? I heard about your ordeal today.'

'I'm okay, I think,' Mary gave a weak smile.

'That is good. I hope the soup will help. It is supposed to be an uplifting dish.' The old chef bowed slightly and shuffled back to the kitchen, Mary's 'thanks' grabbing at his apron strings.

The soup was refreshing. It tingled slightly in the mouth and spring-cleaned the taste buds. Some of the sooty drama of the day seemed to wash away with each mouthful. But while the effect of Pieter's behaviour and the shock of his death were being washed off, the ball of emotions that rolled around in her stomach was one thing that was immune to Solomon's uplifting potion. She could not shake the thought of a widow, one whom she supposedly resembled, being given the news that the road building contract that had taken her husband away from her, had become a permanent role.

She wondered if this widow would feel anything like she had when George left her. Would she have that gnawing emptiness that ate away at ones insides, that feeling of helplessness and defeat, as if you yourself had lost in the struggle against death? She remembered sitting, staring at nothing in particular as the gloom of evening set in like a dimmer switch slowly extinguishing the light of life.

She had thought about phoning Toby back then, letting him know that it was all over, he no longer had a dying father to be embarrassed by. He no longer had a father. George the person had slowly retreated into George the body, until he was just a speck, then he was nothing, just George the memory. He had looked at ease though. He was no longer distorted by his wasting disease. But she had not had the energy to get up and make the call.

The room had got dark, dimly lit by the street lights outside. Voices had walked passed, voices muted by the thick windows. But to Mary it was her numbness that robbed the voices of their clarity.

At last she had moved, closed the curtains and climbed, fully clothed, into bed, pulling the covers tight around her and slowly sobbed herself to sleep.

'How was the starter, madam?'

'Very good. Thank you, Solomon.' Mary tried to look uplifted.

Esther cleared away the dishes and returned with the main course under the watchful eye of Solomon. Once all the dishes were laid out, Solomon began.

'For the main course tonight, we have chicken breast stuffed with a banana and cayenne pepper mash and covered in a cheese, breadcrumb and herb crust; brown rice seasoned with paprika and for the veg-e-tay-bills, we have carrots stuffed with a piquant tomato sauce and cinnamon spinach.'

He smiled, bowed and retreated.

Mary filled her lungs with the rich aromas of the food, letting the subtle textures of sweet, savoury and spice dance playfully in her nose and shimmy through her veins before slowly exhaling and picking up a spoon. As she dished she took further deep breaths, enjoying the new smells that bubbled up as the food was disturbed. She felt herself relax as the culinary aromatherapy took effect. The wine was a perfect introduction to the food. The flavours intertwined in her mouth and flirted with her taste buds, demanding her brain to pay attention. And slowly the memories of the night George died were filed away, each agonising detail put back into its mental box. She knew she would revisit those memories, but for tonight at least, she could put them aside. The food was too life-affirming to be ignored.

There was no dance to be had in the forest that evening. Caiaphas sucked slowly on his lonely cigarette and felt the absence of his partner. It had been a strange day and, although he could not have spoken, Old Man Mawenzi would have known of the events. Stories, especially those like today's would pulse around the community as if the mountain herself was whispering the detail to everyone like a village gossip.

The death of the white man would clatter away in the bars in town, or twitter between the women walking home with the evening's firewood balanced on their heads. Old men would sit together, sipping their home-made beer, click their tongues and shake their heads as the details would be slowly added like the strokes of a brush flicking slowly across a canvas to create an artist's impression of the events. The drama of the car speeding round the bends, then missing a turn and plunging down the ravine, would undoubtedly be the central focus of the work, but the careful observer would notice in one corner of the painting, a couple. The man tall, dark and young, holding a pale, older woman, shielding her view of the drama that was unfolding before them.

Caiaphas gave a half-laugh as he wondered how the story of his role in rescuing Mrs Mary was being told around the mountain. Would he be portrayed as a sort of superhero coming to the helpless white woman's rescue, or would they see him as an opportunist using the woman's fear to get 'in' with her? He did not know if people knew about his bathroom window escapades. It was unlikely that Solomon would have said anything, but he could not be so sure of Esther. He had not picked up any vibes from others whom they knew, so felt sure that talk of his secret had not yet made it beyond the grounds of the lodge.

He drew in a lungful of smoke and held it as the thought of the bathroom window stoked up desires in him, desires now heightened by an embrace earlier in the day, albeit that that had come out of fear rather than affection.

He took another drag and glanced over at the lodge. There was no light coming from the bathroom window and he sighed. Maybe he had missed her. Maybe she had gone straight to bed, exhausted by the day's events.

He heard a noise and turned to see Solomon standing in front of him. He had not heard him approaching. In the gloom he could barely make out the chef's features, but instinctively he knew why he was there. He reached into his pocket, pulled out his pack of cigarettes and offered them. Solomon took one out and waited for Caiaphas to light it. They smoked in silence, then Solomon dropped the butt on to the path, leaving Caiaphas to stamp it out, just as Mawenzi usually did. Not a word passed between them.

TEN

The mountain was restless as the darkness of the night wrapped itself around her. There had been violent happenings and death. She would not rest easy this night. The breeze that usually tickled her playfully as it danced about her surface, was an angry wind that whistled and howled as it screamed out a protest that the mountain should have been subjected to the crass bitterness and senseless death that had stained her with blood. The wind rushed down the road, taking the bends with ease, as if showing how things should be done.

Spirits chattered, an indignant sound, an unwelcoming sound. They did not want the newcomer here. He was not welcome. He was not the one they were expecting. They darted across the surface of their beloved mother mountain, dancing strange dances, trying to exorcise their home of this intruder.

The monkeys hid in their trees. It was not a good night to be out. They could sense the distress of the spirits and it made them nervous. An eerie silence fell on them as they quietly set about grooming each other and picking at the leaves closest to them, not wanting to disturb things by foraging further afield.

In the clearing, the gecko stood at the entrance to its hole, quietly sniffing the air. Its eyes darted left and right but, other than that, it did not move. Going out tonight would not be good, it felt.

Amongst this turmoil, a bewildered spirit wondered. It wanted to shout at the others to stop their chatter, it was unnerving him. It felt that it needed to be somewhere, but did not know where, nor how to get there. It moved uncertainly round the mountain, looking for a way to get away.

The trees around the lodge swayed in the wind and their leaves hissed, frightening dreams away. Inside, a woman tossed in bed, teetering along the line between sleep and consciousness. She tried to grab at shards of dreams that flittered just beyond her reach. Fragments of a father shimmied across the void between consciousness and sleep, but she could not take hold of them.

Then the spirits heard a cough, a loud hacking cough and they knew that the time was close, they would soon welcome the one they were waiting for.

Dawn was reluctant to arrive. It did not want to fight with the wind, nor face the disturbed spirits. It hovered below the horizon for as long as it could, but was duty bound to appear and eventually began its slow thaw of the darkness, quietening the wind and sending the spirits back to rest. In their trees, the monkeys breathed a sigh of relief and began to chatter, quietly at first, as if testing the validity of the new day, but as the first rays of light began to illuminate the mountain, their talk got bold and they began to discuss the frightful night.

Mary opened her eyes and felt the weight of the previous day press down on her. She lay still in the cocoon comfort of her bed, not wanting to move and hoping that Esther's sixth sense about her waking up, was not working this morning. She had not yet fully digested everything that had happened and her feelings were still blurred. The feeling of being violated by the attempted attack on her, blurred with the shock of the news of Pieter's death. There was a sickly sweet taste of relief at his death that was too rich for her palate. The emptiness and sense of loss that the thoughts of Pieter's widow had awoken in her were, perhaps, the hardest of all the emotions to cope with. She wanted to try and sort some of these feeling out before Esther arrived with her morning tea.

'Good morning, Madam.' The door opened and Esther brought in the tray. 'Did you sleep well?'

'Yes, thank you, Esther.' No point in telling the truth.

'The wind did not disturb you, did it?'

'A little.' She could not lie completely.

Esther shook her head. 'It was a strange night,' she said and put the tray onto the bedside table, then paused as if expecting Mary to say something more, but moved off before Mary could speak, closing the door gently behind her.

Mary settled back in her bed and stared at the gloomy ceiling, not wanting to get up. Before she could marshal her thoughts, there was a quiet knock at the door and Esther's head poked round it.

'Oh, madam, I forgot. Caiaphas said that the police were going to come round this morning. It's about that man yesterday. Also, we do have guests tonight.'

The police? Mary wanted to ask why they needed to speak to her, but Esther was gone before she could say anything. She lay back again and sighed, then slowly pushed herself up and sipped at her tea.

Esther was a bit shocked. So this was why the book was so naughty. Mrs Connie had taken all her clothes off and looked at herself, no not looked, studied her naked self in the mirror. That was not normal behaviour. But Mrs Connie had done more than just examine her body, she had analysed it. She had thought that her breasts were like unripe pears, bitter and without meaning. Did European women spend their time worrying that their breasts were like bitter pears? Breasts were for milk, for feeding babies. That was their meaning.

She giggled suddenly as she imagined herself studying her own body in a mirror. What would be the purpose of doing that? She knew what her body looked like, she could see it when she washed, but she had never thought to study it. For a brief second she considered doing that quickly, now in Mrs Mary's bathroom, wondering if she would discover anything in the mirror, but she dismissed the idea as quickly as it arose. Imagine if she got caught. Mrs Mary could come back from breakfast early, or Caiaphas may be outside the window sorting out the fire wood.

She snapped the book shut, not wanting to blame it for Caiaphas' escapades. Surely Mrs Mary had not been standing naked in front of the mirror like Mrs Connie had done? *Lady Chatterley* suddenly felt guilty in her hand. She put the book down quickly next to the bed and hurried out of the room.

Mary did not enjoy her breakfast. The thought of the police coming gnawed at her even though she had nothing to hide. She did not want to tell them about Pieter's indecent and violent advances. Not for his sake, but for his widow. The poor woman did not need to have those sorts of details thrown in the face of her grief, if indeed she did have grief. But what would the police want to know, and what had the waiter up at the hotel said? If he had told the police everything, it would look funny if she did not mention the violence towards her. She chewed on her grilled tomato, oblivious to the delicious juices that squirted inside her mouth.

When she finished her bacon and eggs and was buttering a slice of toast, Solomon cleared his throat and said, 'Madam, it is unlikely that the police will have very good English. Would you like me to translate for you when they come?'

'Yes. Yes, please, Solomon. Thank you.' She suddenly felt much better. She would not have to face the questioning alone. The food's flavours began to break through to her taste buds and she started to enjoy her breakfast. Esther came and cleared away the dishes and, Mary thought, gave her a strange look.

She was not sure what time the police would arrive, so set about trying to have as normal a day as possible. There were no new emails for her, but she did note that the battery indicator was beginning to show that it would need to be recharged soon. She dreaded the thought of having to face Joyce again. She could get away with letting Caiaphas take the machine over to the farm, but had no control over how it would be returned. She closed the machine down, deciding to deal with this issue later.

'Hello? You home Mary?' As if summonsed up by the laptop, Joyce appeared in the doorway. Her face looked slightly drawn and her eyes were red. Had she been crying?

'I just heard about Pieter. They said you were with him.' Her eyes seemed to accuse Mary of something, but she couldn't work out what.

'I...er...I was with him just before...He invited me to lunch to apologise for his behaviour the other night.'

'And what happened?' Joyce made herself comfortable in a chair and Esther brought in a juice and put it next to her. She did not acknowledge this.

'I don't want to talk about it,' Mary said, knowing that this answer would not satisfy.

Joyce glared at her, but she held her nerve. It was none of Joyce's business what happened.

'Why don't you want to talk about it?' There was venom in the question. 'You go off to lunch with him and then he turns up dead. There are a lot of unanswered questions.'

It was Mary's turn to glare.

'And just what do you mean by that?' she hissed.

'Well, why weren't you in the car with him for a start? Why was he driving back alone?'

'Are you saying that I had something to do with his death?'

'Did you?'

'I'm not even going to dignify that with an answer.'

Joyce measured her up. 'He was a dear friend of mine, I think I am entitled to some answers.'

'I had nothing to do with his death. That was his own fault and I'm not saying anything more about it.' Mary felt herself beginning to shake as the anger rose in her, anger not only at the accusing tones of Joyce, but renewed anger at Pieter as memories of his behaviour bubbled up in her mind.

'I don't believe you. You must have done something to upset him.' Joyce's voice rose in pitch.

'How dare you!' The anger tumbled out of Mary. 'How dare you come in here and accuse me! You want to know what happened? Well I'll tell what happened. Your *dear* friend got very drunk very quickly. And then he tried to force me to sleep with him. He was an uncouth barbarian, grabbing at me and trying to take me to a room against my wishes. I managed to pull myself free and ran away, but he came after me. He was angry and drunk and if he hadn't been, he may well have been alive now. So if you think I had something to do with his death, well yes, I did. I didn't just lie down and let him rape me. If I had done so, he would probably be waking up at the Nyala Hotel right now with a huge hangover, but if you think for one minute that I am going to apologise for not letting him rape me, you've got another thing coming. I can't even bring myself to say I'm sorry he's dead. He was a vicious bastard and it's his own damn fault that he's dead okay?'

Mary sat back, exhausted from her outburst, remaining tense and expecting a backlash from Joyce to hit hard, but it didn't.

Joyce seemed to crumble under the barrage and sink deeper into her chair, a sob suddenly escaping from her and this loosened an avalanche of tears.

Mary stared at her. She had not expected this. She felt her anger abate and as the mist cleared, a realisation came into focus.

'You loved him, didn't you?' It was almost gentle.

Joyce nodded and continued to cry.

Mary watched her. She could not bring herself to feel sorry for Joyce, but the anger was gone.

'He wasn't a bad man, but the drink...' Joyce slowly brought her sobbing under control. 'That was his Achilles heel. When he was sober, he was a perfect gentleman. Charming and friendly, but put a few into him and...'

Mary didn't respond, she just watched Joyce trying to cope with her emotions and wondered if she should say anything. *Never speak ill of the dead* she had been taught, but all of her experience of Pieter was ill, so it would be better not to speak. She had said enough already. She struggled to see what Joyce saw in the man. Yes, he had been a bit of a charmer when he was sober and they had met at Annika's place. She would not have agreed to the lunch if he hadn't been, but he wasn't that good looking. It was all a matter of one's tastes. If she was honest with herself, she could see that some people would not have thought of George as good looking. Her friend Karen was surprised when she had first fallen for George, but she found him quite handsome, not in a Hollywood star kind of way, but there had been something pleasant in his appearance. It's all a matter of taste, she told herself. 'Or love is blind, in Joyce's case,' a naughty part of her mind piped up and she had to force herself to pass on a giggle.

'Do you want more juice?' she asked more from a sense of needing to say something than from being hospitable.

Joyce nodded and swallowed hard. She seemed to have perked up a bit when Mary returned from the kitchen to ask Esther to bring the juice.

Solomon sat on a log that lay at the foot of a large tree. He was leaning up against the trunk, his eyes closed. The white kofia cap he wore had slipped a bit and sat at an angle across his forehead. His demeanour suggested that he was fast asleep, but Caiaphas knew better than to believe that.

He was unsure why the chef had stayed up at the lodge after breakfast, especially when Old Man Mawenzi was so ill. Undoubtedly, Solomon would have arranged for there to be someone looking after his dying friend, but it must be something important keeping him here.

Caiaphas busied himself raking the leaves that the wind had strewn over the garden, hoping that the old chef's presence had nothing to do with him. He concentrated hard on the leaves, as if this somehow built up a wall to protect him from any possible trouble that may be heading his way.

Surely his actions yesterday were not being questioned. He had acted out of concern for Mrs Mary. The fact that his concern had stemmed partly from his sexual attraction to the naked figure he had watched through the bathroom window should not count against him. No matter what his motivation had been, the important thing was that he had been there to rescue her.

He gathered up an armful of leaves and took them round to the garden waste dump, or 'compost heap' as Mr James liked to call it. The embrace, holding the trembling Mrs Mary in his arms, came back to him as he held the leaves to his chest. He wondered if she even thought about it afterwards. She was so shaken by whatever had happened that she was probably not aware that she had been in his arms.

He sighed. She most likely had no recollection of it, maybe not even any memory of his role in rescuing her. White people were like that. He was just a servant, someone who was only noticed when they were not there.

He heard a car coming down the driveway and saw Solomon stir from his seat. It was then that he remembered the police were coming to talk to Mrs Mary. He wondered if he would be asked any questions himself.

They looked uncomfortable sitting in the lounge. Perhaps she should have taken them to the veranda where it was less formal. Solomon, refusing to sit, stood beside her like a father watching over his child. She had nothing to hide, but still felt guilty. Were they going to accuse her of not doing enough to stop a drunken man from driving?

So far, the conversation had been in English and she could sense their discomfort with this.

'Solomon is here to translate if that is okay with you?'

The taller of the two policemen, who also looked like he was the one in charge, nodded and smiled a relieved smile while Solomon bowed slightly to him. With the language barrier out of the way, the questions began to flow and, at times, Solomon seemed to answer the questions without deferring to Mary at all. Perhaps he was just clarifying something, Mary thought, but was sceptical with her own logic, as the body language of those involved in the conversation did not back her theory up.

The questions that Solomon did pass on to her were straightforward and there seemed to be no accusatory tones in them. They were just ticking the boxes so that they could complete their paperwork. Mary did stop short of accusing the deceased of improper conduct towards her, and she would not, unless it became necessary. She could always plead embarrassment later. She did get the feeling that the police already knew about what Pieter had been up to up there, however, they were sensitive enough not to press for further details. Alternatively, Solomon was protecting her from this line of questioning.

She found herself wondering what the final report into the South African's death would say. Would it have the unsavoury bits included, presuming that the young waiter from the Nyala Hotel had told the police everything?

She thought again of the woman who would by now know that she was a widow. Was she a sensitive soul who had been charmed into marriage by a sober Pieter only to be bullied and beaten by a drunken one, or was she a tough woman who gave as good as she got? It was possible, Mary thought, that Pieter was a henpecked husband whose drinking problems and lewd behaviour only came to the fore when he was away on business. Was all his macho posing and unsavoury attitude towards women a protest against the pain and humiliation that his wife back home dealt out to him.

Joyce was quite a domineering person. Maybe he had been drawn to her because she was the one who really reminded him of his wife. She thought back to the dinner at Joyce's and recalled how Pieter had cut his groping of her short after a curt word from Joyce. She realised now that Joyce's intervention had not been done to stop Mary being humiliated, it had been out of jealousy and a kind of smugness that she had control over this man.

No matter how she viewed Pieter, she still felt responsible in some way for his death. It was silly, she knew. She could no more have stopped him in his inebriated state then she could have prevented George from shuffling off his mortal coil and the restrictions of his illness. But where George's death had been inevitable, Pieter's had not. Not at this point anyway. She could, she supposed, have hung around at the Nyala and let Pieter have his way with her, satisfied his carnal lusts, then he would probably be alive now. No. That had not, and never could be, an option. She had no real say in Pieter's death, just as she had had none in George's.

Solomon was doing a fine job with the police, but she still wished that George could have been there with her. Or did she? Could she have faced George after being the victim of attempted rape? He had always been a bit conservative about these things. Would he have found her abhorrent, soiled by the ordeal? He wouldn't have, would he? Mary found herself panicking slightly at these thoughts and, catching the suspicious eye of one of the policemen, forced herself to calm down.

Of course, he wouldn't have been concerned about Pieter's behaviour if he had been there because she would never have been groped at Joyce's if George was around. And then Pieter would have had no premise on which to invite her up to the hotel as he would have had nothing to apologise about. And even if he had felt the urge to ask her up there, she would never have gone, not without George.

If only George had been here...

Why did he have to go and die? Look what his dying had caused.

'I'm sorry,' she apologised to the policemen as she reached for a tissue to wipe away the tears that were welling up, 'this is all very upsetting.'

Esther put the plate down and retreated. A slight breeze caught Mary's naked arms as she sat on the small bench at the end of the garden. She picked up the plate and began to chew on the sandwich that Esther had made. The bread here wasn't that great, a little too coarse and not overly flavourful, but she wasn't really tasting.

The police had left soon after the waterworks started. They seemed to scurry away, embarrassed at having upset her. Solomon had been brilliant, escorting them out, then returning to see that she was okay without making a huge fuss. As he cleared away the teacups, he merely reassured her that the police were quite okay with her story and that she would hear no more from them.

She had been grateful for this news, but the bout of depression over George's death had not yet dissipated. It still hung around, a heavy weight on the stomach and a squeezing of the heart. She didn't really want her lunch, it didn't mix well with her emotions but not eating was not an option. Esther would have made too much of a fuss over a 'no thank you', so she had just asked for a tomato sandwich.

She picked up *Lady Chatterley* and began to read. Connie was well into her romance with the gamekeeper Mellors. He had laid out a blanket on the grass and they had made love, but Connie was distant, not living in the moment, letting him have her as she lay obediently beneath him. It reminded Mary of the times she had been a dutiful wife, allowing George to get on with the business while she lay back, her mind on other things.

But after her dispassionate discourse, Connie felt Mellors 'ebbing away'. The phrase fitted well with how she had felt during George's last hours. Well more than the last hours, virtually from the moment he had been diagnosed, Mary had felt him ebbing away. There had been the odd day when hope had reared its ugly head, giving her positive thoughts where none should have been allowed, letting her feel as if this was not happening or that there was a cure just round the corner. False hopes thrust upon her by some unfeeling, sadistic thought imp.

She had always managed to pull herself up again after the down that followed naturally from the false hopes. The positives came less often and with less intensity as George deteriorated, till she felt that she had no choice but to accept the finality of what was happening. George would never be cured, he would simply continue to shrivel up and eventually he would die.

Although it hadn't quite been like that, Mary thought. She sighed and continued reading, hoping to take her mind off George.

Connie was up and at it again. After the initial disappointment of her absentee sex experience, she was suddenly wanting it and Mellors was quite willing to oblige. Mary suddenly lost herself in the scene as the words 'loins', 'buttocks', 'penis' and 'plunging' floated up from the page. This time Connie was there in the moment and Mary went with her, her hand gripping the book tightly till it was over and Mellors withdrew. At that moment, Connie felt what D.H. Lawrence described as 'pure loss' and she fumbled to try and get Mellors back inside her.

Mary fumbled over the phrase 'pure loss'. That was how it had felt when the heartbeat monitor had flat-lined. *Pure loss.* She didn't think she would ever be able to describe that moment, never be able to put into simple words her emotions as the monotonous beeeeeeep told her that her husband's life was over. But here it was laid out on the page for her. *Pure loss.* It had not just been loss, it was pure, unrefined raw and bubbling loss. The word 'pure' somehow made it feel, not good, but more acute. The feeling was one hundred percent loss.

Mary put the book down next to her and soaked in her thoughts.

Caiaphas watched Esther as she played with Thomas. He was hidden from her view by some bushes and she was oblivious to his gaze. He was not sure why he was staring at her, but somehow it made him feel better. It was an innocent scene that played out in front of him. Esther sat on the grass, legs curled up under her. Thomas lay on a small blanket and she would dive bomb his naked tummy with her hand, sending gurgles of delight through his little body.

'She is a beautiful woman,' Caiaphas told himself as he watched, his gaze concentrating more on the mother than the child. He was surprised at that thought. It was not a new thought, but one that had not been used recently. He had had a crush on Esther when they were younger, but she had never shown any interest in him and had eventually married Joshua.

This dusted off thought lingered as he watched, but slowly another, more recently used thought began to take hold. 'She is not for you'. This is what he kept telling himself about Mrs Mary, and now he needed to remind himself of this about Esther. He sighed and was about to move quietly off when Esther began talking to Thomas.

'Ai, my son, what are we going to do about Caiaphas? I am sure he is looking in the bathroom window when Mrs Mary is standing in front of the mirror naked. He is a naughty man Caiaphas. But what can I say? He won't listen to me if I tell him that he is wrong to do that.

'And I cannot tell Mrs Mary not to stand naked in front of the mirror, it is the custom of women in Europe to do this, it says so in her book. They stand there and look for meaning in their bodies. I cannot stop Mrs Mary looking for meaning if she wants to. It is part of her culture and we must respect that.'

She picked Thomas up and held him to her breast, gently bouncing him.

'Promise me Thomas that when you grow up, you will not be like Caiaphas, that you will respect the cultures and rituals of others, and not go looking through windows at naked European women. No good will come of it. You will not be able to help them find meaning in their bodies, they must learn to do that themselves. Instead you must respect women. They are not creatures for you to conquer, they will never love you if you just wish to conquer them. They will only love you if you treat them right.

'A woman's body is very important. Her womb is the first cradle for every person. Her breasts provide everyone's first meals. Her arms are where a child will run to when they are hurt. But most of all, her body belongs to her, not to anyone else. Don't ever try and take her body. It is never yours to take, it is only hers to give.'

She rocked Thomas a bit more and his eyelids drooped. It had been a long lesson for his small mind and it was wearing him out.

'I do not think that Mrs Mary will ever give her body to Caiaphas, so he must stop taking it with his eyes.'

Thomas sighed and closed his eyes, shutting out all bodies.

Rex sniffed the air. He was glad to be out of the lodge. There was too much distress and despair there. It filled the air and irritated his nostrils. He could still sense these feeling in the woman as they walked towards the clearing, but it was diluted by the open air and once they got to the clearing he could leave the woman to her smelly emotions and clear his head in the forest on the other side.

There had been those visitors too. They had arrived in the morning and left later. They were not the usual sort who stayed the night, or that woman with the horse who smelt of loneliness with a hatred of the world undercurrent.

Those odours annoyed Rex and he was glad to be filling his nostrils with the sweet scent of the forest that rode on the breeze. The gecko was there, but Rex could not be bothered to disturb it, he would leave that task to the woman.

He padded quickly across the rocks, not even looking back to see if the woman had settled in her usual spot. When he reached the first tree, he paused to lift a leg against it, then snapped at an annoying fly before moving into the forest. The air was cooler here and spoke to him of normality. The disturbance in nature that the mountain was oozing was a thin scent here and not enough to distract him.

That unpleasant smell had been cloying during the night, but as time stretched the distance between now and the accident, the mountain's distress was subsiding. If only the woman would get over it, then things may smell sweet again.

But, as he picked up the trail of a squirrel and began to move deeper into the forest, Rex recalled the deeper feelings he had sensed in the woman and he knew that those would not be disappearing in a hurry. This latest episode had only served to intensify the funk of the condition she was in when she first arrived.

He stopped and peered back at the figure who now sat on her usual rock. The way she sat confirmed his suspicion; she was still struggling with that earlier problem.

'You know none of this would have happened if you had still been here,' Mary chided the absent George, then as a pang of guilt stabbed at her, she softened a bit. 'I know it's not your fault, I just wish...well you know what I mean.'

She looked around. Rex had disappeared as usual, but she was pleased to see the gecko sitting in its usual spot, his head occasionally turning to check on her.

A thought suddenly struck Mary.

'He's not up there with you, is he?' She had never really believed in heaven or an afterlife, more sort of hoped it existed, but once George died, she liked to think that he was still around in spirit. She drew comfort from the thought. It was soured somewhat now by this new idea that Pieter would share the same afterlife as George.

'I don't think he would be. He wasn't as good as what you were. You would never have done some of the things he did. You were too gentle and you had nothing but respect for women, you were my Gentle George.'

Mary paused again as an image rose in her mind of George meeting Pieter in some heavenly corridor and punching him on his rocky outcrop of a nose.

'That's for trying to get it on with my Mary,' he shouted in Mary's imagined scenario while Pieter lay cowering on the floor, his hands held to his bloody proboscis.

'My knight in shining armour,' Mary whispered guiltily enjoying Pieter's discomfort. As she sat there, she saw George as Mellors rescuing Connie from the frightful Clifford Chatterley, and she stepped into her thoughts and into George's arms. She wanted to make love to him now. Not the grunting, fumbling and detached love of reality, but the intense, pleasurable and meaningful love that the characters in Lawrence's novel made.

George took her in his arms and manipulated by Mary's mind began to make wonderful love to her. Her body swayed gently on the rock where she sat with her eyes closed, enjoying her fantasy, the warm sun that caressed her physical body became George's soft, warm hand that touched the one in her dream and the gentle breeze became sweet nothings, whispered in her ear.

She moved along with her thoughts as they wrapped themselves around her and she gave herself completely to the imagined George.

But suddenly over George's shoulder she saw Pieter leering at her. George faltered in his efforts and dissolved into the clearing.

Mary sighed and slowly adjusted herself to reality again. A strong desire to be held lingered while the rest of the fantasy faded. Just to be in someone's loving arms for a minute or two was all she wanted now, but there was no one around who could oblige.

Then she remembered Caiaphas' strong arms holding her at the hotel. She had felt safe there.

The guests were an American couple who, Mary guessed, were in their mid to late sixties. Bill and Chris. 'Short for Christine,' she explained with a slight southern twang. They had been working with a church charity about a hundred miles away and were doing some sightseeing before returning to the States.

'Jerry and Arlene told us about this place and the fantastic food they had here when they came out, so we just had to come and see it for ourselves. You must remember them, they were here about a year ago,' Bill said as he paced the veranda. He was one of those who did not like to sit still for long.

'I'm afraid not. I've only been here a short while. I'm looking after the place for James while he's sorting out some things back in England. He would remember them, I'm sure,' Mary smiled politely and tried not to giggle at the thought of sieve brain James remembering any of his guests.

'I'm sure he would,' Chris piped up, 'You don't forget people like Jerry and Arlene in a hurry.' She looked at her husband and they chuckled together at some private joke they had about their friends.

Then her smile faded and she said, 'I don't suppose they'll get back here. I know they wanted to, but, well, Jerry had to have heart surgery. He's not been the same since. We're not sure how much longer he's got with us.'

'What sort of work do you do with the charity?' Mary asked and let the long winded answer blow over her. It was far more preferable than hearing about Jerry dying, she could not face talking about that at the moment.

The conversation progressed without touching on death again and Mary found she could relax somewhat. Bill and Chris were pleasant enough and, being American, took charge of most of the talking, allowing Mary to relax and let them do the work. She could scamper off into her own thoughts whenever things got a bit dull.

At five they went for a walk, Chris insisting that Mary come along as guide despite her protestations that she barely knew the surroundings. As they strolled along the path that went in the opposite direction to the clearing they passed a number of locals, women carrying firewood on their heads, men returning from their jobs in town and children come to gawk at the white people. Some of the kids were shy, smiling with averted eyes, while others would sidle up to the three of them and take their hands, walking a few hundred yards or so, laughing amongst themselves.

'Goody morn,' the braver ones would try out their English.

'Oh, it's not morning, it's afternoon. Good afternoon,' Chris tried to correct them.

'Good afternoon,' they would repeat, staring wide eyed.

'Give me my money,' one suddenly piped up and a flood of requests came – 'Give me my pen', 'Give me my sweets'.

'I'm sorry, I don't have anything,' Chris chuckled and held out her empty hands. 'They were like this at the village we were working in. You'd love to give them all a little something, but there are so many. Bill gave out some dollar bills the first day we were here, but he only had a few and they ended up fighting over them. The people who run the charity told us not to give anything as it causes problems, but you end up feeling terrible. We have so much and they have so little, but I suppose you can't give to everyone.

Mary recalled her first day when the deformed beggar had come to the car window. She had seen him a few times in town since then, but thankfully never close enough for him to come begging. The last time she could recall seeing him, he was chatting to Caiaphas while she and Annika had sat on the veranda of the coffee shop. She should, she thought, go and see

Annika tomorrow. She would probably want to hear all about Pieter, Mary guessed.

They stopped at a point that looked out over the valley and watched the sun set, the sky turning a dusty pink and the sun itself became a reddish-orange smudge in the dirty blue sky. It was not a spectacular sunset, but there was something attractive about it. The three of them watched in silence with only the click of Bill's camera disturbing the quiet sound of the breeze in the grass.

'It is so peaceful here,' Chris said eventually, taking in a lungful of air, 'but I suppose we should get back. Once the sun starts going down, it gets dark pretty quickly.'

'Yes, and I'm ready for some of that fantastic food that we've heard about,' Bill added.

They reluctantly turned their backs on the dying embers of the sun that smouldered on the horizon and walked slowly back towards the lodge. They had not gone far when Mary heard footsteps behind them and glanced over her shoulder. In the gloom she could just make out Caiaphas hurrying toward them. She had still not had an opportunity to thank him for his help.

'Madam,' he mumbled as he caught up and then attempted to pass.

'Is everything alright, Caiaphas?' Mary asked. He should have been at the lodge already helping with dinner shouldn't he?

'Everything is fine, Madam,' he mumbled, not looking at her and tried to move on, then turned suddenly, as if realising something and said, 'I was just looking after Solomon's friend who is very ill. The person who was supposed to take over from me was late. I am sorry, madam.'

'Oh. I am sorry to hear that. I hope Solomon's friend feels better,' Mary said, and Bill and Chris nodded their agreement of the sentiments as they let Caiaphas hurry past them.

'For the starter tonight, we have cauliflower florets, coated in a cheese, herb and breadcrumb mix and deep fried. To accompany this, we have a sweet chili and lime sauce.' Solomon placed the dishes in front of Chris and Mary, then returned with one for Bill. Each plate held two golden brown nuggets neatly arranged next to a smear of the orange brown sauce. A delicious aroma floated gently up from the dish.

'This is good,' Bill said, tucking in to the food. 'Jerry and Arlene were right. Particularly after what we have been eating at the project. I don't mean to sound ungrateful,' he said looking up suddenly, 'but one does get a bit tired of, what was that stuff they served us? It was like stodgy rice.'

'Oh,' his wife smiled. 'Ugali I think. Apparently, it was a kind of maize that they grind up, then cook with water. It filled you something, but not very tasty.'

'I've heard of it, but not had any yet,' Mary smiled. She was beginning to enjoy the compliments that Solomon got. It was a sort of motherly pride although she knew that sounded ridiculous. Solomon was old enough to be her father, yet these feelings reminded her of Toby's early years and how she had felt each time he did something clever or special. She could imagine James loving the attention the food got. He would have sat at this table, the centre of attention, bathing in the reflected glory. He would have been in his element.

But, she told herself now – just as she had way back when Toby was the one performing the act getting all the attention – Solomon should be getting this praise, not me. Then she remembered that Solomon did not take kindly to the accolades. She chewed on the delicious starter and another thought struck her. Perhaps Solomon was just being polite, not accepting the praise. He would have been brought up in the old colonial days when the locals would have been complete servants to their European masters. They would not have been allowed to have even a scrap of praise for a dinner well prepared, the greedy Europeans would have wanted it all for themselves. Times had changed, but Solomon was from that old time. It saddened Mary to think these thoughts. She hoped she was wrong.

'For the main course we have chicken cooked with papaya and mustard,' Solomon moved his hand over to the next dish, 'and for the veg-e-tay-bills, we have plantain chips seasoned with ginger, red and green beans with pear shavings and,' his hand hovered over the final dish, 'courgette patties. I think that in America you call them zucchini?'

Chris nodded. Both her and Bill were fixated on the dishes in front of them.

'Baked zucchini with onion, garlic and cheese.' Solomon finished, bowed slightly and departed.

The guests dished greedily, piling the food on the plates in front of them. Mary, who had held back as the host, was a little disappointed that she had not been left with too much for herself, but the Americans were too busy eating to notice.

When Esther had cleared away the main course, Solomon returned to explain the dessert. 'Pumpkin, sweetened and mixed with coconut milk.

'This has all been awesome, Solomon,' Bill bubbled, 'You are one heck of a cook.'

'Absolutely fantastic,' Chris concurred.

The old man bowed graciously, but did not smile, instead he shot the slightest of glances at Mary, it seemed like a reflex, as if gauging the reaction of his mistress, seeing if he was allowed any of the big dish of compliments on offer. It was the first time Mary had noticed this look.

'Yes, Solomon, you have done an excellent job once again,' Mary said and smiled. 'I think this has been your best meal yet.'

Solomon, who had started turning back to the kitchen paused and blinked his rheumy eyes, then smiled, 'Thank you, madam. It has been a great pleasure to serve you.' His voice sounded slightly strange. Was there a hint of tears in his eyes, or was it just their usual wateriness, Mary wondered.

Caiaphas waited, wondering if the old chef would come to the dance again. Esther's words to Thomas earlier had been bubbling away in his mind. He did not believe that he was disrespectful to women, particularly not Mrs Mary and it hurt somewhat that it had been implied that he was. If he did not respect her then he would not have rescued her from that South African man, would he?

But then, his mind kept coming back to this argument, is not looking through her bathroom window every night, hoping to see her naked, is that not disrespectful? He hated the part of his mind that kept telling him this because he knew it was true, despite all the spurious arguments he could raise in his defence.

This discourse had been running through his mind constantly since his eavesdropping on Esther. As had the strange comments about European women looking for meaning in their bodies. Was that what Mrs Mary really could have been doing when she stood in front of the mirror like that. She had certainly been studying her reflection quite intently. It was strange that she was looking for meaning, like what Esther had read in Mrs Mary's book.

Something then registered in Caiaphas' brain. He had been so busy worrying about being disrespectful and all the nonsense about Mrs Mary looking for meaning in her body that he had not registered on the fact that Esther had been reading Mrs Mary's book. Had Mrs Mary allowed her to do so? Or was Esther being disrespectful about Mrs Mary's property?

He was about to start processing this thought when he heard Solomon approaching and prepared himself for the dance.

ELEVEN

The moon cast an inky-blue light around the lodge. The silhouettes of the trees stood guard over the garden, unmoved in the breezeless night. The air hung like a cool lace net over the scene, slightly blurring the straight lines that the walls and roof made amongst the irregular and jagged ones of the trees.

A steady rumble of sound leaked through the window of the guest bedroom, a nasal growl from one of the sleeping occupants of the room. Outside the window a dream giggled nervously, wondering whether to risk entering, worried that the snores would wake someone and catch it before it could settle in a sub conscious.

Unheard by the garden was the tossing in the back room. Another dream peeped through the window and sighed. It would not find a home here tonight, that other noise was preventing sleep back here.

The mountain still felt raw from the recent violence but, the quietness of the air helped her to settle and be calmer this night. The spirits were more relaxed; that stranger who had arrived unexpectedly last night had wondered off the mountain. It would now be the problem of others as it wondered in search of a home.

In a small dark hut, not too far from the lodge, a loud hacking cough erupted and spluttered for a minute before calming to a wheezing, then slowed to heavy breathing before settling into a sleep rhythm. Outside, Death checked the sand timer. 'Not too much longer,' it muttered to itself.

The mountain sensed this impending death but was not distressed. This would be a natural one, a slipping from one state into another. A death like this somehow brought her closer to the creatures that climbed around her every day. They were like her children that she protected whether they were living or spirits.

Even visitors were her children as long as they respected her. She smiled to herself as the snores of one of her guests rumbled around the lodge. She felt sorry for the other visitor in the lodge who was not sleeping because of the noise, but it would only be for one night.

'Very well, thanks,' Mary lied in response to Bill's question of how she had slept.

'You weren't disturbed by his snoring?' Chris asked from the side of the garden where she was admiring some flowers.

'I do not snore!' Bill laughed and cast a greedy look at the breakfast table.

'Oh, he does. I'm immune to it myself, but if you're not used to the noise, it could keep the whole mountain awake.'

'Didn't hear a thing,' Mary lied again and smiled to try and stop the conversation between the husband and wife. If they were anything like she and George had been over this topic, snoring would be the subject of conversation for the entire time over breakfast.

'It's not that bad,' Bill snorted and moved closer to the table, making a show of examining the dishes that were there, trying to give out the message, 'Let's eat rather than talk about snoring.'

'So you admit then that you do snore?' Chris' twang moved on to the next flower bush. 'What kind of flowers are these?'

Mary had to stop herself from chuckling. Neither wanted to cause a scene about snoring so were both trying to change the subject, but they both wanted to get the last word in.

'I'm not sure. We don't get anything like that in England,' Mary said, glancing across at the flowers.

'Everyone snores a bit, you do as well, but you seem to make out that mine causes earthquakes. Is this fruit locally grown?' Bill pointed at the bowl of fruit salad.

'I do not snore,' Chris retorted before Mary could reply about the fruit. 'And stop making a scene.'

'I'm not making a scene, I was merely pointing out that I do not snore as loudly as you make out and that you also snore sometimes, so you can't point a finger at me.'

Mary crept away from the argument, her mind recalling with a strange fondness, some of the disagreements she had had with George over trivial things. She even remembered them having a heated discussion as to whether they were having an 'argument' or a 'disagreement'. It was not so much the bickering that awoke the warm feelings in her, but rather it was the way George would behave afterwards, when they had calmed down. He would never apologise, but did treat her that little bit kinder than usual. Not that he was ever unkind, it was just he paid her a bit more attention, offering her tea and slipping a biscuit onto her saucer, or coming home with a bunch of flowers. Not the big florist 'I'm sorry' arrangements, but just a cheap and cheerful bunch from the garage. He would never admit to her that they were apology flowers, but she knew.

'Madam, would you like to start breakfast?' Solomon interrupted her thoughts and she herded the Americans to the table. They were in the death throes of their tiff and Mary wondered what little things Bill would do to make amends.

She let the guests serve themselves fruit salad first and cleaned up the scraps for herself. The pleasantness of the recent memory of George still clung to her and she took pleasure in watching the elderly couple seek forgiveness for the silliness of their argument. Bill held Chris' hand as they said their grace, she patted his after the 'amen' and they exchanged a smile of the eyes, rather than the lips before tucking in.

As breakfast continued, Mary expected the melancholy or, sometimes, depression that usually followed good memories of George to descend, but it didn't. The warmth of feeling did diminish, but was replaced by thoughts of what she was going to do today rather than the down she usually experienced. Slowly, as this dawned on her, she began to realise that she might finally be on the road to recovery.

Nothing untoward had happened in Mrs Mary's book and Esther put it down and hurried off to do her chores feeling a little cheated. This was supposed to be a rude book and all that happened was that Mrs Connie had gone to pick flowers and found Mr Mellors' hut. She did find it strange that a European man would live in a hut, she was sure that they all lived in houses. But this hut had a key, so it must have been a special one. There was a lot made about the key and whether there was a second one which all seemed very strange. Why would Mrs Connie want a key to a hut when, by all accounts, she lived in a big house? This did not make sense.

She tried to imagine Mrs Mary wanting to go stay in Caiaphas' hut, but could not conjure up an image of this. She felt sure that Mrs Mary would not be spending time in anyone's hut, let alone Caiaphas'. Mrs Mary was not a hut type. There had been one or two guests who had visited the village 'to see how the locals lived'. These had always been awkward times, Esther felt. Why did they want to see our houses? What would happen if all the villagers popped round to the lodge to see how the Europeans lived? That would not go down well.

She giggled, then swallowed her laughter quickly as she realised how unacceptable her thoughts were. She hurried out to the garden to clear away the breakfast things.

Driving down the mountain, Mary locked all thoughts of George and Pieter out of her mind, except the fact that Pieter had died by not driving carefully on these roads. This kept her speed slow and she negotiated the corners with extra care.

Arriving in town she headed into the general store and picked up the items that were on the shopping list, written in Solomon's neat hand. She had hoped that there would be no guests this evening, but a late booking had come in. She had had to put her foot down, insisting that it was no trouble for her to do this. Caiaphas looked a little put out and this reminded her that she still needed to thank him for his help up at the Nyala. But Esther was lurking so it was not the right time.

With the shopping neatly packed into the back of the 4x4 by a muscular young lad from the shop, she drove the 200 yards down the road to park in front of Annika's.

'How are you, love?' Annika guided her into her chair as if she were an invalid. She didn't really like the fuss and was tempted to say, 'I was not the one in the accident. I'm fine,' but held her tongue and just eased herself into the chair and nodded.

'Okay, I think. It was awful.'

From nowhere, tears bubbled up and rolled down her cheeks. She had not really had a chance to talk to anyone who would understand and now, as the opportunity presented itself, all her emotions that had been festering in their mental cells, suddenly broke free and pummelled her senses.

Annika was back with tissues in a second and slowly guided her through the process of stopping the flow of tears, calming the hiccupping sobs and, as Mary reached that calm plateau where one feels numbs and exhausted, was there with a cup of coffee, a biscuit and an ear ready to listen.

It was not a voyeuristic ear that listened, nor was there an 'I told you so' look in her friend's face. Fortified by the coffee, Mary told her all that had happened. Annika shook her head at the right times and patted Mary's arm where necessary.

'Just terrible. You poor thing,' she said when Mary explained about her ordeal hiding in the forest and the anger she had seen in Pieter.

It was nice to be mothered like this. Her own mother would probably have told her not to be such a cry baby and to get over it. She could just picture mum telling her off and Barry, her brother, smirking in the background, enjoying her distress. She wanted to milk this attention, but felt guilty doing so and couldn't say why. So she pressed on with the story.

When she got to the part where she was at a loss as to what to do, and then spotted Caiaphas, she suddenly felt embarrassed, but again could not pinpoint what caused this emotion. Was it the fact that she had been forced to rely on a servant to rescue her? She hoped that this was not the case as she liked to think that she did not look down on those whose position in life were deemed beneath her on the social ladder.

But it wasn't that which caused Mary to stumble in her storytelling. It was the way she had fallen into Caiaphas' arms, like some ditzy heroine in a trashy romance novel where Caiaphas was the roguish bounder whom she loved to hate till fate conspired to thrust her into his arms and be eternally indebted to him.

Mary blanched at the thought, faltered in her tale and grabbed a tissue to hide her discomfort.

'I was lucky that Caiaphas was there at that moment. I don't know what I would have done otherwise,' she concluded.

Annika sat back looking thoughtful for a bit.

'What was Caiaphas doing up at the Nyala?' she asked, then looked up as if surprised that the question had actually been voiced.

'I don't know.' Mary had never thought about that. Why *had* Caiaphas been there? They bought all their supplies in town and, if they needed anything extra, it would be just as quick, and most likely cheaper to go down the mountain than up. What possible reason could he have had for being up there?

'Very strange,' Annika said, a frown flittered across her face and, as if disturbed by her thoughts, she stood up. 'We need more coffee.'

While Annika was inside getting the drinks, Mary tried to marshal her own thoughts. Annika had obviously come up with a reason for Caiaphas being at the Nyala and was not prepared to suggest it. This and the fact that she herself never even questioned why he had been there, left her feeling uneasy.

'I've heard she's coming to Kilimbati today,' Annika said, returning with a fresh French press of coffee, placing it on the table. Her previous concerns seemed all forgotten or well hidden, as if she had stashed them behind the small counter inside, waiting to re-examine them at a later stage.

'Who?' Mary tried stuffing her thoughts into her handbag along with the wet tissue. She didn't want them on display if Annika was not prepared to share hers.

'Pieter's wife. The road company are flying her up here to sort out getting the body back to South Africa and all that.'

Caiaphas and his reasons for being up at the hotel were swept aside in Mary's mind by this newly widowed woman and the emotions she had felt at the time of her own widowhood bubbled back up in her mind.

Caiaphas took the cup from the old man and filled it with water from the jug that sat on the floor nearby. He was a little surprised that Mawenzi was still alive. He was there, but not there, flitting in and out of reality. At times seeming to recognise Caiaphas, then lapsing into a sort of dream where he would mumble incoherently. Caiaphas was not sure, but at one time in a less coherent phase, he thought he heard the old man call him baba, father. This did not feel right, so Caiaphas blamed the harelip and the mumbling for tricking him into hearing something that had not been said.

After sipping the water, Old Man Mawenzi lay back and closed his eyes. His breathing evened out into a regular sleep pattern and Caiaphas sat back against the rough wall of the hut and relaxed slightly. It was always easier watching a man sleeping than watching one who was trying not to die.

He reached into his pocket and drew out his cigarettes, lighting one and slowly taking in the smoke then, resting his head against the wall, blew it out in an almost invisible silver line.

He knew what thoughts were coming and had no idea how to stop them. Would he ever be able to rid himself of the mental picture he held of Mrs Mary in the bathroom in front of the mirror. Could he erase the memory of holding that body that he had seen in all its glory, close to his chest as she had trembled in his arms?

He knew he had to exorcise these thoughts and images. Esther was right, he had no place in this lady's life. It was stupid to think that he would even have a chance. There had been days where he had fantasised that Mrs Mary would marry him and take him with her back to England where everything was brilliant and everyone had lots of money. Then he would pull himself back to Africa and the reality of his life.

Some of Esther's words had helped. What would he know about dealing with a woman who sought meaning in her body? How would he respond if, sitting in their London mansion, his wife, Mrs Mary, said to him, 'What does my body mean?'

He knew what he would like to answer, but also knew deep down that any answer he could come up with would not satisfy the European mind. And this was only one strange thing they had ascertained about Mrs Mary. How many other funny things would be passing through her mind? If she looked for meaning in her own naked body, would she start looking for something in his? He shuddered at the idea of being scrutinised like that. What else would she want to make complex that didn't need to be made so?

He squeezed the last drops of smoke from the cigarette and extinguished the butt. His thoughts now turning to the old man who still lay asleep opposite him. His breathing was regular if not a little bit raspy. A sadness began to fill him at the thought of losing his dance partner. Yes, Solomon had come as a surrogate, but would it be the same? He debated lighting up another, then thought better of it. His guard duty was due to end soon.

He wondered how Solomon was feeling about his friend dying. He was old, he had seen many deaths in his life. Could you measure the length of a man's life by the number of deaths he has seen? How many deaths would he, Caiaphas, have to see before it would be his turn? Death did not frighten him, he was still too young to worry about such things. But he also understood its place in life.

He remembered now a dusty memory, faded by time, how he had lost his younger brother when they were still children. Fragments of the memory popped into his mind as he remembered the way his little friend had slowed down and stopped. How he had been told that his brother had 'gone away' and that he would not see him ever again.

His mother had wept a little and his father had been quiet and serious. But it was only a matter of days before life went on. And that had been how he had approached death since then. There was a short time to be silent and contemplate the event, then you accept that the person had gone away and would not return and life went back to normal.

He glanced across at his dance partner, watching him struggling down that last pathway of life and slowly a thought came about his feelings for Mrs Mary. They needed to 'go away' so that he would never see them again.

The first thing that struck Esther when she resumed reading Mrs Mary's rude book after preparing the guest room was that Mrs Connie was thinking that she married Mr Clifford because she disliked him physically. No wonder European women had such problems in marriage. Why marry someone you dislike, especially physically. Esther thought of her own husband and how he still excited her whenever she saw him.

Her thoughts then turned to Mrs Mary and Caiaphas as they did so often these days. If she was going to understand what was going on there, surely the answers lay in this book. But she was a little confused now. In order for Mrs Mary and Caiaphas to get married, Mrs Mary would have to dislike him physically. It was difficult to say if this was the case. She had not noticed Mrs Mary giving Caiaphas any looks, certainly none that said that she liked him physically. But at the same time there were none that said she disliked him. It was more that she was disinterested.

Caiaphas, on the other hand, judging by his bathroom window escapades, liked what he saw physically. But the rude book never said if the man needs to like or dislike physically. Did that matter though as Mr Clifford was a European man who went round in a bath with wheels on? So he would be very different to an African man surely? African men, from what she had observed, liked to look at their women. They liked to be attracted physically, as an African woman liked to find a handsome man. So, Esther concluded, it was very likely that both men and women in Europe needed to dislike each other physically in order to marry.

The problem here, was that with Mrs Mary and Caiaphas, there was one European and one African and the book gave no indication of what would happen if a European woman thought that her man liked her physically. What problems would that cause? Maybe she needed to let Mrs Mary know somehow that Caiaphas liked her physically and that may stop any relation-ship developing.

She shelved that idea, not sure how she could achieve that without telling Mrs Mary outright. Instead she turned her mind over to the next issue that struck her as strange. It seemed that Mrs Bolton, the servant, was falling in love with Mr Clifford and somehow Mrs Connie did not seem to mind and Mr Clifford seemed to like it. Was it okay for a servant to love a master like this? Was this why Mrs Mary did not have an issue with Caiaphas being in love with her? Esther had to stop reading for a moment to contemplate that thought.

As far as she could tell, Mrs Mary was not even aware of Caiaphas being interested in her. Contrary to her earlier thoughts that Mrs Mary was climbing through the bathroom window to meet with Caiaphas, she now realised that Mrs Mary had not been aware of those prying eyes. Would Mrs Mary have a problem with Caiaphas being in love with her? Esther was not sure.

She did spend a few moments wondering about her own feelings towards Mr James, but there was nothing to explore. He was the boss. A nice man who treated her well (better than Mrs Joyce treated her mother), but there was no love of that kind between them. She chuckled quietly to herself at the thought of even loving him.

Another thing which she read had her chuckling quietly, then stopping suddenly as if embarrassed by her thoughts. Mrs Bolton had told Mrs Connie that all men were just big babies. She thought of her little Thomas and how he was so helpless and so reliant on her for everything.

Caiaphas was not reliant on woman for anything, except maybe someone to cook for him. But he could feed himself and clean himself. Sometimes he was a little bit like a young boy, fooling around, but he was not a baby. And Solomon. He was the furthest thing from a baby, so solemn and wise. As far as she knew, he had never been married and had always looked after himself. He was always neat and tidy and he knew how to cook.

Then there was Mr James. He could not cook, he didn't wash his own clothes and did not even make his bed. About the only thing he could do for himself was wash. She giggled at the thought of having to bath her boss. Of all the men she knew, Mr James was the most baby like. So, she concluded, it must be European men who are babies.

She resumed reading, but then came to a strange expression which caused her to stop and think again. The book talked of success as a 'bitch goddess'. She knew what a bitch was, there were plenty of scrawny ones that scrounged in the village dump, flies constantly trying to feast on the festering sores that dotted their twitching coats. Little brown buttons of teats were always prominent down their ribcage-rippled torsos. She could not see how they could be called goddesses. They were dirty vermin, something you threw stones at to get rid of. You would not throw stones at a goddess and certainly not one that was successful.

Dogs in Europe, she concluded, must be very different. She tried, but could not create a mental image of a dog that could be called a goddess, so dismissed these thoughts and picked up the book again. She had hardly started the next sentence when she heard a car coming slowly up the long driveway. It did not sound like Mrs Mary's car. She hurriedly put the book back on the table, smoothed the bedclothes and went to see who it was.

The woman sat on the veranda staring out at the garden. She had an aura of smartness about her despite her clothes being simple, cheap even. She just knew how to dress well. Her hands were clasped on her lap, as if squeezing out a prayer. Dark rings underlined her eyes and she looked tired.

'She's been sitting out there like that since she arrived, ma'am,' Esther said, peering through the window at the sad figure. 'She has not even touched the tea I made her.'

Mary did not need this. Why had she chosen to come stay here of all places?

'I think she is the wife of that man who died,' Mary tried to sound as casual as she could and, not wishing to discuss this with Esther, headed out to face the inevitable.

'Hello, I am Mary Erskine. Welcome to The Lodge,' she tried to sound as cheerful as she could.

The woman did not seem to hear her and Mary stood for a second wondering if she should repeat herself, or just leave the woman alone. She wanted to do the latter. Leave this woman to her grief. That sort of thing was contagious and she was still trying to get over her own bout of it. But then the faces of those who had shunned her sprang up in her mind and she softened.

'You're Pieter's wife, aren't you?' she said softly.

The woman stirred, looked up and nodded. Her look reminded Mary of how she had felt back when George had gone. There were still many tears in there, but they had lost their way in the confusion of feelings that sloshed around inside her.

Mary eased herself into the chair next to the woman and reached out and took her hand. 'I am so very sorry,' she said gently, and she was. Not for the man who had died, but for the woman who had been left behind.

The woman stared at her hands, then slowly lifted her head and sniffed.

'I'm sorry, you must think me very rude,' she said. Her accent, although noticeable, was not nearly as strong as Pieter's had been.

'No. Not at all,' Mary remembered how she had been when George went. You feel so empty, as if the world around you does not exist. You are that person in the scene, the one where you stand still while everything else speeds by in a blur around you. You are out of kilter with the rest of the world. Later, you wonder how you managed to catch up with the rest, but for that moment, you are on your own.

It would be worse for this woman as she had not been expecting it. Mary at least had known it was coming.

'I'm Mary,' she introduced herself again, this time leaving off her surname. 'I'm looking after The Lodge for James, the owner. He is back in England at the moment for a bit.' She thought it best not to mention why James was there. 'Is there anything you need? Some more tea, or a drink?'

The woman was beginning to speed up and catch up with the rushing world.

'Oh, I'm sorry, I didn't drink the last one,' she looked down at the cup as if seeing it for the first time.

'Not a problem. Let me get you a fresh one.' Mary rose and picked up the cold tea.

'Tanya.'

'Pardon?' Mary paused.

'Tanya. That's my name. Oh, I feel so rude and...' her eyes misted over.

'No, no don't worry. I quite understand. Let me arrange for some tea and I'll be back in a jiffy.

There was something about doing this that made Mary feel – could she call it – important? All she knew was that she had been where Tanya was now. She knew something of what this woman was feeling, she was almost an expert.

Tanya didn't look up when Mary returned, but continued to stare out at the garden.

'It's so peaceful here,' she made a half gesture at the lawn and flower beds.

'It is. James found a lovely spot.' Mary felt that she could not take credit for the peace.

Tanya nodded and remained silent for a long while. Mary felt the need to say something bubbling up inside her, but fought the urge. The talking had irritated her. Everyone saying what they thought should be said, but all saying nothing. And, just like this situation now, the person wanting to say some words of comfort, did not really know the deceased. 'No,' she told herself, 'all this woman needs is someone to sit quietly with her.'

'It is the wife of that man who was killed in the accident. The one that Mrs Mary...' Esther quickly changed course, not wanting to express her thoughts, '...had lunch with.'

She was not sure if more than lunch had been on the menu up at the Nyala Hotel. Caiaphas had never explained what had actually happened up there.

'What is she doing here?' Caiaphas asked after he had put down the box of purchases that Mary had brought back from town. Despite his new resolution regarding Mrs Mary, he was still feeling put out that he was not wanted on the shopping run.

Esther clicked her tongue as if to say, 'why are you so stupid, Caiaphas?' but all she said was, 'She has come to bury her husband.'

'I know that,' Caiaphas' voice glistened with irritation. 'What is she doing here, at The Lodge?'

Esther paused. She had not considered that question.

'Why is she not at the Nyala?' Caiaphas pressed home the advantage he saw that he had, wanting to show Esther that he was not so stupid, he knew why the woman had come to Kilimbati.

Esther clicked her tongue again and turned to dry a dish, not wanting to let Caiaphas think that she had not already pondered the woman's presence at The Lodge.

'Maybe she has come to take back her husband's spirit from Mrs Mary,' Esther was not quite sure what she meant by that, but said it with conviction. It had the desired effect as she sensed Caiaphas falter.

'Why would Mrs Mary have his spirit?' He was not sure how someone could 'have' another person's spirit.

'Do you know what happened up at the Nyala? Do you think that a man and a woman would go there just to eat? They went there for the sex thrill, because Mrs Mary disliked him physically and he had his crisis and he had to grind his teeth till Mrs Mary had her crisis, but Mrs Mary couldn't have her crisis, so she stole his spirit and that is why he crashed his motor car, because his spirit had been stolen.'

Esther felt as bewildered by her explanation as Caiaphas looked, but as the words tumbled out, they seemed to gain strength and by the time she finished talking, she had convinced herself that what she had said was true. She drew a breath, 'That is why the man's wife is here at The Lodge, she has come for his spirit.'

'I just couldn't bring myself to stay there. That was the last place he was before he died. I just couldn't go there, so the company booked me in here.'

Mary nodded, not wanting to think about 'there'. 'There' held horrid memories which she could not discuss with Tanya.

'I know how you feel. I was with my husband when he died and afterwards I just didn't want to be there. But at the same time, you don't know where you want to be. Everywhere seems to be the wrong place.'

Tanya glanced up, her eyes asking questions that Mary knew had burned in her when George had died.

'It's been three months now, he had been ill for a good while before that, so it was a blessing in some ways, but I don't know.' There was no way Mary was going to go into the details of George's death.

'Don't get me wrong, I mean I was glad that his suffering was over. I couldn't bear to see him in pain, but I still can't help feeling sorry for myself. He's free of all this world's problems, but I've got to face them all by myself now.'

She paused, realising that this would not be helping the grieving woman.

'But time, as they say, is the great healer. It doesn't hurt as much now as it did back then.' She did not feel comfortable with what she was saying and fumbled for a way out of this line of conversation.

'What I'm trying to say, I guess, is that it does get better. It is a slow process, but it does get better. You might not think that now. You just need to take things one day at a time and you'll see.'

'Ladies, dinner is served in the dining room. Please could you come through.' Solomon stood holding the door open and bowed slightly at the two women as they passed by into the room from which pleasant aromas had been leaking for the past twenty minutes or so.

'For the starter tonight, we have a cream of tomato soup with croutons,' Solomon announced.

Mary was a little disappointed that it was nothing more fancy or involved. She did want to show off her chef's skills to this new widow and help her cope with the shock she was in, but it was just tomato soup.

They waited silently as Esther spooned the thick orangey liquid into their bowls, steam wafted gently over the dishes and infused their nostrils with delicate scents.

'I love tomato soup,' Tanya said quietly before lifting her spoon. She seemed reluctant to eat and Mary recalled how she had almost starved herself in the week following George's death. It was a natural reaction, a loss of appetite and she was just about to let Tanya know that she didn't have to eat if she didn't feel up to it when her dinner partner, seemingly out of politeness, lifted the spoon and, after briefly blowing on it, took it into her mouth.

It was fascinating to watch the reaction as Mary imagined the flavours spreading. It was as if Tanya were being woken from a dream, a nightmare, to find that all was in fact okay. Life returned to her eyes and the hint of a smile touched her lips.

'Just like mum used to make it,' she said, almost to herself, 'there's even a hint of orange juice in there. Perfect.'

It was not long before her plate was empty and she looked hungrily at the bowl.

'There's plenty more if you want.' Mary indicated.

Tanya helped herself to another bowlful, eating this one slightly slower and as she did, she began to talk. Just general, friendly chatter, with no mention of death.

'For the main course we have cottage pie and green beans with a tomato and lettuce side salad. We also have some garlic bread.' Solomon finished the food introductions and retired as Mary stared after him, a little confused. Why had he suddenly dropped the fancy food?

But Tanya's eyes were bright. 'This is amazing, two of my favourite dishes,' she smiled and began to help herself to a healthy portion.

Over the main course, Mary learned about Tanya's family, her friends, her likes and dislikes, as she chattered away. It was almost as if Pieter was completely forgotten. As she helped herself to seconds, Tanya gave an embarrassed smile and shrugged her shoulders.

'I shouldn't really, but this is so good.'

A sadness flashed momentarily across her face, then she said, 'It has made me feel so much better. And he's used a little bit of paprika. I have always said that a touch of paprika in a cottage pie is what makes it.'

Mary nodded. She had seen the difference the food had made to Tanya, but was at a loss to explain how Solomon could have possibly known that this was Tanya's favourite, or for that matter, that she liked paprika in her cottage pie.

'All we need now is there to be jelly and custard for pudding to make my evening complete. I know it's not fancy. Don't get me wrong, I do like a fancy meal every now and then, but tonight I really felt like a good old-fashioned home-cooked meal rather than those Michelin Chef dishes you get in expensive restaurants,' Tanya paused, thought for a second, then added another spoonful of cottage pie to her plate.

I would not put it past Solomon to have prepared jelly and custard for dessert, Mary thought as she joined her guest in a second helping.

The chef looked tired, Caiaphas thought as he lit up his new dance partner's cigarette. It was more a physical exhaustion than an age-related one, or one brought on by the fatigue of worry. It was as if he had been drained of some of his powers.

There was something in the way he walked and, although it was dark, Caiaphas was sure the old man's hand shook more than usual as he held the cigarette out to be lit, it was the shake of exertion.

But, the rules of the dance stated that Caiaphas could not comment, or offer some kind words of concern. Not that he wanted to, Solomon was not the kind of man you spoke to in that way. In fact he was hardly the kind of man you spoke to at all.

There was, however, something which struck Caiaphas as he inhaled a lungful of smoke. The old man did seem to be slightly friendlier with Mrs Mary than he usually was with Mr James' women. Nothing untoward, but he was being pleasant, talking to her more than just to introduce the food.

Caiaphas shot a surreptitious glance at the old chef, trying in that short time he could run his eyes across the face opposite without staring, to read what he could from the features that wavered in the gloomy murk of cigarette and moon-light. But there was nothing he could see. Just the rheumy eyes and set face that he always saw.

What could be causing this change? Was it whatever had happened up at the Nyala that had softened the hardened rock that is Solomon?

He wanted to risk another glance at the old man's face, but somehow knew that he would not be any the wiser for it and may only cause offence because that was not really a dance step that fitted into this routine.

I don't suppose he's been a dirty old man and been looking through the bathroom windows after chasing me away from them. The thought crept up so suddenly on Caiaphas and seemed so ridiculous that he choked on his cigarette smoke and had to endure the indignity of a coughing fit while his dance partner looked on, unmoved by his distress.

The ceiling of the bedroom gave off a strange aurora borealis light as the dull illumination from the hurricane lamp flicked at it with feather-light touches.

I should go to sleep, Mary told herself, but two things kept poking at her mind to keep her from even feeling tired. The first was the widow, Tanya. As the food had taken effect and she had shaken off the fog of shock, she had chattered warmly.

She had spoken lovingly of her departed husband and Mary found it difficult to believe that it was the same brute who had tried to force himself on her so crudely, but there was something else there, an undercurrent of unease about him.

She was glad that Tanya had not asked any questions about her Pieter. What would she have answered if Tanya had asked if she had known him? 'Yes, and he tried to rape me when he was blind drunk and I refused which made him angry and that's why he's dead.' Hardly the right answer to give, but what if someone else told her that she, Mary, was the last one to be with Pieter. Everyone around the mountain seemed to know, so the chances of Tanya hearing about this were fairly good.

'I must be prepared with a plausible answer when the question comes,' she told herself. But nothing came to mind that sounded suitable.

Mary sighed and rolled onto her side, adjusting her physical position to aid the change of mental path she wanted to take to tackle the second nagging issue. How the hell had Solomon known not to cook the fancy food he usually did? And not just that, he had managed to do Tanya's favourite dishes to perfection, so much so that he had lured the poor woman out of her stupor to a state of near cheerfulness.

It's not like he could have asked could he? She had never seen him address a guest before other than to announce dinner, introduce the food, or give a polite greeting if needed. It surely could not have been coincidence that he just happened to decide to dumb down the meal and this, by pure chance, coincided with Tanya's exact tastes.

No, there had to be something more to it. Maybe the road company had managed to get a message to him to say that's what she would like for dinner. That must be it. Esther always checked the emails for bookings and maybe there were instructions with that which she had passed on to the chef. This theory eased Mary's thoughts somewhat, but with a lingering doubt as to how Solomon had got the nuances of the food precisely right, she leaned over and extinguished the lamp.

TWELVE

A hacking cough echoed in the cool night air. It rose from the lungs and glided freely across the fields where the forest had been cleared on the more gentle slopes. It was a stuttering Morse code message for the ancestors, telling them to prepare a place at their table for there would be a new one coming to them soon. The ancestors nodded quietly as they received it. They knew already, but were used to these reminders that would come from the dying. Sometimes they would start weeks, or even months before the arrival of the new spirit. Sometimes it would only be a few days or even hours before the spirit arrived. All they knew was that someone was coming and they must be ready to welcome the new spirit when the time came. Sometimes they would chuckle quietly amongst themselves, amused that the dying thought they had to remind their ancestors that they were coming. The ancestors knew all.

Time was a lazy thing in their world. It did not adhere to a strict timetable of seconds, minutes and hours. Time would take as long or as short as it needed in their world for things to happen and they all accepted this with ease.

A faint slither of the sound of the cough broke off from the main barrage and went exploring. It caught a light breeze and surfed across the mountain side, gliding just above the trees with a childish abandon, till it reached the neat garden and spotted the lodge. It swooped down, curious to see what secrets the building held.

Outside a window it saw a dream waiting to enter.

'Hello,' the echo of the cough called and waved.

'Shh!' the dreamed motioned for the cough to be quiet.

The cough flew closer and when it got beside the dream it whispered, 'What's happening?'

The dream indicated the sleeping figure in the room that they could just see between a crack in the curtains. 'She is nearly ready to receive me,' the dream said, 'and I don't need a cough waking her at this point.'

The cough nodded and swallowed hard to try and prevent itself from crying out too loudly.

'Are you a good dream or a nightmare?' it asked.

'Oh, I'm very pleasant,' the dream smiled, 'I am a good memory of her father.'

The cough started to splutter with glee, then remembered it needed to be quiet so as not to wake the sleeping woman. It let out a small squeak and fell silent under the reproving glare of the dream

'Can I stay and watch?' the cough asked.

The dream studied it for a while then sighed, 'Okay, but you must be very quiet. I do not want her waking up halfway through. There is nothing more unpleasant than being woken up when you are busy.'

The cough nodded vigorously and held a finger up to its lips. 'Not a sound,' it whispered.

A beautiful day was threatening to leak in through the crack in the curtains, but Mary luxuriated in the warmth and comfort of the bed. She had woken up thinking of her father again and the sheets seemed to be holding her in their arms, the way she remembered her dad holding her when she was a little girl.

It wouldn't be long before Esther would arrive with her tea and this morning Mary did not want the intrusion, hoping to hold onto these feeling for as long as possible.

'Just five more minutes,' she wanted to shout down the passage, the same way she had often begged her father for a little longer in bed when, knowing it would make him late for work, she didn't want to get up to go to school. Even as a somewhat precocious teenager, she would get away with it back then, but only for exactly five minutes. Further pleas would be dismissed until she eventually gave up trying.

She checked her watch, just for fun, to see how long Esther would give her, then went back to her memories of her father. For some strange reason she was recalling the way he would sometimes cough, especially when he smoked his pipe. It was a polite, almost clearing of the throat sound that would invariably be accompanied by a small wisp of smoke escaping from between his lips.

It was exactly five minutes after she had looked at her watch that Esther came in with her tea and to let the sunshine into the room.

It was only as she saw Tanya standing out in the garden that she realised she had, for the first time since his passing, not thought of George when she woke up. And, instead of this making her sad, it buoyed her spirits. She finally felt like she was moving on. She did not have to feel guilty about not thinking of him all the time. It did not mean that she loved him less, nor was she being unfaithful to him or his memory.

Her mind went back to the simple meal of the night before and the seemingly magical effect it had had on her guest. Without realising it, some of that magic had rubbed off on her.

'Good morning, Tanya,' she smiled as she walked out into the garden. 'Lovely morning, isn't it?'

Some of the effect of dinner had worn off, Mary saw that straight away in Tanya's face, but there were still enough leftovers for Mary to work with and, dropping down a gear in her cheerfulness, guided the new widow to the table.

'Better than expected,' Tanya answered Mary's enquiry about how she had slept. Mary nodded her understanding.

'It takes a while. I know I struggled at first.' She didn't know whether to mention that this had been her own best night's sleep since George's death. It would be meant as encouragement saying, 'Look at me, after all I went through with George, I have managed to get to this point.' But it could also be taken as gloating – 'Look at me, after all I went through with George. You've still got a long way to go to get to this point.'

Tanya nodded, lowered her eyes and studied the place mat for a while then raised her head again.

'You were with him that day, weren't you?' she asked.

'Good morning, Madam, what would you like for breakfast? We have eggs, sausage, grilled tomatoes, bacon and hash browns.'

Good old Solomon to the rescue, Mary thought as the chef took a detailed order from Tanya, explaining how she could have her eggs (fried, poached, scrambled, omelette, or French toast) and offering a choice of sausage (pork, lamb or South African boerewors), then discussing what to top the tomato with (herbs, cheese or fried onions).

Mary was sure they did not have any boerewors or lamb sausages. They did not have a freezer (no electricity) to store them, so why was Solomon even offering Tanya these options? But she could not afford to linger on this thought, she needed to focus on answering the question she knew would still be hanging between her and her guest once the old chef had hobbled off to do his cooking duties.

'Pork sausages, please.'

Solomon nodded and, even though his face was impossible to read, Mary felt sure that he had known the answer before even asking the question. He nodded, first to Tanya, then bowed slightly to Mary and in doing so seemed to pass the message that he had done what he could to give her time to think. It was over to her now.

'Yes, I was with him, we were having lunch.' She did not want to be asked the question again, scared that this may throw her back to that unprepared moment when it first came.

'We had met at a dinner party a few days earlier. There's a farm not too far from here run by an English couple and they love entertaining the ex-pats.' Mary felt she had better explain.

'Ray and Joyce?' Tanya asked.

'Yes,' Mary nodded.

'Pieter told me about them. Said they had sort of adopted him like he was an orphan. He always spoke fondly of them. I'd like to meet them if I get the chance. You know, to thank them for...' her thought got cut off by a lump in her throat.

Mary waited a moment while her guest calmed herself.

'Well, at the dinner, we had a...a disagreement. It was nothing really, silly.' Mary suddenly realised she had not though this one through properly. 'Anyway,' she acted as if she didn't want to dwell on something so trivial, 'I guess he felt bad and wanted to apologise.' It was sort of the truth. 'He really didn't need to.'

'He was such a gentleman,' Tanya smiled.

Nodding is lying, Mary told herself as she pictured a memory flashing through Tanya's mind of a time when, perhaps, Pieter had really been a gentleman.

They fell silent and listened to the wind making a low whispering sound as it tickled the trees which shuddered in delight. The birds chuckled at the spectacle, unaware of the strange, unspoken tension between the two women on the lawn.

'Your breakfast, madam,' Solomon said, placing the plate in front of Tanya. 'And for you, madam.' Mary got hers. 'Please do enjoy.'

He bowed slightly and hobbled over to his usual sentry post. Mary watched him move off, thinking that he looked weary. She had not noticed it earlier. But she could not dwell on this, her mind was telling her to brace herself for the next question Tanya would ask – why hadn't she been in the car with Pieter?

Caiaphas glanced at the woman who sat at the breakfast table with Mrs Mary. She was a white woman, but not from Europe. She was African like him. He wondered if she would, like Mrs Mary, be worried about meaning in her body and having a crisis and gritting teeth. Would an African white woman be different to a European white woman?

When he had spied through Mrs Tanya's bathroom window last night, she had not even hinted at the strange rituals that Mrs Mary had. It was just brushing teeth and then off to bed. But there had been one night when Mrs Mary had done that, so he couldn't be sure.

But there had been, and even now at breakfast, there was, something similar about the women. It was more pronounced in Mrs Tanya than in Mrs Mary, but the white African carried a sadness around with her which he had seen in Mrs Mary, more so when he first picked her up at the airport. Now, as the two sat at breakfast, he could see that Mrs Mary had lost a large part of that burden. There were still vestiges of it floating around her, like a bad smell that you knew was still there, but you had got so used to it that your mind had all but shut it out.

Around Mrs Tanya, it was like the mist that sometimes covered the mountain when you could hardly see the next bend on the path. But already this morning she had changed since her arrival yesterday. The sun was beginning to illuminate the mist. You still could not see the next bend, but you felt safer approaching it.

The reason for Mrs Tanya's sadness surely had to be that her husband had just died. That sort of sadness was visible on black Africans too when they lost loved ones, but it did not seem to be as thick a fog, nor did it cling so closely to the person. Death is more important to the Europeans, he concluded.

He glanced across at the women again. They were talking in a friendly manner as they ate their breakfast. Mrs Mary was finding out what Mrs Tanya was going to be doing during the day and she replied that the road company was sending someone to pick her up to go sort out her husband's affairs. Mrs Mary asked if she wanted someone to go with her and Mrs Tanya shook her head, smiled and said, 'Thanks'.

The conversation continued and Caiaphas lost interest and returned his eyes to the flowerbeds and getting rid of some weeds. His mind, however, lingered on Mrs Mary. The sadness he had seen in her when she first arrived had definitely faded. It was the same sadness that Mrs Tanya now had. Slowly his mind made the connections. Mrs Mary's husband must also have died. He looked up again and studied the women. Maybe, he thought, that was why Mrs Mary was looking for meaning in her body. Did she think that it only had meaning when she had a husband?

His eyes took in Solomon as the old man moved slowly to the table to enquire if the ladies wanted anything else. Solomon was a wise man. Maybe he had worked out that Mrs Mary was looking for a new husband. What if his strange, almost friendly, behaviour towards her was him trying to become Mrs Mary's new husband? Surely that could not be!

Caiaphas stood up and moved quickly to tell Esther of his new theory.

Mary was glad that Tanya had not wanted her to go with. She had felt obliged to make the offer, but really did not want to go see Pieter's body in the morgue. A large part of her reluctance stemmed from the fact that she did not want to ever see Pieter's face again. She was seeing enough of it in her mind, she did not want the added intrusion of seeing it in the flesh.

But there was also a part of her that did not want to be in a morgue. The thought of this had already brought back too many memories of George's death, she didn't need any further prompts on that front especially now that she was finally beginning to feel that she was over the worst of it.

Despite this, she could not help her mind bringing up George's body after he had gone. It was as if he had just gone to sleep, drifting quietly off as if he were slowly floating from her grasp. She had wanted to reach out and pull him back, to chide him – gently of course – for even thinking of deserting her.

She put down her teacup and stared out at the garden. Instead of the tears she expected on her cheeks, she felt the corners of her lips being tugged gently upwards, like a flower bud stretching towards the warmth of the sun. The smile felt warm, as did the memory. He had looked so at peace. The grimace of pain that had plagued his last days had just melted before her eyes. How could she now begrudge him that release?

The sun was beginning to make its way across the garden and she felt its warmth tickling her bare arms. She glanced down at *Lady Chatterley* next to her, but this was not a time to be reading about an unfaithful woman. She was feeling more devoted to George now than when he had been alive. In life, the daily chores and, in the latter days, the taking care of him, had taken up too much room for devotion. But now, she had all the time in the world.

She knew there was no Mellors out here for her. And even if she did eventually find someone else, or even fell for James, she knew that she would never be unfaithful to George. She glanced up and saw Caiaphas coming round the side of the house. In terms of occupation, he was probably the closest person to Mellors, but he held none of the attractions that the gamekeeper had for Connie Chatterley.

'Oh, Caiaphas. Could I have a word?' she called over to him.

Solomon and Mrs Mary? That was just too much for Esther. She did not dare share the rumour with Thomas. He was too young for such scandalous a story. She busied herself tidying the kitchen and ignored his mumblings from the cardboard box where he lay.

What would Mrs Mary want with Solomon? Or he with her for that matter. He was an old man and she was still young. Not young like herself, Esther thought, but too young for the old chef.

She knew that Mrs Mary liked the food he cooked, but a woman, if she was married, was expected to do the cooking. In Africa anyway. Why would Mrs Mary marry Solomon when she would have to start cooking and he would have to stop? Perhaps in Europe, married men did cook. But Mr James didn't, although he wasn't married. Neither did Mr Clifford in the rude book. But then he lived in a bath with wheels, so how could he cook while sitting in the bath? Esther was still not sure if married white men cooked given that those she knew were either not married or not able to cook because of injury.

Then she remembered Mr Ray, Mrs Joyce's husband on the farm. He was a married European who was not injured and he never cooked, so, she concluded, married European men did not cook. Therefore, should Solomon ever marry Mrs Mary, he would have to stop cooking, especially if they moved to Europe. It would not do to live in Europe and have the husband cook.

She shook her head and clicked her tongue. This was all too much. Solomon was a cook through and through, he would surely not give this up for Mrs Mary. What else was there to Solomon other than his cooking?

She glanced over at the box where her son lay. His life was so simple compared to a European one and, so far, had had none of the complexities that the European presence in Africa had brought. She picked up the child who gurgled and smiled at her.

'I will do everything I can to keep your life simple,' she promised him.

Caiaphas smiled to himself as he made his way over to Old Man Mawenzi's place. It was his turn to watch over the dying man, but his thoughts were nowhere near his old dance partner. Nor his new one whom Caiaphas was sure would be the one on duty who he would be relieving.

His thoughts were back at the lodge with Mrs Mary and her formal thanking of him for his part in her rescue up at the Nyala. He could tell that she remembered the embrace and he could tell that she didn't particularly want to. Her strange embarrassment at this, as if it were somehow something unclean and to be disapproved of, had done wonders in helping him forget the crush he had had on her. This was not the sort of woman he desired. He was, and always would be, a servant in her eyes. He was just doing his duty in rescuing her; he could never be a knight in shining armour no matter how valiant he was in his deeds.

As he strode along the footpath around the side of the mountain, he felt relieved of a burden. The feelings that had built up in him about the white woman were gone. They had been a passing moment of insanity on his part.

It was not that he felt that she was too good for him. She was too complex. A funny creature running hot and cold, wanting to find meaning in things that were just there, so linked to life that to search for a reason in them was meaningless.

She had hinted at what had happened at the hotel. 'That horrid man' and 'what he tried to do was despicable,' were phrases that dripped with clues. Caiaphas knew Esther would love to be privy to these droplets of information but, he decided, that he should not mention them. Despite her quirks, Mrs Mary had been good enough to offer him heartfelt thanks for his help and, he felt, that deserved some recognition on his behalf. She would not really like everyone knowing about what had transpired.

He also did not judge Mrs Mary too harshly for her treating him like a servant. He could tell that she didn't really want to do it, that her human nature was telling her that it was wrong, but she felt compelled to obey some unwritten law. A law that was born in the minds of Europeans who were so caught up in the complexities of life that they had created for themselves that they could not see a way past it.

In fact, he found himself feeling a little sorry for Mrs Mary. She was the one missing out. By adhering to those rules of the mind, she could never get to know and appreciate the warmth and friendship that most Africans had to offer. She was a servant too. Her master was the ideas and norms of her society and it was a harsh master.

The way she carried the death of her husband was further evidence of its harshness. The Europeans seemed slow and sluggish to move on from the loss of a loved one. They dwell on it and carry the load around with them long after they could convert it to a memory and not be oppressed by it. Memory was good, it was light to carry, especially if you chose the nicest bits and threw all the baggage attached to it away.

Caiaphas began to whistle a happy tune as he made his way to look after the dying man.

The gecko nodded a greeting as the breeze ran in and out between the woman's ankles, like a playful kitten. The warmth of the rocks rose to form a pleasant pool for her to wade through. At the far end of the clearing a rabbit watched wearily, keeping a close eye on the dog which trundled on floppy paws next to the woman.

They reached the rock that Mary liked and Rex looked around slowly, sniffed the air, then seemed to make up his mind about something and looked at the rabbit before settling down with a sigh near Mary's feet. *Sod natural instincts, I'm feeling too lazy to be asked*, he thought.

He lay his head on his paws, then as if hit by an afterthought, lifted it suddenly and feigned to lurch towards the rabbit. The latter, not wanting to take any chances, disappeared into the forest and Rex put his head back down, a smug grin tickling the edge of his mouth. Oh yes, he still had it.

He settled down again, enjoying the warm sunshine on his back. He had sensed a change in this latest visitor to the lodge. The dark aura that had clung to her when she first arrived still had some lingering mist, but the thunderclouds had passed. Rex felt more comfortable sitting near her. She did not reek of desperation as much.

The old chef had been up to his tricks again, Rex thought. He could always detect something in the food aromas. A somewhat unidentifiable smell in there that was a balm to the soul. It was not often that he smelled these. Occasionally when that other bloke, who had been missing for a while, was stressed or upset, Rex had detected a shift in the food that brought calm to the man. But these were always very subtle, sometimes almost undetectable. But last night it had been in your face, or in this case in your nostrils.

Rex did not bother himself with the whys when he detected these strange scents. He did find that they disturbed him somewhat as they arose, but he would quickly settle into the rhythm they seemed to exude and would relax. The best thing about this potion was that it made the humans who ate the food more bearable to be around. The air of unrest that shrouded them would dissipate and Rex found himself less troubled by the odours.

He was glad of the old chef doing his magic last night, particularly with the new arrival. She was so drenched in blackness that he had, much to his chagrin, left the veranda and found refuge near the bench in the garden, most upset to have been forced from his favourite spot.

He sighed again at the memory of that eviction, but then his nostrils picked up the scent of the rabbit again as he lay at the woman's feet. There was nothing to it now, he had to give chase, he could not let the rabbit get away with this act of defiance.

A cloud had lifted from Mrs Connie and that was because she had had sex. Esther found this a strange thing. Was it because she had had sex with the gamekeeper, or was it just because she had had sex? The book was not clear on this. Casting her mind back to the earlier sex scene where Mrs Connie had made the man grit his teeth till she had her crisis, Esther realised that there was none of this with the gamekeeper, so perhaps it was this man Mellors, and not the sex that had lifted the cloud.

The cloud had come about by Mr Clifford telling Mrs Connie how much she meant to him. She had been distressed by this. A very strange reaction, Esther thought. Why would a woman be distressed if a man showed interest in her? Most women she knew enjoyed the attentions of a man. And, this attention was coming from a husband; how much more precious that was to come from the one you had married.

Had she been Mrs Connie, she would have still been flattered by the expression of devotion from her husband even if she was seeing another man. It made a person feel good to be wanted. But this Mrs Connie did not feel good, she felt distressed.

Esther moved her thinking on to the situation at the lodge. Mrs Mary had had Caiaphas interested in her and, while this was the case, she had seemed maybe not distressed, but rather unhappy. But now, according to Caiaphas, it was the old chef Solomon who was showing interest in her and Mrs Mary appeared happier, as if a cloud had lifted from her. If the book, which was now living up to its reputation as being rude, was a reflection of how European women reacted, then surely this proved that Mrs Mary and Solomon had had sex. This Esther struggled to believe. Solomon was too old to have sex. And Caiaphas was not Mrs Mary's husband.

So what was happening? Esther straightened the bedclothes in the guest room and began to tuck the sheets in. She had left off tidying the room for as long as she could in favour of reading more, but the question her reading had raised about Solomon had distracted her too much. Could he possibly have been responsible for the cloud rising?

The woman who had arrived yesterday had also changed overnight. There had been a lot of cloud lifting going on last night. Given that she had just lost her husband, she must have had lots of sex for there to have been such a change and Esther could not even begin to imagine that Solomon could possibly have supplied this.

She was missing something, she thought as she flicked a duster round the guest room, surveyed it to check that she hadn't omitted any task in the preparation of the room, then moved on to clean Mrs Mary's.

As she walked down the short, dark passage that connected the rooms, a thought struck her. What if Solomon had been responsible for lifting Mrs Mary's cloud while Caiaphas had been busy lifting Mrs Tanya's? She clicked her tongue. Men! If they are not having to grit their teeth, they are busy lifting clouds.

Joyce, who arrived at the lodge just as Mary returned from her walk, was her usual self.

'The widow's staying with you, isn't she?'

'The widow? You mean Tanya.' Mary was in no mood for this rudeness and answered with some force.

'Oh, she's Tanya, is she? You two are getting right pally, aren't you?' The sneer on her lips rubbed off on the words. 'Esther! Juice!' Joyce slumped into a chair and slung her legs over the side, dust from her riding boots puffing up as the heels deliberately hit the side of the chair.

'Do you have a problem with that?' Mary half growled, glaring at the boots which tapped away on the clean material against which they sinned, in clear defiance of Mary's look.

'Oh, no problem,' Joyce waved away the non-existent problem, gave a horrid smile, then went in for the kill. 'Not surprising really, you two are so alike.'

'What's that supposed to mean?'

Joyce's eyes lit up. She had baited Mary and now the trap was sprung.

'Well, you are both wishy-washy, insubstantial little women. I don't know what on earth James sees in you.'

Mary stared, too shocked to answer.

'Oh, come on,' Joyce stretched the 'on' to breaking point. 'Don't tell me you didn't know. He's head-over-heels in love with you. Always has been, always will be. You're all he ever speaks about. This lovely woman, Mary, that he knew in England. Mary, the perfect woman, Mary the one for him, Mary this, Mary that. That's all you ever heard from him. Mary, Mary,

Mary. He's obsessed with you. Now I see it.' She sat up, pushing her heels vindictively into the side of the chair to help herself up.

'Yes, that's it. He's just as wishy-washy as you, hence the attraction. He could never handle a real woman like me. No wonder he kept turning down my advances. At first, I thought he was gay, but now I know, he just knew he not could handle someone like me, someone with a bit of spunk.' Joyce looked triumphant now.

Mary felt her strength for this fight going when a movement on the lawn outside caught her eye. Solomon was walking very slowly across the grass, presumably heading to the kitchen to prepare dinner. The thought of his food and in particular the simple meal he had prepared last night, returned to her with some force and suddenly she felt her strength return. However, before she could speak, Joyce fired off another triumphant sounding shot of, 'Esther! Where is my bloody juice!'

'That's enough!' Mary expected it to come out shrilly, but it was an order barked out by an army sergeant. 'I'll not have you talking to Esther like that. If you want a juice that much, then at least have the decency to ask nicely. I do *not*,' she spat out the word like a gunshot, 'want you speaking to Esther like that again.'

Out the corner of her eye, she caught sight of Esther standing at the kitchen door, a glass of juice on a tray, her eyes wide in shock at the scene. Joyce had not seen her and Mary wished she could communicate to Esther to return to the kitchen, but could not do so without alerting Joyce to the young woman's presence.

Thankfully Esther, on assessing the situation, decided that the kitchen was a better place to be than out there and quietly retreated.

Mary stood glaring at Joyce who had shrunk back from the onslaught. She wanted to continue shouting at this obnoxious woman, but regret at having done so was already beginning to mingle with uncertainty as to what to say next. Before she could do anything, however, the shock on Joyce's face faded and was replaced with a nasty smile.

'Well, look at you all forceful and everything,' she stood up slowly. 'James won't like that now will he?' She tutted, 'he likes his women watered down, like that god-awful juice that Esther serves here.' She moved to the doorway and turned to face Mary.

'Well, you can keep your horrid juice and your wimpy James. Me, I'm off to find another real man. One like Pieter. You couldn't cope with him because he was a real man, he knew how to fuck a woman properly. James wouldn't know a woman's arse from her elbow, but Pieter, he knew where my arse was.'

She spun on her heel and stared straight into the icily calm face of Tanya.

Esther hoped that Solomon would leave his post for just a minute so that she could update Caiaphas on what the white people had been up to. She had such a juicy story to tell, but the old man sat quietly at his post and she knew he would not leave until his job was done.

She looked over at him and on seeing how he was, she got a slight shock. He sat with his eyes closed, his hands resting lightly on some of the ingredients he had called for, but he was not moving. For a second she feared he had died, but as she examined him more closely, she could just detect the slight expansion and contraction that breathing did to the frame.

There was a fluttering of the eyelids and his lips now twitched in what seemed like a soundless prayer. As Esther stared, she began to get a nearly uncontrollable urge to move towards him and touch him, feeling that there was something happening to him that she needed to be part of. The kitchen dimmed and all she saw now was the old man surrounded in a light that she could only call angelic.

But Solomon was not an angel, was he? How could he possibly be? Angels were white men in white clothes, that's what they had led her to believe at the Catholic school. Her mind hung by a thread to this thought as the light drew her closer, she reached out her hand to touch the old man, but his eyelids fluttered again and opened, the light faded and Esther quickly lowered her hand and turned to the sink. He had seen her trying to reach out to him, she knew he had, but tried, by wishing hard, to believe that he hadn't. There had been a strange look on his face, not an unpleasant one, it was almost bemused. Esther burned with embarrassment.

'Mint!' he commanded as if nothing had happened. Had anything happened? Esther paused for a moment, then glad of the distraction, stepped out the back door. It was still warm out there and a breeze played gently in the trees. She found the mint plant easily in the moonlight and picked a sprig of it. The air cleared her head and, even though she hesitated slightly before going back inside, she felt relieved of all the strange feelings the episode had stirred up. She was glad that the old chef had needed the mint. The little excursion outside had been just what she needed.

Solomon was busy chopping some vegetables with his usual slow clunk, clunk, clunk of the knife on the cutting board and all felt normal. She put the mint down next to his hand and went through to set the table.

The slap seemed to still be echoing in the room and each time it reverberated in her mind, Mary had to stop herself from giggling at the image of pure shock on Joyce's face as her cheek had reddened from the blow. But laughing wasn't the right thing to do, especially as Tanya had disappeared into her room after dealing the blow while Joyce had stormed off in the opposite direction.

She had not been sure what to do with Tanya, leave her be, or try and comfort her? She chose the former, recalling how she had felt when the women in the village had given her an icy reception. No amount of attempted placation by anyone – had there been anyone to attempt it – would have worked for her. She just needed the time alone to cool off before facing the world again. She hoped Tanya felt the same way and wasn't wondering why she, Mary, hadn't come knocking on her door.

She caught the movement at the door out of the corner of her eye a fraction of a second before she heard the throat being timidly cleared.

'I'm sorry about that,' Tanya stood in the doorway, seeming reluctant to come into the room, 'It's just that...'

'No. No need to explain,' Mary interrupted, 'Come, sit. Do you want some tea?'

There *was* a need to explain, Mary knew this. She also knew that there was a need for her to say that there was no need.

Declining the tea, but accepting the offer of a gin and tonic, Tanya eased herself into the chair and sat quietly as Mary arranged for Esther to fetch the drink.

Once she had the glass in her hand, she started to make the unnecessary explanation.

'I knew he wasn't faithful to me, but somehow thought that if I just pretended he had never strayed, I could believe it and have happy memories of him. But that woman...who was she anyway? She just ruined it for me.'

Mary nodded her understanding, then said, 'Try not to let Joyce get to you. She's the one Pieter wrote to you about, remember, the couple who he had become friends with. She is the most obnoxious person I've ever come across. Pay no attention to her.'

It was easier said than done as Mary well knew. Thoughts of James and his obsession with her, if Joyce was to be believed, had not been far from her mind since that awful encounter. At least her bombshell had been a pleasant one compared to Tanya's and she had been thinking of James in a warm light since then. But she couldn't continue that now, not with Tanya being around.

Her guest sat quietly for a minute, slowing nodding, as if trying to convey to her heart what her mind knew was sensible – she should not let Joyce affect her like that. At length she looked up at Mary.

'What did she mean when she said that you couldn't handle Pieter?'

The old man was busy making the pudding and the mint lay unused beside the chopping board. Esther was sure that he would use it, even if just to put it on top of the dessert as decoration. The white people liked that sort of thing. But there was a nagging thought that sending her outside to get the mint had not been because he needed any. She recalled how that little excursion outside had cleared her head of the strange experience.

Had it not been for the mint still lying there, she would not have given the 'angel' image she had had of Solomon another thought. It was as if the fresh air had blown it out of her mind.

But that little green sprig next to the chopping board hinted at strange happenings, but, Esther's mind was a little blurred in the detail.

'Thank goodness for Solomon,' Mary thought and not for the first time in recent days. He had forgone his five-minute warning that he usually gave two minutes before announcing dinner and went straight in with, 'Ladies, dinner is served.'

He had once again given her the precious gift of a little time to prepare an answer for a question she had expected but was not prepared for.

'The starter this evening is poached egg on garlic toast with a bacon and red wine sauce.'

They were back to the fancy food and Mary eyed her guest to see what her reaction would be.

'Your chef seems to be able to read my mind,' Tanya said, leaning over her plate to take in the visual presentation of the food, almost reluctant to tuck in and destroy the picture on the plate. 'I did feel like having something a little bit posh tonight.'

Mary nodded as the realisation that she had a hankering for some bacon, began to filter into her mind. She began to think of the other dinners she had eaten since arriving at the lodge and how, each one had satisfied an unexpressed need or particular flavour she was craving. How could Solomon have known every time?

But she could not dwell on these thoughts as she had Tanya's earlier question to deal with, and it would not go away. Probably better to come forward with the information than hold back and appear as if you were hiding something.

She let her guest have a few mouthfuls of the starter and enjoyed some herself before she cleared her throat and said, 'You asked about what Joyce said earlier regarding me and Pieter.'

Tanya paused in her chewing and nodded slowly. There seemed to be a little reluctance to pursue the question now but, Mary knew, an answer would be required at some point, and what better time than now when they had the good food to sweeten the bitter story she had to tell.

She began slowly, telling of the dinner at Joyce's and how a drunken Pieter had made 'inappropriate advances'. She thought it best to omit the groping; it was bad enough talking about that evening without going into the sordid details. The food, however, seemed to give her tongue impetus and guide it in what to say.

They ate as they spoke, Tanya nodding slowly as the antics of her departed husband were revealed. She was, Mary thought, surprisingly calm, but as Mary examined her own feelings, she felt at peace getting the ordeal off her chest.

'What happened the day he died?' Tanya asked. The starter had been cleared away, but before Mary could answer, Esther appeared with the first dish of the main course, a rich aroma wafting into the room with her. Solomon followed and after all the dishes were placed on the table, began the introductions.

'For the main course tonight, we have chicken, baked with lavender, cheese and a little bit of chilli. We also have sweet potato, baked with ginger and honey. For the veg-e-tay-bills, we have green beans cooked in a light lemon sauce with hazelnuts. We also have a salad of beetroot, apple and orange with sun-flower seeds and a fruity vinaigrette.'

Once again, the old man had given Mary time to formulate her answer. How did he do it? And the food? Judging by the way Tanya's eyes lit up, she knew that the main course was hitting exactly the right note. They helped themselves to generous portions and as they tucked in, Mary again felt her tongue loosen and she found she could tell of her ordeal up at the Nyala Hotel without it affecting her. Tanya absorbed the story with a sense of sorrow and sympathy for Mary. The food seemed to neutralise the anger and bitterness of the words without ever losing any of its flavour.

Over dessert of a rich chocolate orange brownie and mint custard, they changed the subject and spoke of the mountain and the beauty of the surroundings. The dim light of the hurri-cane lamps brought their widowed spirits closer and Mary felt as if the mountain itself was cradling her as she talked of its beauty. She now knew why James had fallen in love with the place and, for the first time since coming to the lodge, the thought of staying and never going back to England began to form in her mind.

The old chef did his job at the dance, but again his heart did not seem to be in it. He looked eager to move off. Caiaphas was not too concerned, he wanted to be places himself. The bathroom window was calling him again and he could not find the strength to fight the urge. He matched Solomon draw for draw on the cigarettes, perfectly in step.

His eyes became drawn to the red dot burning at the end of the old man's cigarette, watching it brighten and fade with each puff. And slowly as he watched, he felt himself being sucked into the burning glow. He was shrinking, being rolled into a small ball and wrapped in the blanket of warmth at the end of the cigarette. The rich aroma of the tobacco caressed his nostril and eased his mind.

The light of Solomon's cigarette began to pulse on and off in time to the blood moving through his brain and this slowed till he could not feel his own thoughts. Somewhere in the distance, he knew he had a cigarette, but his mind could not command his hand to bring it to his mouth.

And then the light was gone. Caiaphas blinked and looked around. He could not see Solomon anywhere and when he looked down at his hand, he held a lit cigarette that had not been smoked. Somewhere in the back of his mind he thought there was something he had wanted to do, but couldn't remember what that could be. He took a drag on his cigarette and moved off slowly towards his home.

THIRTEEN

A gentle breeze blew around the mountain, tickling her so that she smiled. She was in a good mood. The distress of the recent violent death had been all but eradicated and those visitors who were ailing about it, slept peacefully. Good dreams were skating around her surface and all was well.

The hacking cough that had not abated during the day continued into the night, but this did not disturb the mountain. It was a natural passage being followed and she knew that the rheumy eyes that now watched over the coughing man would be there to oversee his journey across to the spirits of the ancestors. The time was close.

The breeze squeezed under the door of a hut and tiptoed across closed eyelids. It giggled in a childish way at what the eyes behind the eyelids had seen through windows they were not supposed to be looking through. It knew that those eyes would not be drawn towards that forbidden window again. Things had altered so that the urge was no longer there.

The breeze journeyed further on around the mountain and found a room where a mother lay sleeping with her child lying in a cardboard box nearby. The child's eyes were open and looking fearfully around in the dark. It would not be long now before he cried out, so the breeze jumped into the box and cuddled him till he sighed and closed his eyes again.

The mother, hearing the sigh, turned in her sleep, but did not wake. She had been troubled too. A book had been messing with her mind lately and she had witnessed something today that she could not really explain. But as she lay sleeping, the breeze knew that she was slowly dismissing all the strange thoughts that the book had stirred up in her mind and that she would show no more interest in it. The events of the day that she could not fathom, were responsible for this, but she could only make the vaguest connection.

At the lodge, the breeze could sense the peace of the occupants. The one so recently bereaved was sleeping well, a calm aura floated around her and her dreams were lavender scented. The other occupant of the house also slept. She too had fragrant dreams, more savoury than sweet – onions and bacon frying – and a homely aroma clung to them.

But as the breeze slipped into the room through the small crack left open in the window and rippled through the light curtains, it suddenly sensed a lingering tinge of hurt in the woman who lay sleeping in the bed. The breeze made a light circuit of the room, flicked briefly through the pages of a book that lay on the table next to the bed, then suddenly it smiled as an idea struck it. And it was a good idea. The breeze did a gleeful loop-the-loop then squeezed out through the small opening the window had left and darted joyfully across the mountain in search of the rheumy eyes.

Tanya does not look like a widow this morning, Mary thought as she watched her guest walk across the lawn towards her. Breakfast was already laid out on the table and Mary had had to exert a fair bit of constraint to not start before Tanya arrived. She looked almost younger than she had when Mary first saw her sitting on the veranda, her whole body shining with a youthful glow.

'Morning, Tanya. Did you sleep well?'

It was a stupid question that did not need to be asked as the answer was written all over Tanya's face.

'Very well, thanks,' Tanya smiled and eased herself into a chair. 'In fact, I have not slept that well in a long time.' She looked up, a flash of guilt raced across her face then disappeared. 'You know,' she started, then stopped, contemplating if she should say what she was thinking. She gave a 'what the heck' shake of the head and went on. 'You know, with Pieter gone, I feel like a weight has been lifted off of me. I kept telling myself I loved him and that everything would be all right but I always knew deep down that it wouldn't be. But I was too scared to do anything about it. Too scared of what he would do.'

She stopped and began to dish herself some fruit salad. Mary waited for her to finish before dishing her own.

'It's going to be strange getting home and knowing that he will not be coming back, but I'm well provided for. The road company had a great life insurance policy on him so I don't have to worry about that front, but I think the most difficult thing will be realising that I don't have to live my life in fear. Sometimes his emails hurt more than...' she paused again and Mary could almost see her mind remind her that she could say what she liked, he was not there anymore, '...than when he would hit me.'

Despite expecting the comment, it still jolted Mary as if the vocalisation of it made it more real. She had never had to worry about George being violent with her. That had never been in his nature, for which she was grateful. He had even died peacefully.

Her thoughts were interrupted by Esther asking Tanya what she wanted for the cooked part of breakfast.

That's strange, Mary thought, *Esther hasn't been around to take the breakfast order for a while, I hadn't noticed that before.*

The young woman looked – Mary searched for the word – peaceful, that was it. There had been an air of fretfulness about her these last few days, but now she was calm and happy.

Come to think of it, Mary's inner voice was talking again, *that's how I feel. Calm and happy.*

Like the evening before, the conversation lapsed into a relaxed and pleasant one and breakfast was over too soon. Thoughts of deceased husbands were wrapped up and stored away.

'I'd better go finalise my packing,' Tanya said at last. 'The car to take me to the airport will be here soon.'

Mary knew as she watched her guest walk across the lawn that she would miss her.

Esther picked Thomas out of his box and held him close to her. The child gurgled happily. It had missed its mother. Not the physical presence of her being, but the attention he used to get had not quite been there of late, as if she were distracted.

There had been some nagging thought in Esther's mind as she had tidied Mary's room, like a chore she had forgotten to do, but she could not quite place her finger on what it was.

She had straightened the blankets again, then returned to the bathroom and looked round. The toilet bowl sparkled, the basin gleamed and the shower floor glistened. There was soap in the wire rack in the shower and another bar next to the basin. Mrs Mary's creams were neatly arranged and her toothbrush and toothpaste stood like a couple in love in the small glass by the basin. The glass itself was clean and shiny.

She returned to the bedroom and looked round. What was it she had forgotten? The floor looked clean, the small rug next to the bed lay perfectly straight. All the cupboards were closed and the extra blanket that Mrs Mary liked was neatly folded at the bottom of the bed.

Esther shook her head to rid her mind of the strange doubt. There was nothing wrong. She had done everything as usual. She absent-mindedly straightened Mrs Mary's book on the bedside table and returned to the kitchen eager to see her son.

James' email had been sad, but there was also a sense of relief. It took Mary's mind off the recently departed Tanya.

'Mum has gone.'

'Gone' not 'died'.

'She went in her sleep last night. A blessing in a way as she was really struggling with the pain. There'll be a small funeral next week, then I'll be coming home. Of course, you are welcome to stay on as long as you like. Will let you know the dates once I know. Hope all is well there. Love James.'

Mary cried gentle tears, but did not feel sad. James' mum had been there for her when her real mum hadn't so there was a definite sense of loss, but her overall feeling was one of gratefulness for this surrogate mother.

She had just blown her nose, wiped the tears away and was starting to contemplate the prospect of 'stay as long as you like' when she heard a knock at the door.

'Hello Mary.'

It took a moment to realise that it was Ray, Joyce's husband. He had been quiet and reserved at the dinner party, so much so that the dim impression he had made on Mary that evening had faded quickly and she now struggled at first to recognise the tanned and slightly rugged man that stood politely outside the door.

'Ray?'

He nodded as if confirming that she had got his name right. 'I was wondering if I might have a word?'

'Um, yes. Yes. Shall we sit on the veranda, it's such a lovely day?'

They settled themselves into the chairs and Mary waited for him to speak. He was the complete opposite of Joyce, quiet, polite. Mary wondered how they ever got together.

Ray made a start, but was interrupted by Esther who had come to see if they wanted anything to drink.

'Coffee, please. Thank you, Esther,' Ray said and gave a gentle smile.

Once Esther had disappeared he turned back to Mary.

'I just wanted to let you know that you can still send the laptop over to be recharged, but I'm afraid that Joyce will no longer be able to fetch and carry it for you, you will have to send someone round with it. I am sorry about this, but I really don't have anyone to spare at the moment.'

Mary nodded slowly. There was bound to be some fall out from all this nonsense with Joyce, but she could not help feeling pleased that her life would no longer be intruded upon by someone so rude. She just hoped that James would not be too put out by this.

'I am sorry Joyce feels that way,' Mary began, then stopped as Ray raised a surprised eyebrow.

'Joyce? This was not her decision,' he interjected.

'Oh. I see. Well then, I'm sorry you feel this way, but I do think Joyce went a bit too far.'

It surprised Mary that Ray was the one being vindictive and why didn't he go the whole hog and stop re-charging the battery altogether? The thought had hardly finished when she realised that she still had the wrong end of the stick.

'A bit too far?' Ray looked puzzled, 'I'm sorry, but I'm not following. Did you and Joyce have a disagreement?'

Mary half shrugged her shoulders and half nodded her head in an attempt to communicate that yes, they fought, but no, it was really nothing.

'She...um...' Mary had to tread carefully here, 'she...er... insulted one of my guests.'

'Pieter's wife?' Ray raised an eyebrow again and Mary nodded. The nodding seemed to catch as Ray's head began to bob gently. The penny had dropped on at least one side of the conversation.

'I guess Joyce bragged about her affair with Pieter in front of her?'

Mary kept nodding, fearful of saying anything at the moment.

'Did Pieter's wife say anything?'

'No, she just slapped Joyce.'

Ray nodded, almost smiled, Mary thought, then went on. 'That would explain why she was so hyped up when she got back yesterday. She came flying in, ranting about "that bitch" and then she let slip "I loved him more than she ever could," she said. She didn't even realise what she had just admitted to. It was only when I asked who that she suddenly stopped and tried to back track. But the cat was out of the bag and I made her tell me everything.'

He paused for a moment, perhaps reflecting on whether he had done the right thing or not.

'I had had my suspicions, she just confirmed them. So I've sent her packing. She leaves for England tomorrow and I've contacted my solicitor back home to start divorce proceedings.'

'Oh! I am so sorry,' Mary began.

'No, don't be,' he waved his hand as if to ward off her sympathy. 'It's something I should have done years ago. It's my own fault really. Joyce didn't want to move here but came along because she loved me back then. She wasn't always this nasty you know, but she changed after we got here. At first it was just with our staff, but then it got worse and soon everyone seemed to get the brunt of her tongue.'

He paused and fiddled with the brim of his hat for a while, making it do a quick revolution, then continued as if a new idea had occurred to him. 'I suppose that was what made me suspect that she had a thing for Pieter. She was never rude to him.'

His hat ticked round another twenty seconds in his hand.

'Anyway, I just wanted to let you know about re-charging the computer. I am sorry, but I really have no one to spare at the moment to bring it back to you. Things are a bit hectic on the farm. I hope to get some more staff on board soon, then I'm sure normal service can be resumed.' He smiled, then stood to leave.

'No need to apologise, that's quite alright. I'm sure Caiaphas can pop round to fetch it.'

Ray nodded.

'Any news from James?' he was almost at the door when the afterthought struck.

Mary paused. Should she be the one to let Ray know about James' loss? She had no idea how close he and Ray were.

'I had just finished reading an email from him when you arrived. His mother died yesterday,' – 'died' not 'passed away' or any other softer word – 'he will be coming back soon.'

Ray nodded thoughtfully. 'Please send him my condolences when you reply to him. You two should come over for a drink or something when he's back.' He said this as if she and James were already a couple and his look seemed to confirm what Mary read into the voice.

Caiaphas watched Esther's bright eyes as she told him the good news. Mrs Joyce was going back to England. Thomas, feeding at her breast picked up on his mother's joy and gurgled contently.

'She will no longer treat my mother so badly. Mr Ray is a good man and my mother will look after him so well now that Mrs Joyce has gone.'

Caiaphas struggled to share Esther's joy. Mrs Joyce had been a non-entity to him, just another white woman who ignored him after he had been 'conquered' by her. That was before he knew that she had no sway with Mr James. 'You will sleep with me or you will lose your job,' she had said. So he had obeyed. He probably would have slept with her anyway, even if his job wasn't at stake as, back then he had been curious about what white women would be like. But now, as he remembered that episode, he knew that he would not allow himself to be used like that anymore. Something in him had changed and he felt more grown up and able to understand the way things worked in the world. Yes, there was still a lot to learn but he had taken a giant leap forward in the last few days, although he didn't quite know what had caused that.

He nodded at Esther to express his happiness at her joy, but did not respond verbally. Something inside him told him that words were not necessary at this point. He then watched as Esther, smiling brightly and humming gently, eased Thomas off her breast and, after bouncing him a little in the air, much to the young child's delight placed him into his cardboard box cradle and set about cleaning the kitchen with a lightness to her touch.

He picked up the list for the required supplies that Solomon always left for him and stared at it for a long time. It was not nearly as detailed as usual. Instead of the list of ingredients that were required, the old chef had just listed a brief description of the starter, main and dessert that was planned for the evening meal. Caiaphas began to ask Esther if she knew what was going on, then stopped, studied the list again and slowly nodded his head.

'She was only here a couple of days, but I feel a bit lonely now she's gone,' Mary confessed to Annika.

The Swede studied her with bright blue eyes that sparkled in the well-tanned face.

'But?' she asked, sensing there was more.

'But at the same time, I don't feel as depressed as I did before she came. It's funny really, when I first saw her I expected that her grief would open up old wounds for me, wounds that had not properly healed. I thought I would end up more depressed as her loss would remind me of my own. But, I don't know, I feel more at peace now with George's death. It's not completely gone, but Tanya seemed to take Pieter's death so well that I almost felt guilty about being so miserable.

'I keep feeling that I will return to my depressed state, but there is a little something, I can't really explain what, that is telling me I'm over the worst of it. Does any of this make sense to you?'

Annika nodded and gently patted Mary's hand which lay on the table.

'I know exactly what you are talking about. When I got here, I was still all shook up by Nils' death. I don't even know how I managed to buy this little shop,' she gestured round the small veranda, 'but I sort of stumbled along and got things done. And then one day, I just snapped out of it, like a switch had been flicked. I remember the day well, I was sitting out here like we are today, sipping on a coffee. James had had me over to dinner the night before and that old chef of his, Solomon, he cooked all of these old Swedish recipes. I don't know how he managed to know them, but they were just perfect, reminded me of my mother's cooking. Anyway, I was sitting out here, remembering how good the meal had been when suddenly it struck me that I was at peace with what had happened. I was no longer bitter that Nils had left me alone. I understood that what had happened was all part of the cycle of life. I still don't stop missing him, but I guess you could say that that was the moment I realised that I had accepted what had happened.

The two women sat quietly for a bit, Mary contemplating what Annika had said and relating it to her own feelings about George. *Acceptance of what had happened.* She could accept that George was gone and that it was for the best that he no longer suffered, but there was still a nagging issue about George's death that she could still not come to terms with and, she knew that that was what those women back home were so upset about. However, she was still not prepared to discuss this with anyone.

'You should come have dinner one evening,' she changed the subject, 'I could get Solomon to do Swedish food again.'

'Yes, that'll be nice.'

Mary's nagging thoughts slunk to a small corner of her mind as the conversation moved on to lighter things, but even as they did so, she knew this was just a temporary respite.

Old Man Mawenzi was there, but not there. The rheumy eyes watched from the corner of the darkened room as the dying man lay on his crude bed, rasping breaths came sporadically from the prone figure accompanied by the occasional cough.

The mind behind the rheumy eyes knew that the time was close, but would the woman be ready? Was last night's meal good enough to prepare her? He would know the answer soon.

After lunch, Mary decided to go to the clearing again. She had not been for a few days and, despite the clouds building up, she wanted the solitude of the place so that she could think. There had been a lot of things going on – some explained, some not – and she needed to try and order her thoughts on the various matters.

Rex looked at her when she asked if he wanted to come with, then he looked at the sky as if to say, 'Are you mad? You want to go out now when it's going to pour with rain later?' Then he sighed and put his head back onto his paws.

'Suit yourself,' Mary said and headed out the door. Despite the weight of the issues she wanted to think over, she felt good and hummed quietly to herself as she made her way along the path.

It was still sunny when she laid out a towel to stop her dress getting dusty, settled on her favourite rock and breathed in the warmth. The gecko nodded a greeting, then turned its eyes to the approaching clouds and mentally calculated how much basking time it had left before the rain would arrive.

At the edge of the clearing, a rabbit twitched its nose, checking to see if it could detect the scent of the dog.

Mary stretched her legs out and leaned back on her hands, her eyes closed against the bright sunlight. She relaxed her mind and let thoughts pass lazily through it.

She liked the idea of James coming back soon, although it would be a bit strange seeing him in this different environment. It had been quite some time since they had last met up, probably before he bought the lodge, she thought. She wondered if he had changed much since she last saw him and imagined that he would be, despite his recent time in the UK, quite tanned. A bit like Ray. You can't live in a country like this where the sun shines a lot and not get somewhat brown.

She opened her eyes and studied her legs which stretched out below the knee-length cotton dress she wore. They were definitely browner than when she had first arrived, as were her arms.

Without really leaving her darkened skin completely, she tried to think about Tanya and the mysterious, one might almost say miraculous, healing that took place in the few days she was here. She had gone from being completely cut up and at a loss over the death of her husband to being relaxed and at peace with it. There was little doubt in Mary's mind that Solomon's food had something to do with that, but she could not answer the 'how?'

But why had it taken until now for him to start working his magic (if that was what it was) on her? Surely James must have explained her situation to his staff before heading off?

She hitched her skirt up to a just on decent level to allow her upper legs to get some of the sun that still shone. The clouds were closer now, but had a little while to go yet before they blocked off the light.

James could be a bit of a scatterbrain at times, so perhaps he had not told them anything. Maybe that was why Solomon had never served her 'healing food' before. Maybe she had just benefitted from partaking in Tanya's meal by accident. Maybe she could just pull her dress up a little higher, no one was around.

The sun felt good, but it was not letting her concentrate. As she settled back down again after pulling her dress right up and tucking it into the bottom of her knickers, she thought again of James and reminded herself that she was here to think, not sunbathe.

Should she take him up on his offer to stay on? What would happen if she did? From the things she had heard in the past week or two, James was still in love with her, but she was unsure of her feelings towards him. She loved him like a brother, but could there be anything more? George had arrived on the scene just at that time in her life when she was beginning to see men as more than just brothers. What if she had never met George? Could she have bestowed those same feelings of love that she developed for her husband on James?

The sun was now gently caressing her thighs and she wanted to be annoyed at its interference with her thoughts, but couldn't. It was like an amorous and persistent lover, slowly seducing one into the mood when the thought had not been near your mind to start with.

Oh, sod it, she thought and gave in to the sun's demands. She stood up, hesitated for a second to dismiss a tiny bit of self-consciousness (no one ever came to the clearing, did they?), then lifted her dress over her head and settled down again in her underwear. She was not totally giving in that easily, playing hard to get. She lay on her stomach now, letting the sun massage her exposed back while she tried to reel in her thoughts.

The sun, however, had other ideas. Its time for fun was limited as the clouds rolled ever closer.

'I will be a little late getting back,' Solomon spoke rare words to Caiaphas when he arrived to take his turn at watching over his dying dance partner. Normally something like this would have irritated Caiaphas, but he felt strangely relaxed about it. For the first time, he actually felt that the old chef was trusting him to do something. It was strange, but he sensed that this watch over Old Man Mawenzi was more important than previous ones.

Somehow he knew that the old man would not die until Solomon returned, but there was something about the next few hours that made it necessary that he, and not Solomon, was there.

He nodded to Solomon as if dismissing him and assuring him that everything would be fine. He felt oddly mature. He was no longer a young man despite what his body said. His mind felt ordered as if he knew things about the ways of man that he had not known before and yet he had no idea how he had acquired that knowledge. But this did not trouble him, it was as if it was destined that one day he would wake up with such knowledge.

He checked that the cup next to the old man's bed was full, then settled into his usual spot to watch. Solomon had gone off to see Mrs Mary. No, not see, help. Caiaphas knew that, but did not know how he knew.

Old Man Mawenzi seemed as peaceful as a man in his condition could be. His breathing, although rasping and coming in long intervals, had a regular rhythm to it. Rasp in, wait, wait, wait, rasp out, wait, wait, wait, rasp in.

Things were changing. He could feel it. The mountain in its mysterious way was moving into a new phase. Caiaphas put one hand onto the floor of the hut and felt though his palm the slow steady heartbeat of the mountain, his home. He was joined to her by some invisible umbilical cord. He could go wherever he wanted in the world, but would never find happiness away from her. It would be on her slopes that he would live, until his time came.

The thoughts flowed through his mind like a kind of energy and it filled the air in the hut, causing the old man to stir.

He gave a low cough, drew in a ragged breath, then in a barely audible voice said, 'Solly?'

Caiaphas hesitated.

'Solly,' the voice came stronger and the old man was now trying to sit up, his eyes opened and he looked around, the hut, searching. They landed on Caiaphas and seemed to light up. 'Solly,' he said again, this time with some conviction.

Caiaphas moved to ease the old man's head back onto the crude pillow. Air hissed out from the harelip in a relieved sigh, followed by a warm, 'Solly' as his eyes closed, but his hand, rough and dusty, sought Caiaphas' and grasped it in a surprisingly strong grip.

Caiaphas looked down at his hand which the old man held. It tingled slightly as if energy was flowing through it to the wizen body on the bed. He felt as if this was keeping the old man alive.

So this was what Solomon had wanted from him. He had to keep Mawenzi alive for a while longer. He squeezed the old man's hand gently and placed his free hand on the floor to draw energy from the mountain.

'I am here, Mawenzi,' he said.

'Solly.' The voice was as gentle as mist.

Mary glanced round. The clouds were not too far off now, but the sun still played with her skin, enveloping her in a comforting warmth that was somewhat sensuous.

A slight shudder of pleasure ran through her body which seemed to jolt her mind. I must think, she told herself and sat up, trying to force the fuzzy warmth from her mind.

'James,' she said his name out loud, hoping that actually hearing it would focus her mind to think. 'James, James, James what am I going to do?'

What should she do?

He didn't answer. How could he? He was thousands of miles away.

She sighed and gently massaged her naked legs as if rubbing the warmth into them. No, James could not help her with this decision. Even if he was here, he would be biased. She needed to decide for herself. Something inside her was saying that if she did stay on when James got back, it would be a permanent arrangement.

She wondered, just for a moment, what her mother and brother would say.

'Dear Mary, mother and I are thrilled with your news. We hope you and James will be happy.'

Or in the words of the youngsters – *'whatever'.*

And Toby? Her own son. He would probably reply, *'whatever',* which she would take to mean *'I am thrilled with your news, I hope you and James will be happy. PS. Can I have the house?'*

She smiled quietly at the thought which a few weeks back would have hurt, but which she now felt oddly at ease with. She accepted that she had not been the best mother and it was unfair of her to expect Toby to be the best son. Trying to make him into a good, loving son now was not right. In fact, it would probably drive him further away from her. No, the best course of action, should she decide to stay, would be to offer him the house without him having to ask, but make it look like he would be doing her a favour rather than the other way round.

Besides, she did not want to go back to the house. The village was full of judgement against her. The Mrs Cobblers and Hazells of this world would still be there when she got back. They would still be going out of their way to avoid her. Some of them still deliberately crossing on to her side of the road, just so that they could make a show of crossing back again as they got near her.

This thought brought her round to George. Should she consider what his opinion of the matter would be if he were somehow paradoxically still there to give his view on what she should do now that he was no longer there? They had never discussed this. You don't usually discuss death with the one you love. When he fell ill and they began to realise that he was not going to recover, they did not talk about it. He was too busy being ill then and she was too busy looking after him.

Even when he put forward the idea of ending his life, he did not talk about her future without him. She hadn't really thought about what would happen to her when he was gone. There was little space for thoughts of that nature in a head that was a tempest of emotion. The push-pull of not wanting him to go, but also not wanting him to suffer, sloshed back and forth in her mind with vicious, sea-sickening force.

She had arranged the trip to Switzerland at George's insistence, not telling anyone, not even Toby, what they were planning. But it had not been 'they' that were planning, George was planning, she was carrying out the third part of her now out of date marriage vow – love, honour and *obey*. Although she could hardly say her compliance was out of a sense of being tied to words she had shyly uttered years ago. Caring for him had worn her out to the degree that she merely did as she was told without too much thought.

Mary was too deep into her current thoughts to notice that the sun had been tapped on the shoulder by the clouds and that she was now with a different dance partner. Despite the shade the clouds brought, the air was still warm.

There had been counselling, lots of it, but she quickly became good at looking like she was taking it on board and understood everything that they were about to go through, but the truth of the matter was that she could not recollect a word of what was said back then. The words the counsellor spoke had floated like feathers falling to the ground, too light to disturb the air they fell through.

And then it was time. She had held his hand and sat with him till the nurse came and guided her away. 'He is at peace,' the nurse had said, not 'died'.

She hadn't cried until she got back to the hotel and sat alone in the room as it slowly got dark. The muffled sounds of the street outside as fuzzy as her mind. At last she had cleared her head enough to phone Toby to let him know.

They figured it out, the village. When she returned without George and had to let people know that he had passed away, they knew. Rumours started and, Mary suspected, were confirmed by Toby. They came to the funeral when George's body got back, but she could feel the daggers being glared at her as she sat alone at the front of the church.

Even her mother and brother picked up on the vibe. They joined neither side, preferring to remain neutral. It was as if they could not bring themselves to condone what Mary had done, but at the same time were bound by ties of blood to not take up arms against her. One consoling thought that passed through Mary's mind as she had sat in that church was that at least there were no surviving family members on George's side to have to deal with.

The cooling of the air as the sun had disappeared, now made itself known to Mary and she looked round. The gecko, seeing that she was with the living again, nodded quickly to bid her good day, before it scurried into its hole in the rocks just as the first rain drop landed with a 'splat!' just next to Mary. The second one hit her naked shoulder.

She stood up quickly and, as she began to gather clothes, a scene from *Lady Chatterley* came back to her. When she had read it, she had loved the way Connie had thrown off her clothes, inhibitions and cares in that dreary world she lived in and ran naked in the rain. Yes, there was Mellors to tease with her nudity, but, Mary felt, the scene was more about the freedom that Connie gained than anything sexual. And how she craved freedom from the guilt that still gnawed at her about helping George to end his life.

She glanced round the clearing as the rain began to gain momentum, then moving quickly, she stripped off her underwear and shoved her clothes into her bag, hauled out the waterproof raincoat she always carried, and wrapped the bag in it.

She stood, letting the warm rain, which had quickly turned into a solid downpour, wash across her body, feeling the slickness it brought to her hair and the slippery layer it added to her skin.

For a few moments she just stood, letting the rain soak her through, her face lifted to the sky, her eyes closed. She wanted the rain to wash away her sin. The sin of being alive when George was dead, the sin of having helped George end his life when all around her said she could not, the sin of wanting to be happy in a post George world.

She had tried hard to believe that these were not sins. She kept telling herself over and over that she had done nothing wrong. But her powers of persuasion had met with the backlash of a community that had poisoned her to the core. The dark stain of guilt was etched on her like an immoveable tattoo.

As she stood in the rain now, she did not feel naked. The shame of sin cast a heavy cloak over her as she stood exposed in all her glory. How she wanted to be free, to cast off this unwanted garment.

Her body swayed slightly, then as the scene from *Lady Chatterley* played through her mind again, she was off and running, her feet surprisingly nimble over the uneven rocks. If she just ran fast enough, maybe she could outrun the sin.

She reached the edge of the forest and darted to one side like a trapped animal desperately searching for some chink in the cage to escape by. She ran the length of the border between the forest and the clearing, feeling the rush of air against her wet, naked skin. She doubled back, her lungs beginning to burn, but the sin burned more and she could not stop until she had escaped it.

She had tried so hard to hide it, bury it deep inside herself and try and show the world that she was not guilty as charged. But she could not shake the feeling that she had done wrong. And it must show. Why else would those women in the village be so intent on reminding her?

She hurtled towards the cliff face that fell off sharply in a forty foot drop. The air screaming a protest as she crashed through it, causing it to scatter as the chickens in front of the car had done on her first day here. The cliff edge yelled out a warning and she stumbled slightly, then righted herself and veered off in a new direction.

Her heart thrashed in her chest as she headed across the clearing again, but now her legs were beginning to weaken. She started to feel the rain again and a slow, drip-fed message was getting through to her mind that she could not outrun it like this. Lady Chatterley may have had her carefree run in the rain, that moment of freedom and joy, but things had quickly turned grim after that.

Mary slowed and as she did, she instinctively headed towards the little bundle that held her clothes. On reaching them, her legs, unused to this sort of exercise, melted under her as she collapsed onto the flat rock, curled herself into a protective ball and handed over control of her body to her grief, letting it shake her naked form in gasping sobs. The pregnant raindrops battered the side of her face, each one a new death, reminding her so acutely of that one death that had been so controlled and clinical that it had sliced through her heart with scalpel-like sharpness, leaving her open and bleeding before she even knew that she was wounded.

FOURTEEN

We are born, tiny microscopic dots slowly unfurling within a protective watery womb before sliding out into the harsh glaring light of the world, our tiny eyes are screwed up tight against this unwanted intrusion. We writhe, slowly feeling our way, groping through this first terror. We know nothing of death, even those for whom life is but a few brief seconds, do not, cannot, grasp what is happening.

We grow. We live. Some more than others. We devour knowledge, some with greater appetites than others. We explore, we invest, we create, we investigate. And yet, at the end of it all, when we breathe our last, we are still no wiser about that phenomenon that ends our journey, that thing we call death.

There are few among us who have no fear of it. Even those that choose to have some control over when it arrives are not without fear, they just have a greater fear of continuing life.

George had been like that. She could see it in his eyes. The constant pain, discomfort and lack of dignity that his illness had brought, scared him. The fear of living day after day with this condition slowly built up in him. Each stab of pain, each laboured movement, each time someone had to help him go to the toilet, all this slowly tipped the scale, adding more weight to the fear of life side. The fear of death on the other hand, never diminished in weight, but it was losing the battle to stay lower than the other pan on the scale, till finally it tipped enough that George, dear, poor dependable George, rock solid George, wracked with an overwhelming fear of life, colluded with the only person he could turn to and arranged to rid himself of that fear.

She had done her duty. She had been a good wife and made all the arrangements despite her mind screaming at her not to. She had loved, honoured and obeyed. Why could she find no peace in that? Why was she tortured every morning by that slight shudder that went through George's body as it expelled his last breath? Would she ever be able to remember that and not feel guilt?

A fear rose in her that this guilt would slowly tip her own scale. The fear of having to live every day as a reject from society, spurned by those who had never experienced seeing that imbalance in a loved one, that scale so firmly down on the side indicating a greater fear of continuing to live, far outweighing that in-built fear of death. They would never know what it was like and yet they felt morally superior to judge her and carry out that judgement with such wrath, as if she had somehow personally offended them just by loving her husband enough to aid him in this ultimate act.

The intensity of her thoughts slowly eased as if running out of fuel. They would be back, she knew, they just needed to re-fuel and they would be back. The rain, which her distress had blocked from her mind, was slowly beginning to register on her prone, naked body, tapping out a rapid Morse code to her brain to return to the present. She knew she should open her eyes, uncurl her tightly wound up body and be born again into the world, but for the moment, she felt safe in this mental womb, her fear of what lay beyond the back of her eyelids prevented her from obeying the call to slide into life again.

She felt the last sob leave her body and lay perfectly still. The rain was still heavy and cool on her skin.

And then it stopped. Abruptly. Too quickly for it to have been natural. Her eyes forgot their fear of the future and opened wide, glanced towards the sky but saw only the concave innards of an open umbrella. In a mad panic they followed the handle down to the dark, wrinkled hand, then flew across to the statue like face with its rheumy eyes averted.

Esther watched Caiaphas with suspicion.

'Solomon said he would be late,' was all he had said and now he sat at the old man's seat looking slowly round the kitchen. There was something new about him, an air of maturity, an air of authority.

Could Caiaphas actually cook? She had never seen him do anything like that and, from what she had heard round the village, he still went home to his mother for his meals. Esther held Thomas closer to her breast, a little scared at this change.

Slowly Caiaphas reached out a hand and touched the potatoes that lay beside the chopping board. He rested it lightly on each one, as if it was listening to them, hearing them put forward their case as to why they should be chosen over the other for dinner. When he had heard each one's plea, he made his selection and began to peel in slow, deliberate movements.

Should she say something? Tell him to stop messing around. Solomon would be here soon and would not be pleased to see the young man in his seat. She could not imagine what Solomon would do or say. She had never seen him get cross or even raise his voice, but there always seemed to be a threat about his manner that you never felt brave enough to chance your luck against it.

But there was something now in Caiaphas' demeanour that sent out the same message. *Don't mess with me* clung to him like a dark aura. She quietly clicked her tongue and set about her chores. If Caiaphas wants to mess with Solomon, let him. He would have to deal with the consequences.

'Salt.' The command came in a younger man's voice but with an older man's authority and Esther instinctively fetched the condiment.

She should have been burning with shame. Everything about the situation screamed that at her as she dried herself with the towel Solomon offered and then slipped into her clothes which had remained remarkably dry in her bag wrapped up in the raincoat. The rain had eased and passed almost before she had accepted the rough old hand to help her to her feet.

Where was the shame? She could not answer that. Despite being so close to her and helping her up, Solomon had kept his eyes averted enough and his stony face was still indelibly etched with a sense of indifference to her nudity or strange behaviour. To him she was and had always been fully clothed and had not been curled up naked on a rock in the middle of Africa, bawling her eyes out.

Despite this sense of ease and lack of embarrassment, she had no idea what to say to him other than to thank him for the towel. But how had he known she was here? How had he known she would need a towel? The questions burned on her tongue but she could extinguish them.

'Madam,' he said once she had finished straightening herself out and running a comb through her hair, feeling it lie like damp seaweed against her skull, 'you need to come with me.'

She did not protest, she had not a voice to protest with and legs, still aching from their recent exertion, that were too tired to argue, so politely followed behind the slow shuffling gait of the old man who walked so much like her father had. Her voice, numbed by the recent eruption of emotions, did not even try to give form to the question that thundered somewhere in her lava covered mind. 'Why? Why must I go with you?'

The path, hardened by a thousand journeys up and down the mountain, was slick and the water still ran freely over its glistening surface. A damp funk rose from the sodden leaves on the floor of the forest and floated in the no-man's land between perfume and stench.

Mary concentrated her mind on her footsteps. Slow, methodical left, right, left. The rhythm stamping on thoughts that she wanted desperately to think and yet in equal measure wanted to forget.

The forest thinned and a watery sun gave off a lukewarm haze in the early evening. She permitted herself to hear the sounds of the birds as they bustled about in the sky, sharing their evening meal and the gossip of the day. And still she followed unquestioningly behind the old chef whose body rocked gently side to side like a retired ship's captain, struggling to cope with a steady surface to walk on.

As they neared the village, the sun dropped like a pink pearl into the hazy dark pool of the horizon, momentarily sending up a muddy splash of rusty reds into the sky which all but disappeared as they walked along the hut-lined path. Mary was just vaguely aware of the stares she received from women hunched over steaming pots that stood on small fires. Small children ran around them, but stopped to stare silently at her, fingers in mouths, eyes wide yet strangely accepting of this strange sight on their turf.

Solomon slowed and then gestured for her to enter a rundown hut at the far end of the village.

She is not back yet.

Esther wanted to voice her concerns to Caiaphas, but this was a new, strange Caiaphas, one that she felt she could not talk to in the way that she had in the past. She could not talk to him in the same way that she had a few weeks back when Mary had gone out for a walk and discovered the clearing. She could not, she felt, even hint at the possibility that Mrs Mary had done what Mrs Judith had done. Not to this new Caiaphas.

She wiped a clean plate and placed it quietly on the table in front of Caiaphas as she had been commanded to. He continued to chop at some vegetables with slow deliberate clunks of the knife on the chopping board.

Esther sighed, then glanced nervously over at Caiaphas, expecting him to admonish her with a look, but instead he laid the knife to one side and then smiled at her.

'Mrs Mary is fine, she is with Solomon. They will be here later.'

Esther nodded, but her face still showed concern at this strange new maturity in him.

As if reading her mind, he broadened his grin.

'I do not understand it yet either, but one day we both will. Today I have to be Solomon and do the cooking and maybe tomorrow too and the next day. I do not know for how long. He has given me a...' he stopped as he searched for the right word, '...a ziwadi, a gift.' He gestured at the food he was preparing, then his smile faded. 'I guess there is more, I can feel inside me that there is, but I don't yet know what that may be.' He looked thoughtful for a moment, then reached for the knife and began to chop again in the same slow, rhythmic beat that Esther was so used to.

Esther stared for a moment longer, then slowly nodded her head and smiled as things fell into place, then glanced over at the cardboard box where Thomas lay sleeping.

'One day, my son,' she whispered in her heart, 'one day you will be given the gift of Solomon.'

The light inside the hut was a gentle dull orange and was supplied by a small kerosene lamp. An elderly woman sat in one corner, her eyes glued to the prone form at the opposite end of the room.

On seeing Mary, she shifted uncomfortably, but nodded politely then slowly raised herself to her feet. She moved to the door, half curtseyed to Solomon who shook her hand and mumbled something in Swahili that, although Mary did not understand the words, she realised it was a deep, heartfelt thanks and also noted that it was quite likely that a few shillings had changed hands in the exchange.

When the woman was gone, Solomon gestured to a small rickety looking bench made of a few planks nailed together which stood against the wall near where the woman had been sitting.

'Please,' he said, inviting her to sit. Mary eased herself onto the bench, half expecting it to break under her weight, but despite the unevenness of its legs, the construction of it was solid.

It was then that the prone figure coughed, a raw hacking sound that seemed to erupt from deep within the lungs. The figure convulsed in time to the throbbing cough and as its face moved in and out of the light, Mary realised with shock that this was the deformed beggar that she had been confronted with on her first day in Kilimbati. She recoiled slightly on the bench, then aware of Solomon's presence, settled down, squashing the thoughts of revulsion that threatened to bubble up.

Solomon seemed not to notice her flinch and he slowly squatted near the beggar's bed.

'Why has he brought me here?' The question screamed in Mary's mind, but she could not form it with her lips. She watched the old chef slowly settle himself, an impatience burning inside her, but she knew that Solomon never rushed things. She knew she would have to be patient.

When he was ready, Solomon reached out and took the beggar's hand.

'This is my friend Mawenzi,' he said, each word stood separately like the posts of a fence. The beggar coughed as if in response, as if saying 'Hello, pleased to meet you.'

'He is dying,' Solomon went on, his tone had its usual flatness, but somehow Mary felt the emotion.

She could still not fathom why Solomon had brought her here. She tried not to appear like she was averting her eyes from the beggar and looked across to Solomon, her eyes asking the question, but the old man was not to be rushed. He held his friend's hand, his face set as if to say that the words 'he is dying' should explain everything.

At length he seemed to notice her gaze and looked up. Did a brief flash of exasperation cross his face? It was hard to tell. He returned his attention to his friend but addressed her.

'You are mourning your husband's death, are you not?'

The question surprised Mary, but she nodded, then realising that the old chef wasn't looking at her, mumbled a 'yes.'

Solomon acknowledged her answer with a slight incline of the head, but continued to concentrate his gaze on the prone figure which seemed to be breathing slightly more regularly and less jaggedly.

'James must have told him,' Mary thought, 'but why does he bring this up? What has it got to do with him?'

'You feel guilty about his death.' It was not a question and was delivered in such a way that Mary knew she did not need to confirm it.

There was a long silence as Solomon watched his friend's frail body ration out its last few breaths in slow gasps, interrupted by long silences as if savouring each one.

The guilt Mary had stored up over taking George to Switzerland bubbled up in her mind as it had done so often, causing a sense of dread and an ache. She was beginning to resign herself to the fact that it would be a weight she would have to carry with her for the rest of her life.

'The guilt you feel is not yours,' Solomon still did not look up at her. 'It is a false guilt that your society has put on you. They feel that you have let them down because you did not stop your husband from dying.'

Could he know what Mary had done? No, she told herself, there is no way he could, James didn't even know. She had been careful not to let him know. Unless...

She thought of the women in her village. Those with stares and glares that had accused her every day. Could one of them have possibly let James know that she had helped George to die? There were a few of the ladies who knew James, one or two had even visited the lodge. She could imagine the email carrying the phrase 'black widow' rushing through the cables, or bouncing off the satellites, or however it was that emails travelled.

No, calm down, she told herself. *What did Solomon actually say? 'You did not stop your husband from dying,' not 'you did not stop your husband from killing himself.'*

As she calmed her mind with this thought, Solomon looked up at her from his patient and slowly shook his head while looking her in the eye.

Again her mind was set racing. Had he read her thoughts? The co-incidences were piling up too much for her to dismiss this thought as foolishness and her tongue began to fumble with the question forming in her mind. How?

'He does not have long to go now,' Solomon indicated the old beggar with an incline of his head and Mary's tongue stopped mid-fumble. His shake of the head had been for the dying man, not from reading her mind. Surely.

'We here in Africa do not have the doctors and medicines you have.' The old chef continued in his slow, precise manner. 'It seems to me that, with the advances in science people have come to believe that all disease can be cured. You have television programmes where doctors always find the answer and save the patient's life. Your world keeps telling you that death is a bad thing and should be, and can be, cured. One day, I think, you will make dying illegal.'

He stopped and gave a small chuckle at his joke, his rheumy eyes losing some of their age and, just for a second in the dim light, he looked young. Mary, despite still trying to digest what Solomon was saying, managed to realise that this was the first time she had heard him laugh or seen him smile.

But the humour did not last long and the watery glaze returned to the eyes.

'Here in Africa, we have not yet got the doctors or the medicine that you have,' he paused then added, 'or the television programmes. We have not yet been made to believe that we can escape death. We still accept it as natural and a part of life.' He gave Mary some time to contemplate this.

After a period of silence he said, 'Come, hold his hand,' and indicated for her to join him next to the beggar. Still somewhat dazed by what he had been saying and not really giving a thought to the deformities that had so upset her on their first meeting, Mary took Old Man Mawenzi's rough and dirty hand.

The dying man sighed as if satisfied, breathed in a ragged breath then slowly released the air from his lungs and did not breathe in again.

Mary felt the man's life leave him, just as she had with George, but she did not squeeze the hand now as she had back then. With George she had wanted to, and still wanted to hold him back, keep him with the living. But now, she felt completely at ease letting the old man go.

Of course this is different, she told herself, *I loved George and spent a good part of my life with him, whereas I hardly knew this man. It is so much easier to let go.* But even though she told herself this, she knew there was more, something profound had happened.

It was not the death itself that was the prompt for this feeling, it was the reaction of Solomon. He stared for a good while at his friend's body, then gently laid the hand he was holding across the dead man's chest in his slow, deliberate manner. He took the other hand from Mary and also laid that on the man's chest.

And then, he smiled.

And it was not a sad smile.

There was a kind of joy in the old chef's eyes.

At first, Mary was puzzled. In the few short moments she had seen Solomon and Mawenzi together she had known there was a strong bond of friendship between the two men and yet Solomon almost seemed pleased that his friend had gone.

'He is truly at peace now,' the old chef again seemed to answer her thoughts. 'He struggled all the way through his life, but now he can relax. Look how calm he is.'

Mary stared at the beggar's face. In death it did not seem as grotesque, in fact it had softened and seemed to almost have a soft glow of serenity. In an instant she recognised that change as being the same she had seen in George as his grip on her hand had loosened despite her grasp of his tightening.

'If my friend had been born in England, he would not be dead now,' there was a hint of pride in Solomon's voice. 'He would have been kept alive for as long as possible with machines and pills and medicines. And the doctors would be saying what a great job they are doing in fighting off death. But Mawenzi would not have wanted that. He wanted to go when he was ready.'

He stopped to smile and look at his friend again, as if recalling a conversation they had had a long time ago.

'I know he did not want to die. No one wants to die, but he knew he had to and he did so when he was ready. Fighting nature is fighting a war that you can never win. It is foolishness to fight when there is no way you can win. It is better to surrender and not have to go through the pain of battle. The problem with people is that they seem to think they can win. But if you surrender when the time is right, then your enemy will give you better terms.'

Mary nodded slowly. It was beginning to make some sense; it was not about giving up, but about knowing when to stop fighting. If George had not arranged to end his life, then his death would have been worse, both for him and for her. He would have had to endure the ongoing pain and further decline in his ability to do anything, coupled with the mental anguish of having to try and cope with the way people would look at him and have to care for him.

And she would have had to stand by and watch this continual worsening of his condition. It had been bad enough watching him slump to the point it had. How much worse it would have been if she had had to watch this slow decline for who knew how long? There had been nothing she could have done to stop it and that sense of helplessness ached as much, if not more than the despair at losing him had.

Despite this, she still could not bring herself to smile and feel the strange happiness that Solomon seemed to exude.

'You need to truly let go,' the old chef continued to confuse her with his uncanny ability to answer her thoughts. 'You in England have a saying, may he rest in peace?'

Mary nodded. There had been a few who had mumbled this to her at George's funeral, but at the time they felt like obligatory words mumbled by mourners there for good form. They were as meaningless as a 'how are you?' asked by a telesales person, used to goad you into buying insurance you did not need.

Solomon seemed to wait for her to go through this mental process then said, 'But how can anyone rest in peace if they are worried about you. If you have concerns about a friend, or if your child is sick, or your husband or wife is acting strangely, do you sleep well at night? No. You cannot rest if you are worrying about someone. So too your husband cannot rest in peace until he knows that you are at peace about his death.

'Mawenzi here, he used to say to me, "Solly, when I die, do not lose sleep, for if you do, I will not be able to sit down and relax with my ancestors. I will be too busy worrying about my friend Solomon and why he is not sleeping. I will not be able to sit down with my father and my mother and tell them all that I did when they left because they will see in my heart that I will be torn between sitting there with them and going to see that my good friend Solomon is okay. And my mother will then not be at peace because you know how much she loved me. Despite all my problems, she loved me so much and when I go to my ancestors, she will want to spend a lot of time with me so I cannot be worrying about you". That is what Mawenzi said to me just one week ago, when he knew he was dying.'

Solomon paused and a cloud seemed to pass across his face, only to be chased away by what Mary thought was an extreme effort.

'It's not easy,' she told herself, 'but it makes sense.'

'I will be sad, there is nothing wrong with being sad. But I will not be a good friend if I let Mawenzi go to his mother and father still worrying about how I am coping with his death. I will sleep well tonight so that Mawenzi can be at peace.'

He looked down at his friend again and studied him thoughtfully, then looked up at Mary.

'Your husband cannot possibly be at rest with you still worrying about his death. When he died, it was past the time that nature had granted him and I think that he knew that. You need to smile about the good times you had with him, he would like that. You can miss him, there is nothing wrong with missing him. A man will have his pride and missing him will say to him that he was good to you because you would not miss a bad man. So miss him, but do not let that take over your life. If you let yourself become too upset, he will not be happy because you are not happy. Do you understand what it is that I am saying to you?'

Mary felt the teardrop roll down her cheek and she wiped it away with the back of her hand, then gave a sob-laugh and sought out Solomon's hand which she held tightly.

'Yes, I do understand what you are saying, Solomon. I can just picture George now, sitting up patiently waiting for me to sort myself out so that he can go and rest. He was such a patient man.'

They sat quietly together for a bit and Mary began to feel a kind of peace descend on her.

'Goodbye George,' she whispered.

The boy walked quickly along the path, stopping occasionally to check that the mzungu, the white woman, was still following him. He was not very good with the torch, allowing it to flick on and off the path at will, but the mzungu seemed to be doing okay. She was humming quietly to herself. The boy thought of the 200 shilling coin in his pocket. Easy money. Just show the woman to the lodge, Solomon had said.

They had not allowed him into the hut where the Mzee Kichaa, the mad old man, was and the other boys were sure that that old man had died. They would know soon enough, word of these things travelled fast.

He recalled, with a slight pang of guilt, the overripe tomato that he had hurled. He had been a hero that day for the bull's-eye that he scored on the old man's back. Even after Mzee Solomon had caught them, the others had still congratulated him on his shot when they were sure the old chef was nowhere to be seen.

He tried not to think too much about this now. If you disturbed the dead with thoughts and worries about them, they could not rest and if a spirit could not rest, it would certainly seek out and disrupt the life of the one who is not letting it rest. His mother had told him that.

He felt safe with the mzungu woman walking quietly behind him. Mzee Mawenzi would not do anything with a mzungu around, he was too polite to do that. It was the walk back to the village that he was not looking forward to.

When he had seen the mzungu woman safely to the front door of the lodge, he walked to the back, trying to put off the inevitable return journey and hoping that Caiaphas who sometimes gave him left over food would be around this time.

Caiaphas was at the open kitchen door, a more mature mind would have said 'waiting for me', but this thought did not occur to the young boy, he was too busy being grateful for the company.

He greeted Caiaphas respectfully and exchanged the pleasantries that adult men usually did, giving him a sense of importance that he was being treated like a grown up.

Caiaphas asked the questions with adult words but a child's tone.

'My mother is well. My father? He is well too, his crops are growing nicely and our cow has not yet given birth.'

When they were done with the business of exchanging news, Caiaphas held out a packet.

'There is not much today, but this is very important to help you grow.'

The boy took the bag and, well trained in his customs, did not peek inside until he had finished his conversation and moved a little distance from the lodge. The reason for the custom, he had been told, was that you do not open a gift in front of the giver in case you are disappointed and this shows in your face. It was good that he had remembered his traditions as there were just tomatoes in the bag. They had plenty of tomatoes at home.

Then he remembered the words Caiaphas had said, 'This is very important, they will help you grow.'

He stopped on the path as a soggy missile flew across his mind and splattered on the back of a dusty shirt. But unlike the reality of the other day, this vision played out differently. The owner of the shirt did not stand waiting for another direct hit, but turned slowly and where the young boy expected to see a disfigured face, found that he was looking at a healthy face and a pleasant smile. Old Man Mawenzi nodded at him, touched his healed lip as if trying to believe it himself, then turned and walked slowly away without limping. 'I was once young too' a voice floated back.

The boy stood rooted to the path until the departing old man had dissolved into the dark of the night then slowly reached into the bag and took out a tomato, biting into it and letting the juice squirt down the side of his mouth. Then, feeling like a man, he walked down the path without fear.

'For the starter tonight, we have a yam, carrot and paprika patty with a creamy chive sauce.'

It felt strange having Caiaphas introduce the meal, but at the same time it felt right. The dish he placed in front of Mary looked beautiful, the carrot flecking the white fleshy yam, which was slightly fried to a rich golden brown. The sauce seemed to ooze lovingly from the centre of the patty, and a small pink flower sat gently on top as a colourful garnish. The aroma floated softly from the dish and tickled Mary's nose. She half expected Caiaphas to wait and watch her taste this first dish he had prepared, but he bowed slightly, as Solomon used to do, and retired to the kitchen.

Mary enjoyed the ambiance of the food for a moment longer before finally picking up her fork. She was feeling profoundly at peace with everything. George was now a memory to be treasured, not something to fret over or be ashamed of. He needed his rest and she could now grant him that. It felt strange to let go and yet in doing so she had secured him to her forever.

She ate, letting the food dance a salty tango with her taste buds. It had that same magical quality that Solomon's did, but there was a slight undertone of sexiness about it. Her thoughts turned to *Lady Chatterley*. It was supposed to have been a sexy book, filled with naughtiness, but was in some ways a sad tale of missed love. She and George had loved each other in their strange way. But now, unlike Lady Chatterley, she did not think the one giving her this freedom would object to her choice, should she decide to make it. Clifford did not approve of Mellors, but, Mary felt sure, George would have approved of James.

She lifted the last forkful of yam, pausing slightly before putting it into her mouth, a gentle smile playing on her lips.

The mountain felt the warm night breeze dance gaily on its slopes. It heard the excited chatter of the ancestors welcoming a new one into their company and the gushing exuberance of a mother reunited with her mzee child.

In a clearing, a gecko sat quietly absorbing the fading warmth of the rocks. The mountain felt its quiet, beating heart and listened to its reptile thoughts and nodded its agreement.

Dreams, coughs, birds, rabbits, breezes, forgotten conversations caressed the paths, rustled in the trees and scurried in the undergrowth.

Then everything went quiet and still. The gecko turned its head slightly, the dreams paused, the coughs were silent and the forgotten conversations died away. Even an old, world-weary dog, head on paws, deigned to lift a lazy eyelid, just for a moment.

Into this calm came a slow, steady footfall as it made its way down the path towards the town of Kilimbati which slept at the foot of the mountain.

In a brief opening on the path where the trees were not so thick, the old figure paused and turned to look back towards The Lodge. The moonlight glinted in the watery eyes of the figure, catching a wry smile.

Solomon nodded his satisfaction with events, then turned and slowly faded into the darkness of the mountain night.